The Naked Way

Chris Henry

ISBN: 0989553116
ISBN 13: 9780989553117

TABLE OF CONTENTS

Chapter 1

THE CATHEDRAL, SPRING 1992

I don't want this century anymore. I don't want the next one either. A future of endless possibilities has no meaning for me now. I only want this: the hot red stone of the piazza under noonday sun. Kaleidoscope light through stained glass on my face. Another civilization. Perfect marble altars, centuries old. I worship the bones of Italy's saints, unknown to me before today. This is what I want: Siena. Tomorrow, Florence. Then Arezzo, Volterra, Perugia, Pisa...

I don't want the world anymore. I want Gwen. I looked for her in the tourist crowds today. She's halfway around the world, but I see her everywhere. When I close my eyes, the fragile darkness gives way to memory: I see snow falling, the gray eternity pressing in on the windows of the tiny apartment where she stayed with me. Her scent blows on the summer breeze, past museums and tour buses, just beyond my senses. Singsong Italian speech mixes in the air with rumbling German and shrill Midwestern American English; I only hear her voice.

I wander into the cathedral, a straggler from the group. The holy water in the little marble basin is cool on my fingertips. I cross myself as I enter the sanctuary; this may be as close to heaven as I'll ever get. Black and white marble columns, out of all proportion to tiny human form, shoot up to secure the grand vaulted ceiling, higher than my hopes. The floor is an explosion of geometric possibilities: checks, squares, floral patterns, snaking and weaving lines. Sounds of shuffling feet and whispers from the distant apse almost break up altogether in the vast space, reaching my ears as one harmonized, echoing hum, ongoing and without a definite source. I'm drawn in further. There are scores of paintings on the walls, multiplications of the saving image. Christ in agony. Christ in glory. Glory in every brushstroke.

There's a girl with the right hair — wavy blonde past her shoulders - looking at paintings. Her back is to me. Could be the right shape. Probably too tall. She turns. Not Gwen. But very pretty. She walks past, returning my curious look. Blue-green eyes, like mine, like hers. But not Gwen.

I stand where she was and look at the paintings. Each image resonates in deepest memory. I read their titles from a guidebook: "The Slaughter of the Innocents." The sword slashes out, blood runs red. Arrogant soldiers march on. How many more times? Forever, infinite repetitions of the slaughter, I now know. "The Nativity and Visitation." "Arrival and Adoration of the Magi." Who is the holy infant, Gwen? Who was born again, you or I? I'm a midwife, I once wrote to her. *I brought you into the world in my bed.*

I wander off and find a pew where I sit down and put on my headphones. I mean no disrespect by it. It's a tape of my friend Brandon's old band, The Naked Way, recorded on cheap equipment at a basement show back in Denver. I press the 'play' button and a soaring voice rises above a churning ritual beat in my head. I look up to see a tortured crucifix; the voice of the singer could be the sacrificed god's. *"Pulling the sun down..."* the voice wails. In my mind I see him: his long, lean body wrapped perversely around the microphone stand, lion-like golden hair to his shoulders, head thrown back to howl.

Brandon was the drummer. He's here in Italy, in the cathedral with Kate, looking at a mosaic of The Flight into Egypt. They turn and see me. I smile at them. This trip was Kate's idea. It's a class, really, with grades and everything. Her art history professor put it together for a reasonable price, and god knows I needed to get away. The history of Tuscan art is saving me.

Brandon and Kate walk over to me. "What do you think?" he says. We all laugh. We've only been away from home for a week, but it seems like a different life. Brandon points out busts of the popes lining the inside of a high dome, and nearby statues of prophets and patriarchs, with gold stars on a field of blue behind. Gold angels hover over us; there is gold everywhere.

Men aren't allowed to wear shorts in most of the holy sites in Italy. But the ticket-takers never say anything about Kate's shorts. They show off every inch of her long, tanned legs and then some. She poses on one leg, then the other, snapping her bubble gum and giggling. "Oh my god you guys, isn't this divine? Wait, I made a pun!" Her laughs end in little pug-nose snorts that make Brandon smile. Brandon has two modes when he's with Kate: smugness or existential despair. When the slender brunette is happy and loving him, he can't hide his self-satisfaction. When she's pissed-off, moody, playing the brat or just making him work for it, Brandon's face turns to ash.

Brandon can be smug now. Kate is happy. She is Brandon's girl, so I try not to think about the shape of her lips, and the way they look as she puckers up to apply her shimmery pink lipstick right here in the church. Kate's wearing a t-shirt with Andy Warhol's pop-art print of Marilyn Monroe; she perfectly imitates the star's sultry expression. The transcendent majesty of the church is just a novel and exotic new setting for Kate's show, a show that never ends. So is all of Italy, for that matter. "It's so beautiful, you guys!" she says. "I'm gonna turn Catholic or have an orgasm. Or both!" Again with the snort.

"Feels like another world, doesn't it?" I say. But there are some things worth saving from the old one. I pass over the headphones to Brandon. He grins ear to ear when he hears the music start. I leave the walkman with him and wander on.

My footsteps echo across the vast interior of the cathedral. I'm drawn to a door in the opposite wall and I follow the impulse. I pass through into a little round room, a chapel to the Virgin Mary. An image of her face is the center, abundant red roses around her, her baby boy on her lap, white candles burning beneath, sweet frankincense in the air. An old Italian widow draped head to toe in black sits up front in a little pew, praying and softly weeping. I sit down silently in back and stare at the Queen of Heaven. I've never been one for organized religion, but I know the Goddess when I see her. I close my eyes, and in my mind the image before me shifts through her different faces and incarnations and masks across time and cultures: Gaia, Shakti, Venus, Mother Earth. All the while she sits serene on her throne in a child's sentimental imagination of paradise, revealed behind Michelangelo's billowing clouds.

Mostly I pray for Gwen. Much as I want to, I can never hate her. I only love her more and more. She loves me too - this is by far the hardest thing. It wasn't lack of love that made her run, but the overpowering weight of an opposite force: something alien, cruel, insatiable, hidden in total darkness. Or at least that's what I tell myself. Mother Mary, take her pain away. I couldn't.

As I walk out of the chapel, I push the mop of brown hair back from my face. A longer, shiny, raven-black hair catches in my fingers. It must have stuck to me when I kissed Grace goodbye this morning. I stretch it out to its full length and curl it playfully around my finger. I can still smell her faintly on my fingertips.

Chapter 2

THE MARKETPLACE, FALL 1991

As Eli made his way down Larimer Street, a towering dark form emerged from an alley through a cloud of septic steam, almost colliding with him. There was no chance to look the other way or pretend he hadn't seen him. Eli accepted a brief embrace from Xavier's open arms.

"Dude! Long time no see!" he enthused, his face too close to Eli's. His breath was rank; a pale winter sun reflected in the lenses of his shades. Xavier wore a variation of his usual streetpunk uniform: black boots, ripped jeans, deathrock tshirt and several rattling necklaces under a thin and tattered overcoat, with an oversized sailor's hat on his head, apropos of nothing. "You been out to see any bands lately?" he asked. "We gotta catch a show!"

Eli looked at him through squinting, skeptical eyes. "I'm around," he said noncommittally. Xavier was a notorious scammer, hangeron, petty thief, and selfstyled gypsy; always trying to sell a hit of acid or a stolen trinket for cigarette money, inviting someone to other people's parties where he himself was not welcome, working some angle or another with a huge manic grin on his face. The joke in town was that you should never say Xavier's name three times, or he would materialize as if out of thin air.

"Eli, my man, my brother!" He shoved a hand in his pocket and put another on Eli's shoulder. "Got something for you, bro. You're gonna love this."

Eli started walking again. "I'm not buying any hot CD's today, X."

Xavier followed, dodging cars and bicycles to keep up through an intersection. "No dude! This is special for you, because I know you're all spiritual-like. This is *holy*!" He passed over a cheap gold necklace with a locket. "Check it out!"

"Forget it, slick. No sale."

Xavier's eyes grew big. "But *look,* man." He opened the locket. "See? It's the Virgin Mary. She's cool...she's, like, the Queen of Heaven and stuff. Five bucks."

5

Eli glanced at the bauble with disdain. "This is a new low even for you, Xavier. What'd you do, steal it from a church or something?"

"I didn't *steal* anything, Eli. I found it up at the cathedral cafeteria after the free lunch, okay?" He shook his head. "You've got me all wrong. You think I'm a criminal or something. I'm...I'm a *trickster*, like in the old myths. Wherever I go, strange things happen. Little miracles. Unforeseen circumstances." He made a sweeping theatrical gesture with his arms, nearly hitting an old lady walking the other way down the sidewalk. "Fortuitous meetings!"

"Natural disasters," Eli suggested. He turned into *The Marketplace* café, housed in one of the oldest buildings on Denver's oldest street. With an espresso bar and a deli, nestled into a tree-lined downtown historic district, it served as Eli's daytime headquarters, a home away from home. He cut through the crowd of lunching business people and students nursing coffees, looking for a friend to sit with, an exlover to avoid, any way at all to ditch Xavier.

"I can forgive you for the bad vibes, Eli," Xavier said, still on his heels. "It's hard to lose a reputation in this town. But I need to ask a favor. Can I crash on your couch tonight?"

"Never," said Eli. He stepped up to the espresso bar. The barista was putting the finishing swirl of whipped cream on a cup of hot chocolate. Five fingers reached out, closed around the handle of the mug and picked it up. The fingers were on a hand at the end of an arm attached to a shoulder that belonged to the most beautiful girl Eli had ever seen. Their eyes met just before she turned and walked away. "Never," he stammered, "never have I seen a creature such as this!"

Though she was dressed simply in jeans and a sweater, wore no makeup, and had her long blonde hair back in a modest ponytail, the girl was so beautiful that most all the men in the room turned their heads in unison to watch her go by. She sat down at one of the little round wooden tables in the back, took out a book from her backpack, and looked again in Eli's direction.

"Dude! She's *fine*," raved Xavier. "She's crazy fine, dude!" His eyes bugged and his hands held onto the brim of his sailor's hat as if to keep it from flying off his head. Eli ignored him, staring across the room. The table next to hers was empty. "Three bucks!" Xavier said. "Give her the locket! As, like, a token of your friendship and eternal worship!"

Eli pushed some money over the counter. "A coffee for him too, please," he said, indicating the wayward punk pilgrim with his thumb. He took his own cup, put his mouth to Xavier's ear, whispered "take your coffee and fuck off," and walked toward the back of the café.

The table next to hers was still empty. *Should I sit against the wall?* he thought. *On the opposite side, facing her? Too obvious.* As he approached, she looked up from her book. She looked up at him and smiled, an easy and open smile, her long eyebrows arched hopefully, her bright blue eyes fixed on his. She smiled at him as though he was her guy and she'd arrived early for their usual coffee date, just to see him come bounding in right on time. He smiled back. The empty table was forgotten, all scheming and plotting became impossible, and, as if in a slowmotion trance, Eli took off his coat and sat down at the table with the impossibly beautiful girl.

They stared. For a long time. In her hand was a pen, its tip resting on a page of the book: a journal. She let it drop, closed the book. Eli realized speech would be necessary eventually. "What's your name?" he said.

"Gwen." She offered a hand. He took it.

"Gwen," he echoed, "I'm Eli."

"Hi, Eli."

"Hi."

She let out a laugh, breaking the tension. He laughed too. They shifted in their seats. She lifted her cup to her lips, took a sip, set it back down. He watched her full lips curl back into the devastating smile.

He said, "You're not from here, are you?"

She laughed again. "How did you know?" He shrugged. She pushed a strand of hair back from her face. "I'm from Maine," she said. "I came here to ski! I'm going to live and work in Vail for the winter. I don't start work for a few days so I took a bus down to see what Denver was like. Do you ski?" He shook his head no. "You live in Colorado and you don't ski? I *love* to ski," she said. "I'm working for the resort so I get a free season pass. I ski free all winter. Isn't that great?"

"That's fantastic," he agreed. Actually he had always loathed skiing, ski towns, the whole wealthy, smug ski culture. But for Gwen's sake he was willing to try a more positive attitude.

"What about you?" she asked. Her brow furrowed slightly. "How old are you?"

"Twenty. You?"

Her face relaxed again. "I'm twenty also. You don't believe me!"

He laughed. "Sure I do. Why wouldn't I?"

"People think I'm lying. They think I can't be that old. But I am! It's true."

"I believe you. You look all grown up to me."

"Good," she laughed. Her innocent grin turned a little bit sly. "Where do you live? Here in Denver?"

He nodded. "The milehigh city."

"With your parents?"

"No, I have my own place."

"Cool. You go to school?"

"Yeah, right down the street at City College. Probably do an English major."

"I'm an English major too! So where do your parents live?"

Eli shifted his weight in his seat. He cleared his throat and ran his hands through his hair. He looked past Gwen, over her shoulder to the front door, as though his parents might walk into the café at any moment. "It's a long story," he said. "I'm on my own." He brightened up, with evident effort. "What about you?" he asked, shaking it off. "What's your family like?"

"Just normal," Gwen said. "I can't stand them. But I love 'em. I guess." The gorgeous smile wrinkled into a frown. "My parents are divorced. My dad is a suit. A real estate developer. He couldn't be tied down anymore, so he traded Mom in for a newer model. Disgusting. Then again I can't totally blame him, because Mom is insane. They both think I'm crazy to leave school for a year to come out here." This thought brought the smile back. "Oh, and I have *three* brothers." She rolled her eyes.

"Older or younger?"

"I'm the baby, remember? Can't you tell?"

"You don't seem like a baby to me."

Her fingers rested on the colorful fabric covering the bound journal on the table. Eli dared to reach out and touch the other end, tracing a line around the edge of the cover. "You were writing," he said. "Impressions of your trip?"

"Not exactly." She looked skyward. "Just about...well..." She fixed his gaze. "Just about how everything is relative. Everything! There is no objective reality. You know what I mean?" He loved it. Beauty and brains, and just goofy enough for him to handle. "It's all perception," she continued. "Impressions, thoughts, images. Nothing else. At home I'm surrounded by shiny, happy people living shiny happy lives - until you look a little closer. Then you see everybody is a wreck inside and nobody knows what it's all for. I mean the truth behind things can never really be pinned down, don't you think?"

"Big question. I suppose not."

She nodded, encouraged by his agreement. "Who knows if any of this is really happening?"

"Definitely not. You've come to the right town, we excel at contemplating the void here," Eli deadpanned. They stared for a while and said nothing. If it was just a sensory illusion Eli was seeing, it was a very pleasant one. "Do you have plans for the rest of the day?" he asked. Her eyes widened and she shook her head. His directness took the talk out of her for a moment. "Come with me," he said. She nodded yes, staring, mute.

Before they left, Gwen asked for directions to the restroom. He watched her walk away until she was out of sight.

Xavier pounced immediately, pulling up a chair and sitting too close. "Dude, she's *rad*!" Eli just smiled. "Hey, do you have a cigarette, bro?" Eli shook his head. "Oh right, you don't smoke, what was I thinking? How about your friend you think she has one for me?" This brought an impatient frown. "Okay, all right, I get it." He stared down at the locket necklace still in his hands, rubbing it between his fingers, then looked back up at Eli. "Hey, did you hear? Alexander is in jail, man!"

This got Eli's attention. "Jail? I didn't even know he was back in town."

"Denver City and County jail, out by the airport."

"What for?"

Xavier narrowed his eyes to knowing slits, looked left then right as if making sure no one could overhear. "Don't know."

"Trouble finds him. Or he finds trouble."

"It's a hard world, dude." Xavier tipped his cap. "I gotta go. Have fun with your lady friend!" He bounced away, laughing for no apparent reason, asking strangers for cigarettes on the way out.

So Alexander was back in town, and locked up. Eli should probably go see him. But the thought didn't hold. The café had filled up since he'd sat down with Gwen. She had taken her backpack with her, leaving nothing at the table. Maybe she'd put that backpack over her lovely, slender shoulder and walked right out the back door into the fading November afternoon light. No hard feelings. He would have even admired her style: a clean break, no awkward good-byes, off to her ski slopes and new adventures. He would forget her soon enough. But if she did come back to him, he knew, everything would change.

Chapter 3

IN NO HURRY

She did return. On a whim Eli suggested they go to Denver's art museum. "Not one of your world's great museums but a lot of cool Indian stuff." He congratulated himself on the tactical genius of the invitation. The longish walk to the museum would give them time to talk and get acquainted. The art could foster an open, creative, spontaneous mood between them. And the museum was in the same general direction as his apartment.

She liked the idea, and they walked down the long pedestrian mall that formed the backbone of downtown. A free shuttle ran the dozen blocks from end to end but Gwen preferred to walk, saying "We're in no hurry." So they strolled through the town. These were the worst years of Denver's infamous brown cloud of air pollution, and the light of the setting sun through the haze had a way of making the present moment look like a wistful memory or a fading photograph. In front of boardedup storefronts, newsstand headlines claimed a new recession had just hit. When did the last one end? Eli and Gwen passed through waves of bodies: wellscrubbed yuppie commuters, swaggering bboys with pants sagging low, defeated urban elderly, wheelchair convoys, waddling overweight tourists, babyfaced skate punks. Was he ever a skater? she wanted to know. Never, he swore it. "Good!" she said, shaking a finger at him in mock rebuke.

Eli found it impossible not to notice all the heads turning for his new friend. She didn't seem to notice at all. He pointed out some of the more distinctive regular street characters, like the Vietnam vet street preacher - a short, stocky guy who wore the same red Marine Corps jacket, camouflage cap and pants and black military boots every day. He alternated hellfireandbrimstone demands for repentance with frothing tirades against homosexuality, rock and rap music, and Communism, all in the same

11

angry bulldog voice. He'd been preaching on the mall for years. Hadn't anyone bothered to tell him the Cold War was over?

"I went up to him one day," Eli said to Gwen as they passed him on the street. "He had his camouflage cap on real low on his forehead, just raving away, and I said, 'Where do you guys get all this stuff about a wrathful God? Jesus Christ was the first nonviolent revolutionary.' It must have hit some kind of nerve, because his eyes totally bugged out, he was shaking, he obviously wanted to kill me right on the spot. But instead he started yelling, 'I don't listen to Satan! I don't listen to Satan!'" Eli leaned close to Gwen's ear. "Turns out I'm Satan," he whispered in a conspiratorial tone. She laughed.

They cut through a run-down park between large government buildings. Eli waved away kids selling dime bags of weed. The last sun glittered on the gold dome of the state Capitol building to their left; on their right, crews were already setting up a gaudy life-size plastic Nativity display on the steps of City Hall. The art museum loomed ahead like a surrealist fairy tale castle; asymmetrical narrow slit windows in gray Dada Disney towers watched their approach with interest. A punk-rock girl with a shaved head, nose ring, and big chest stomped towards them across the dead grass in black Doc Martin boots. As she passed, she looked Gwen up and down, licking her lips. She grinned a wicked congratulation at Eli. He tried not to look at her tits, but the words on her tight-fitting t-shirt insisted on being read: *Love Kills*.

As they entered the museum and Eli paid their admissions, he stole a lingering glance at Gwen. She had taken a huge leap of faith by following him through the streets of a strange city. What did she see in him?

They rode an elevator to the Native American exhibit on the fifth floor. Stepping from the elevator, they were met by a tall glass case alone in the middle of the gallery floor containing a long white ceremonial robe, hung as if draped over the invisible body of a serene holy man. Spotlights bathed it in an other-worldly glow. The two of them stood silently beneath the ghostly outstretched arms. It was as though the disembodied priest had been waiting for them, over centuries of ritual time, to join them in a strange, improvised ceremony.

"I think I have goosebumps," Gwen said. Eli laughed. She looked up at him, her fresh red lipstick pursed into a wry smile. "I can see your thought bubbles," she said.

"You can see my what?"

"Thought bubbles!" She traced an irregular cloud above him with her finger. "The thought bubbles over your head. Like in the cartoons. I can read your mind. I know what you're thinking."

"Is that right? That's a very impressive talent you have, Gwen! So what *am* I thinking?" he asked.

She laughed and shoved him away with both hands.

They shuffled through the exhibit together and apart. The floor was practically deserted; they had the gallery to themselves.

When she drew to his side again, he fought the urge to stroke her hair, hold her hand, kiss her. Common sense and restraint were breaking down; time was slipping off the track. Soon words would start coming out of his mouth that he wouldn't be able to control. Unable to face each other, they stared at an elaborate beaded horse dressing marked with stars and flowers and suns. "I like it," she said.

"I like you, Gwen," he said.

She blushed majestically, turned away and walked to the next display, biting her lip. He turned and tried to look at some paintings. His heart pounded. There was nothing else to be done. He turned back to see where she'd gone. She was standing still in the middle of the gallery, holding her coat in her arms with her long blonde hair illuminated from behind by spotlight, head cocked a little to the side, looking at him. Just looking at him, waiting. He walked to her. She froze, her gaze dropped to the floor. He stopped in front of her and with a finger under her chin, gently tilted her face up to him. She looked up, eyes searching. He pulled her to him by the waist and kissed her.

Chapter 4

THE TELEGRAM

Eli lived in Capitol Hill, a neighborhood of students and artists and yuppies and urban poor all jumbled together, just south and east of downtown. He walked Gwen home past used book stores and record stores, decaying Victorian houses spilt into little apartments, and elegant, well-kept turn-of-the-century mansions glowing like giant Japanese lanterns in the gathering darkness.

Eli had a corner studio in a 1930s red brick apartment building. It had white walls, hardwood floors and lots of windows. A futon on the floor, snug with Indian blankets and Midwestern patchwork quilts, shared a wall with a stereo and a sprawling LP record collection. Eli sat down in a big brooding red stuffed reading chair to take off his boots as Gwen shuffled around looking at his things. A meditating Buddha hung on a print over the bed; a reproduction of a Matisse painting was on the wall behind the stuffed chair, its circle of faceless nudes joining hands to levitate into the air in the blue room of the painter's imagination. On a frayed and tattered black and white poster, Lakota prophet Black Elk stood over the rim of a canyon, arms raised to the sky, offering prayers to the void. The *White Album*-era Beatles solemnly watched over the scene from their separate 8x10's, arranged in Eli's carefully considered order of preference: John, George, Paul, Ringo. Among ferns along the windowsill sat a halfdozen Mexican prayer candles, the tall glass cylinder kind, with pictures of saints on the front and prayers in Spanish and English across the back. Eli lit them one by one with matches from an American flag matchbook. "Make yourself at home," he said.

"I think I like it," Gwen said. "I like it here." Eli smiled and went to the kitchen. But when he brought out two cups of steaming hot tea, Gwen was sitting at the edge of the couch, coat still zipped up, backpack on her lap, looking like she was getting ready to leave instead of having just arrived. Eli stopped in the doorway, a cup in each hand. John Coltrane rumbled soulfully from the oversized speakers. "Listen, I know this all must seem incredibly random," Eli said. "I didn't mean to cajole you into coming over here if you didn't want to…"

"No!" She looked herself over and laughed. "I'm sorry. I'm acting like a baby." She set the bag aside but left her coat on. "I know I'm being a freak. I'll be okay in a minute."

He handed her a teacup and sat down. "I like freaks," he said, and kissed her, just a heartbeat longer than in the museum. They held hands and stared. They kissed some more. After a while Gwen took off her coat.

Love was in the room. It descended upon them in the café with a muffled thunderclap. It walked with them through the streets and the crowds and into the museum, darting here and there amongst the relics. Love ushered them home through the dusk and made them forget they were strangers. Now it filled the little apartment to bursting, throbbing in the music and in their touch.

But love is not a solitary emotion. It draws every other human emotion to itself, fires every synapse, releases every memory. All manner of hidden things rise up out of darkness to meet it. Wherever it goes it brings along a legion of attendant emotions, bickering and quarrelling among themselves; love summons all of its anteced-ents and opposites and offspring, without which it cannot exist.

The lights went out. They tumbled onto the bed in a state of advanced liplock. Everything Eli wanted, everything he needed, was now in Gwen's face, in the weight of her body next to his. His memory didn't suggest an unfavorable comparison with a past lover. His heart didn't slink away into shadows, leaving his body to advance alone, as it had so many times before. Everything in him said yes, yes, yes.

Eli felt Gwen's body unclench with a sigh. He eased her back unto the futon. Hands roamed. Buttons were loosed, zippers unzipped. A pile of clothes grew at the foot of the bed. U2's *Achtung Baby* churned and moaned on the stereo. How far would it go? Candlelight flickered and blazed, flashing frantic kabuki theater silhouettes on the dark walls. Eli tugged on the top button of Gwen's jeans.

All of a sudden she went cold all over. It was impossible to miss. Her limbs stiffened and the breath tightened in her chest. She clenched Eli's hands at the wrists. "Please stop," she said. He stopped.

"What's wrong?"

"I think I have a problem," she said.

"That's okay." He looked into her eyes, trying to catch a glimpse, but they were unfocused, glazed, wouldn't meet his. He brushed the hair back from her forehead. A cloud came over her face. Eli became aware that he was lying on top of her, pinning her flat. Something told him to roll off. "Do you want to talk about it?"

"I don't know…no. I just have a problem."

He lifted her hand to his lips and kissed her fingertips. "It's okay. We don't have to do anything. I'm just glad you're here."

"Me too."

Gwen asked for a glass of water and Eli brought it from the kitchen. She was visibly shaken, brow furrowed, eyes shut. He just wanted to hold her, to gather her up to himself and make it better, but he felt her shudder at his touch. He held on, gently, but she was in the grip of another embrace. Something – maybe the strange synchronicity of the day - had carried Gwen over an invisible barrier, further and further inside herself, to a hidden, troubled realm. Already Eli was imagining the worst.

Slowly, she began to speak from her darkened state. "All my life…all my life, people…*men*…have wanted something from me." She shook her head. "Even when I was little…just a little girl. Is that right?"

He saw the leering eyes in his mind. "No. No it isn't."

"I remember, in first grade…every day after school the boys would catch me… they held me down on the sidewalk…" She was choking back tears. "They wouldn't let me up!" Over the next few hours, in stammered, broken phrases, in a voice clenched tight as a fist, a young woman told the terrors of a girl's life. The litany went on, jumping from year to year; disconnected memories, a story with no plot but a very definite theme: endless harassment, pursuit, irresistible force. Eli's eyes never wandered from her face, but after a while his mind lost focus on her words. He heard only their tone, their slow halting rhythm, a lamenting music that pierced him to the core, a dirge as old as the world. He knew what she was going to say.

Time blurred. He ventured a glance at the clock and saw it was past midnight. He'd known her less than half a day and already he could hardly remember who he'd been, what he'd felt or thought about before they met. Now here she lay in his bed, writhing in the secret pains of her soul. He sat with her, offering and withdrawing his hand - sensing now a want of comfort, then a certainty that any touch would be violation.

Suddenly Gwen sat up and opened her eyes, her spell past. "I think I was raped," she said. It was news to her, as shocking as if she'd just been handed a telegram in an old-fashioned movie. "I was raped." She looked at Eli with a start, like she'd forgotten he was in the room.

———

Gwen spent the night. She said she didn't remember anything about the rape. Nothing. Not who or where or when. She only knew that it had happened. Had she talked about this with anyone else? "No one. No one knows but you." Eli didn't press for information. Gwen slept with her clothes on, even her thick sweater. Eli wore boxer shorts. He whispered every assurance he could think of. He would never pressure her for anything. He only wanted to make her feel safe and happy. He would support and help her any way he could. Anything he could give, anything he could do, she only had to ask. She listened to all this in silence, blinking bleary eyes reflecting faint fluorescent streetlight through the window, clinging to him trembling, burying her face in his broad chest. Then turning away, out of his embrace, really afraid of his arms.

Chapter 5

WHO ARE YOU?

They awoke late in the morning to pale sunlight streaming through the windows. It was a new morning, a different world than the one they'd woken to separately the day before. Gwen was okay. They were together. They had survived the night.

No mention was made of the night's shocking revelation. Bringing Gwen breakfast in bed earned a smile. While Eli took a shower, she poked around the apartment, thumbing through his CDs and LP records, perusing his bookshelves, looking at his things and acquainting herself with his world. "You have a lot of Kerouac," she called to him from where she was crouched with a pile of books.

"You like him?"

"Oh yeah. *Dharma Bums* was my favorite. Do you like Allen Ginsberg?"

Eli grinned to himself in the bathroom. She was too perfect. "Of course."

"I read his poem 'Fuck Me, Jack,' in high school English class. I think my teacher had a heart attack. I was wearing my cheerleader uniform that day. Can you believe I was a cheerleader?"

"Actually, I think I can," Eli said as he dried off from the shower. When he emerged from the bathroom shirtless in his jeans, drying his hair with a towel, he found her standing by his desk holding a sheet of construction paper with a newspaper article pasted to it.

"Oh my god!" she said. "Is this you? It *is* you!"

He laughed. "It's me. This past summer." A blackandwhite photo showed Eli in shorts and a rain parka slumped against a NO PARKING sign, looking dazed, and an equally disheveled girl sitting on the curb next to him. The headline read SEVEN SURVIVE LIGHTNING STRIKE IN WASHINGTON PARK. "My summer job. The office director pasted that up and gave it to me. Don't I look like hell? like I just sat through seven consecutive Metallica concerts or something."

He put his arms around Gwen's waist and nibbled on her ear while she read the article. It revealed that Eli had been working for an environmental group called Green Future, leading a crew of door-todoor fundraisers on a campaign against toxic chemicals. Clouds rolled in as the crew stopped to eat lunch in the park, but there was no rain. Suddenly, a bolt from heaven. It struck the tree they sat under, burned down its bark and then around the circle of seated bodies, sending Eli, his crew of eco-warriors, and their clipboards full of petitions flying. Then came the downpour of rain. No one was seriously hurt.

Gwen laughed incredulously. "Oh my God. You were struck by lightning. I've never met anyone who was struck by lightning before." She put the article down and turned to face him, suddenly serious, staring deep into his eyes, searching. "In fact, I've never met anyone like you at all." She reached out a tremulous hand and spread her fingers against his chest, over his heart. Desire, wonder and fear mingled in her face. "Who are you?" she asked.

For the first time in his life he had an answer to that question. "Someone who cares about you very much," he said. She fell into his arms, releasing the heavenly weight of her body into his.

Chapter 6

SCARRED FOR LIFE

They walked to a hip vegetarian restaurant in the neighborhood for breakfast. Eli had thought there was something of the sheltered rich kid about Gwen, a suspicion that was confirmed as they walked through the city. She stared, truly shocked and perplexed, at the ragged homeless people who were commonplace to Eli. They took an alley shortcut, stopping to look at a graffiti mural of Jack Kerouac.

"Those eyebrows," Eli said. "So involved in the troubles of the world."

"I've never been in an alley before," said Gwen. "So, this is like, your neighborhood, huh?"

"Yep. I'm what a princess like you would call a 'townie.'"

"Shut up!" she said, and punched him hard in the shoulder.

He laughed.

"So, are you, like, a tough guy?" she asked.

He shrugged and smiled, then self-consciously straightened up his gangly six feet. "Who, me? Nah. I'll look out for the people I love, though."

She kissed him, arms wrapped around his neck. "You think you're the new Jack Kerouac or something, don't you?"

"This was his 'hood once," Eli said, pulling her close to him. "Now it's ours."

During breakfast they stared at each other like crazy people. The width of the table between them seemed cruel. Their conversation was slow and disjointed, as in a dream. It was the dream of being twenty years old and having breakfast for the first time with your true love. Eli's fork found his plate through the mist; Gwen only picked at her food.

Eli took her to his favorite used record store on the way home. He tugged her by the arm to cross the street so they wouldn't have to walk past the porno shop.

Inside the record store, Latin jazz boomed from the speakers. Shelves and stacks were crowded with records; CDs and cassettes filled the shop to bursting. Posters of classic rock legends and flyers advertising underground local shows papered the walls under dingy yellow lights. The old bearded beatnik who ran the place peered over the lenses of his glasses to watch Gwen walk past. She pulled a Jane's Addiction record out of the bins as Eli thumbed through the blues section. "Do you like them?" she asked Eli, holding up the Jane's record.

"Love 'em."

"Even though they're transvestite drug addicts?"

Eli laughed. "Especially because. First time I saw them live, Perry Farrell stuck a tampon up his ass during the spoken-word break in *Pigs in Zen*. I'm scarred for life."

It was Gwen's turn to laugh. "Me too. Vicariously scarred. I think I like them even more now that you've told me that."

Back at Eli's apartment, cold winds began rattling the windows as the afternoon expired. Gwen curled up on the couch, brushing out her long blonde hair. She made no sign of leaving. "Can you stay the night?" Eli asked. She nodded and smiled. "Can you entertain yourself for a little while? I know this is going to sound strange, but I have to go see my friend in jail." Gwen just kept slowly, rhythmically brushing her hair and staring at him with her big blue eyes. "Just before we met, I ran into a mutual friend who told me he was there," Eli said. "He didn't do anything really bad. Probably. Maybe he ran out on a cab again like last time."

Jail. Gwen had probably never known anyone who'd been in jail, let alone visited one herself. Neither had Eli, until he met Alexander. But she made no protest and told him she could keep herself company while he was gone. After the last twenty-four hours, nothing seemed strange anymore.

Chapter 7

THE MUDDY RIVER

The jail was two bus rides away, out by the airport, and Eli had time to think. His mind wandered back to how he'd met Alexander, the singer of his friend Brandon's band, The Naked Way, as he stared out the window of the rumbling bus and watched the city go by.

Brandon's dad worked for an international firm that kept his family on the move throughout his childhood. When his dad was transferred to Denver, Brandon wound up being the new kid at Eli's high school at the beginning of senior year. Brandon was handsome with angular features, expressive brown eyes and bleached out hair. Eli commented on his rare R.E.M. t-shirt in their AP English class on the first day of school, and they became fast friends.

Eli was the established brainy bad boy of the class — the kid who wrote brilliant English papers, aced Ancient History exams that gave everyone else nightmares, and never met a classroom debate he didn't like, but who ditched class to smoke weed and get blowjobs in the parking lot at every chance, who chased freshman girls and drank until he blacked out at house parties every weekend, who made himself a legend of argument, contradiction, trouble, rebellion and fun at every turn.

Brandon had a winning shy smile, listened more than he talked, and became part of Eli's crew of hard-partying popular kids. Instead of doing their homework, they read Kerouac and Henry Miller and mythologized their own bumbling adventures, sexual exploits and hard-partying epiphanies as if they came from the pages of classic literature.

They bonded over music. Brandon played guitar and drums; Eli's head rang with music at all hours of the day, but he couldn't play more than a few chords. Eli, who grew up on 60s rock and electric Chicago Blues, turned Brandon on to the majesty of

23

Led Zeppelin over joints in his blue station wagon in the school parking lot. Brandon led Eli deeper into 'alternative rock,' past R.E.M. and U2 to bands like Pylon, Drivin' & Cryin', and Mary My Hope. They rocked out to Guns and Roses. For Eli, it was a guilty pleasure; Brandon had grown up loving KISS-style glam-rock and saw nothing ironic about Axl and Slash's act. When friends told them The Cult was the greatest hard rock band in the land, they snickered and told them to look up Jane's Addiction. They ate mushrooms and went to see the moody Cowboy Junkies sing *Sweet Jane*. They consoled one another when R.E.M. released *Green*; the band's betrayal of jingle-jangle mysticism for shrill plastic pop seemed like the end of innocence. 'Alternative Rock' would soon become just another category of corporate music - but not yet, not quite yet.

When they finished high school – for Eli, more of a tumbling out the other end than a graduation – they stayed in the city while most of their friends went away to college. Eli got an apartment. The Berlin Wall fell and the Cold War ended; anything seemed possible. Eli took classes in Zen Buddhism, but found his unquiet mind wasn't ready for the meditation mat. Brandon played drums for a classic rock cover band with guys twice his age, sneaking in back doors of bars and clubs to play despite being underaged. They both took classes at the city college, where Eli joined liberal activist groups and neglected his studies once again. Brandon got a job in the kitchen of an all-night café called *The Muddy River*, which became the hub of their night life.

Located in a run-down industrial area on the outskirts of downtown, *The Muddy River* looked from the outside like an old abandoned warehouse. On the inside, gloom gathered to the two-story ceiling above tables lit by candles and feeble old lamps. Goth kids built little bonfires in their ashtrays. Beautiful middle-class high school girls from the suburbs, with hair and make-up just so, drank cappuccinos and smoked clove cigarettes and flirted with the rough-around-the-edges city boys. Punk rock city girls sneered at their suburban counterparts. Old hippies reeled in anyone they could to hear their tales of beatnik glory. Mohawked punk-rockers and anarchists nursed coffees for hours, laughing at the waitress' glares. A few young women in their mid-twenties ruled the roost, running the place from an elevated espresso bar, serving half as managers, half as den mothers to the motley assortment of orphans and misfits. An upstairs loft held a used bookstore and a secluded carpeted nook where confessions and cigarettes and kisses were exchanged. Perversely nostalgic muzak from an AM radio oldies station murmured in the background. The street gypsy Xavier squatted like a gargoyle on the steps to the loft, scanning the crowd for a friend with money to lend or a joint to share.

Most nights Eli and Bobby held down a booth. Eli fanned away Bobby's prolific cigarette smoke as they argued good-naturedly about books and philosophy. Bobby was a year older than Eli and Brandon. He cut meat in the butcher department of the grocery store where Eli and Brandon had worked after school as seniors. Bobby was short and wiry and fidgeted constantly as he talked, brushing curly sandy-brown hair out his eyes. His fidgets had fidgets. He'd recently been in rehab, but promptly fell off the wagon and drank and partied as freely as ever. He poured whiskey from a flask into his coffee, barely bothering to conceal it in the bohemian café.

Eli and Bobby paid court to the "Feminist Committee," as Bobby called them — Camille and Bethany. Eli first knew Camille as his downstairs neighbor in the Capitol Hill apartment building where he lived. Camille was a walking firestorm of indignant outrage — an outspoken feminist, anti-capitalist and environmentalist. She mimicked Sinéad O'Connor's militant look by shaving her blond hair down to stubble. The aqua-green scarf she wrapped around her skull matched her eyes. She denounced 'The Patriarchy' at every turn, seeing its vast conspiracy behind every injustice, large or small. A blue-green Planet Earth was tattooed on her shoulder with the inscription: *Love Your Mother*. If her dad would just release her trust fund, she vowed, she would go live in a tree with Earth First radicals defending ancient redwood forests from clear-cutting in Northern California. Or else follow the band Skinny Puppy on tour. One or the other.

Bethany was a statuesque brunette who went to an exclusive private college. Bobby had met her in rehab. She came downtown on weekends sometimes to hear his confessions and his drunken visions, to lean in close and tell him to clean up and come back to a twelve-step meeting. He'd read to her from Bukowski and she'd laugh. He'd read to her from Dostoevsky and she'd sigh. But she never went home with him at closing time.

Bethany befriended Camille at *The Muddy River*, and was often to be found at her right hand, nodding in affirmation of her rants. Visually, they made an odd pair: Bethany, articulate but stiff and soft-spoken, prim in suburban sweaters and designer jeans; Camille, pounding the table in worn-out overalls with punk rock t-shirts and black combat boots. Camille made grandiose proclamations about art, culture and politics, delivered with self-deprecating laughter that was not to be confused with license to disagree. "*Do the Right Thing* is the most important movie in the history of film! May *Birth of a Nation* rot in its grave! *Gone With the Wind* right next to it! Fucking racist patriarchal propaganda!" Bobby sometimes tried to make the case to the Committee for why he and Eli were Good Men and Not Like the Others. Eli avoided the trap, and let Bobby dig himself deeper. "You don't read women authors, do you?" demanded Camille.

Bobby, the most voracious reader any of them knew, searched his memory. "I loved Judy Blume as a kid," he offered with a shrug.

Camille scoffed and shook her head. "That doesn't count!"

Eli pretended to pick up a phone and put it to his ear. "Are you there, God?" he asked. "It's me, Bobby. Camille is about to kick my ass, get me out of here!"

For all her man-bashing and gender identity angst, Camille was an avid, practicing heterosexual. Eli noticed a series of boys, each scruffier and hipper and sadder-looking than the last, coming and going from her apartment. They were broken, lost boys who she tried to fix. The sisterhood only went so far. "I tried licking pussy once," she admitted once in an unguarded moment. "It wasn't for me."

"Maybe you just need to find the right flavor," Eli teased. "Keep trying. It's too good to give up so easily. Nobody likes a quitter!" They laughed like brother and sister.

One night the four of them shared a table, smoking and talking while a dread-locked Jamaican singer with an acoustic guitar performed on the café's tiny stage. Eli was trying to lend Bobby an introductory Buddhist text for the umpteenth time; Bobby insisted he had already conquered the topic by reading Hermann Hesse's *Siddhartha*. "Bobby, you can't learn Buddhism from a fucking German!" Eli exclaimed to general laughter. "The first thing he does in that book is split the Buddha in two — no! Buddha taught that suffering comes from the illusion of separation. All one! Get it?" He appealed to Camille and Bethany for support with a look.

"Eli, only Mother Earth can make us whole," said Camille. "As far as I'm concerned, Buddha, Yahweh, Zeus, Ronald Reagan...they're all just disguises for the patriarchal Santa Claus father-god." Bethany nodded earnestly.

Eli laughed and threw his hands up in exasperation. "What if it's not all about sex, what if it's not all about gender conflict? What if..."

"Wait," Bobby said. "That's him."

"Who?" Eli asked. "The patriarchal Santa Claus father-god?"

"No, more like the fucking opposite, in the flesh. The singer in Brandon's new band. Alexander." Eli caught sight of a long, tall figure walking to the back of the café just before he passed out of sight.

"Brandon has a new band?"

Bobby nodded and fidgeted with a lighter, trying to spark a smoke. "He's playing drums. Said a guy he works with in the kitchen plays guitar. Says he's incredible."

Eli watched the door to the kitchen. Brandon came out, tossing an apron into a hamper. He looked different than in high school; he'd buzzed off his surfer-boy hair and started doing a ridiculous number of push-ups every morning. His face had developed a new hardness to match his body. A few guys followed him out of the kitchen over to the friends' table. Brandon introduced them as they pulled up chairs.

A kid with dark floppy hair, Chuck Taylor tennis shoes, ripped cargo pants and a Ramones t-shirt nodded. "I'm Ear Wax," he said. "I play bass."

Bobby laughed out loud. "Ear Wax?"

"Yeah. Like, too poor for q-tips. I grew up, like, punk rock, all the way."

A stocky shorter guy stood beside his chair, pulling a off a cook's hairnet and shaking out his long, straight brown hair. Muscles rippled as he replaced the hairnet with a Japanese silk headband. He reached out to shake hands. "I'm Marco. Just got to town a few weeks ago. God told me to move here, he didn't say why."

"To start a band with me, mother fucker!" It was Alexander. He was beautiful, with a chiseled, noble face and wavy blond hair past his shoulders. His body was lean and lithe, a head taller than Eli's six feet. He was all bohemian glamour, shirt-less with beaded necklaces under a long black leather thrift store coat, smelling of patchouli oil. He carried himself like an actor on a stage - graceful like a prince, supple like a cat. One moment his big brown eyes radiated love, narrowed into judgment and contempt, then exploded into generous mirth, before settling back into mocking irony. He made an exaggerated bow to the Feminist Committee. Bethany squeaked out a "hello." Camille rolled her eyes. But Eli noticed her cheeks flushed red.

The singer shook hands with Bobby, then turned to Eli. "Let me guess...*Eli*." He stretched the name out with a mixture of curiosity and mockery. "Brandon tells me you're quite the scholar. Of history, literature, music, politics...and vagina."

"Guilty as charged, sir."

"Well, why don't you share your accumulated wisdom with us, young master Eli? Your thesis statement on the fairer sex, perhaps. Please, enlighten us about the deeper mysteries of woman-kind."

Eli ignored the mocking tone and played along. He stood up and cleared his throat theatrically.

Bobby laughed. "Oh, this'll be good!" He clinked a spoon on his water glass to get the rest of the table's attention.

"Gentlemen…and ladies," began Eli, "the female orgasm is the highest purpose and organizing principle of all creation." Hoots and howls rose from all sides, but he waved them away. "I'm serious! The female orgasm raises the sun in the morning and puts it to bed at night; it makes the grass grow and the birds sing and the flowers bloom. It hangs the moon and the stars in the night sky. It expresses our highest aspirations and heals our deepest wounds. Take care of the clitorises in your life, dear friends, and everything else will fall into place. The female orgasm is the crowning achievement of 10,000 years of human civilization. *That*," he said, looking at Alexander, "is the sum total of any wisdom I've gained in my years of study and contemplation."

He sat down to laughter and snorts. The Feminist Committee applauded earnestly. Camille laughed and squeezed Eli and purred and rubbed her bald head against his shoulder. Ear Wax pounded the table and whistled, until Marco shot him a withering look. "Ah – *ahem* – very good," Ear Wax said sheepishly.

"Hippie carpet-muncher," Marco grumbled.

Alexander slow-clapped. "Bravo, young master Eli!" he said. "Well played! Another convert to the vagina cult!" His grin was wry and inscrutable. He leaned in close and put his arm around Eli's shoulder. "Brandon wants you to love our music," he said in a quiet aside. "Your approval is important to him."

"I'm sure I'll love it. What's it like? Who are your influences?"

Xavier had been watching from his perch, and now pulled up a chair into the circle. "Hey, were you guys talking about *orgasms?*" he asked excitedly.

Alexander ignored him. "Influences? Do we even have a name yet?" he roared to his bandmates.

"The Four Horse Cocks of the Apocalypse!" replied Marco.

"You see, Marco is a good Christian boy," Alexander said, "quick with the biblical references. Our influences? Super-8 porno movies from the seventies. Serial killers. Televangelists. The French Revolution. Vampires."

Eli laughed incredulously. "Vampire rock?"

"Yes my boy! You know how many books Anne Rice has sold? I have a theory - in the future, American pop culture media will be dominated by vampires. That's how degenerate and polymorphously perverse our society is becoming. Blood sacrifice is the only thing America really understands. It's 1990 now…in 20 years, fourteen year old girls will be creaming for vampires, mark my words. Books, TV shows, movies, lunchboxes. Vampires will be the new rock stars, the ultimate pop celebrities."

Xavier nodded, eyes wide in wonder and awe at the prophet's vision. "Yeah man!" he said. The Feminist Committee scoffed in unison.

Alexander paid them no mind. "I'm serious, Eli. The human mind craves what it can't have. The thrill of the forbidden. You've read your Freud, haven't you lad? Super Ego versus Id! It's a twenty-four hour battle, every fucking day. Underneath it all, we're all just naughty who children who want to break the rules, aren't we? Let's give the people what they want, Eli. We're letting the monster out of the crypt. The Stones said it twenty years ago: rape, murder — just a shot away!"

"Rape, murder?" Eli echoed. "I don't believe that's what people really want."

"No?" The singer cocked his head sarcastically. "What do they want, professor?"

"They want love! They want to get healed. They need a hug. Even Bobby here, he just won't admit it." Bobby laughed. "You need a hug, Alexander?" Eli asked.

"Depends." Alexander turned away from him and locked eyes with Bethany. "Depends what you mean by *hug*," he said with a leer, stretching the word out somehow into a profanity. Bethany was stone-faced but didn't turn away. Alexander looked back to Eli; the leer slowly transformed into a mad, joyous grin as he spoke. "You're right, Eli. People want a hug. They need to get healed. We're going to purge the devil out of their hearts. We're going to touch people where they really live. We're going to act out everything people keep bottled up in darkness in the depths of their souls. We're gonna rock the fucking skeletons out of the closet! Lust. Disgust. Danger! Blessed incest…"

"SHUT THE FUCK UP." Bethany had risen to her feet and was leaning over the table pointing a finger in Alexander's face. "You fucking asshole! Shut your fucking mouth! You have no right…You have no right to throw that word around…" She was red and stiff with rage. The room went silent and still; all eyes were on Bethany. Her face was inches from Alexander's. He slowly lifted two fingertips to his lips, kissed them, and put them to Bethany's painted, trembling mouth. She slapped his hand away, grabbed her things and stormed out the front door.

Alexander shrugged back into his chair. "What's with the valley girl?" he asked no one in particular. "Up both your holes, Princess!" he hollered over his shoulder.

Xavier stood up to follow Bethany out the door; his tattered, second-hand cowboy hat fell off his head. Eli grabbed him by the arm as he leaned over to pick it up. "Maybe...maybe she needs someone to talk to," Xavier stammered. Eli frowned and shook his head. Xavier slowly sat down.

"Show's over, folks," Bobby said. "Nothing to see here." He passed around his flask of whiskey. The reggae singer started back up and the buzz of normal conversation in the room resumed. Everyone poured a little whiskey into their coffee except Alexander, who drank right from the bottle. "Drink up, calm everybody down a little," said Bobby. His twitch flared and his soft hurt brown eyes bulged and winked. "You really have a way with people," he said laughing to the singer.

"Must have hit her pretty close to the mark to get her all riled up like that, huh kid?" said Alexander.

Eli slid over to the chair Bethany had vacated, next to Camille. He expected Camille to explode at Alexander, but she was oddly calm. She leaned in and whispered to Eli. "See Cleopatra over there? With the kid?" Eli saw a beautiful buxom young woman in Egyptian-style goth make-up and long, jet-black hair worn up, tied and adorned with elaborate braids and jewels. She held a blonde infant wrapped tight in a white blanket against her breast. Her pin-up calendar cleavage heaved as she rocked the baby back and forth. Her eyes locked onto Eli's. "Babylonia, she calls herself," Camille said.

"Babylonia? What is she, Prince's back-up singer?"

Camille nodded at Alexander, who smirked at them from across the table. "His ex," she said quietly. "Like Babylon, capitol of sin and vice. Thinks she's goddess of the goth girls, or queen of the damned, or something. Just another stupid bitch from the 'burbs, really," said Camille with a sneer. "Her real name is Marcy or something. That's Alexander's baby she's holding."

"No way."

"Serious. They fell in love, it was magical, they fought, he knocked her up, they fought some more, the police came. Now they just stalk each other from a distance until the restraining orders expire."

"You know Alexander pretty well?"

Camille's rosy cheeks turned a little rosier. "I know him." She pulled out her pack of Marlboro Reds and lit one. "Bobby! Whiskey? Please?" Bobby passed her the flask and she poured a stiff shot in her coffee cup. "I'm the one who brought him to town. We met at a party after a show in Seattle. He stole my heart and said he'd love me forever. Lived with me for six months. Until he left me for the hooker of the Nile over there, right before you moved into the building. Later he told me he'd been fucking her all along, since the day after he got to town. He picked her up while he was buying cigarettes at the 7-11 down the block. Gave her a bun in the oven pronto. Isn't that romantic? She looked almost ready to bust by the time he finally left me. And when the baby came, she named him Morrison. Just to fuck with Alexander."

"Huh? I don't get it."

"Jim Morrison. The Doors. He fucking worships Jim Morrison. His whole act is based on him. Alexander isn't his real name either. He's got the Alexander the Great haircut, just like Jim Morrison. Haven't you read *No One Here Gets Out Alive?*" She raised her voice enough for Alexander to hear. "The fucker isn't original enough to come up with his own shit. I told him he's a *hotel lounge singer fucking Elvis impersonator!*"

"Oh, burn!" said Xavier, jaw agape.

Alexander snickered and blew Camille a kiss. "Just a little homage, darling Earth Mother. That reminds me, when do I get my notebooks back? I need those lyrics and poems."

"When hell freezes over." Camille turned back to Eli. "He's a slut. Lucky thing the only STD's he gave me were curable. Now he's a got new woman…poor thing."

"Hi guys!" A perky, cute brunette with long, curly hair wrapped herself around the singer from behind; her southern accent made "hi" come out as an elongated *ha*. She wore a form-fitting black business dress and clutched a day timer in her hand.

Alexander stood up to introduce her with an exaggerated bow. "Ladies and gentlemen, this is my love, Amelia. She hails from the lovely white supremacist republic of Texas…"

"Hey!" she protested with a playful shove.

"She'll be in charge of fulfilling all my personal needs, wants and desires…" Amelia rolled her eyes but her grin betrayed pure pleasure. "She'll also be managing our band. What are we calling ourselves, boys? The Mighty Phalluses?"

"The Donkey Kong Giant Dongs!" offered Marco.

"Ear Wax and the Three Dwarves!" chuckled the bass player, wiping chocolate milkshake from his lips.

Brandon realized everyone was waiting on him for a quip. His eyes narrowed. "I guess Led Zeppelin is already taken?" he said.

"I have a better idea," said Alexander, pulling Amelia into his lap. "We'll give my little tart here a microphone too – we'll call the band *The Sid and Nancy Experience.* Right, darling?"

She squealed with mock-terror and pounded her fists on his chest as he picked her up in his arms, swinging her around and biting her neck. "No hickeys!" she shrieked. He dumped her roughly in his chair, pulled out a pair of dark wraparound shades from his jacket, and clambered up onto the table, sending coffee cups clattering to the floor.

"Get the fuck down from there!" shouted a red-headed manager from behind the espresso bar.

"Asshole! You're gonna get me fired!" growled Marco.

Alexander paid them no mind. He threw his head back and began to sing.

"Can we dream

in my wonderland?"

His voice was rich and sweet, and showed much more tenderness than Eli would have expected.

"cry happy and smile for the love we had

looking through our madness beyond good and bad"

For the second time that night, Alexander hushed the whole *Muddy River*. He spread his arms as his voice climbed and filled the room.

broken hearts overripe, we'll fly another night..."

...as suddenly as he'd begun, Alexander quit the a capella performance at its yearning peak, the sweet voice giving way to maniacal laughter. He jumped off the table. Marco got out of his chair and grabbed his singer by the collar, berating him for making a scene. Over their shoulders, Eli saw Babylonia pack up her things and leave out a side door with her child in her arms; he watched her heart-shaped bottom swish back and forth until the door closed behind her. Camille blew smoke at Alexander and Marco as they stood arguing. Marco's face was red and the veins bulged out on his neck as he poked his finger into the taller man's chest. Alexander took off the shades and pulled Marco into a bear hug. He winked at Camille and Eli as Marco struggled to escape his embrace.

Camille shook her head and stabbed out her cigarette. "Stupid fucking poser," she hissed.

Chapter 8

THE SWEETEST THING A GUY EVER WROTE FOR A GIRL

A couple weeks later, Eli got a call to meet Brandon and the guys in the band for drinks downtown after work. Eli and Brandon had bought fake Ohio ID's from the same high school friend, so they didn't worry about getting in. They went to *Calvin's*, a seedy downtown pool hall and bar. Eli and Brandon walked in together to find Marco and Alex sitting down with a pair of sexy but dour heavy metal girls Eli hadn't seen before. The place was empty except for a couple of old men shooting pool in the next room.

A flamboyant gay waiter sashayed over to the table. His eyes lingered on each of the young men around the table and then fixed on Alexander, who returned his leer. Finally the waiter snapped his gum scornfully at the metal girls and spoke. "Girls, I'm going to need to see your ID's. Guys, what can I get you?" Eli and Brandon cracked up as the girls made noises of complaint but shuffled through their purses for their own fake IDs. Marco glared at the waiter. "Jäger shots are a dollar for happy hour," he offered by way of conciliation, tapping his pen on the table impatiently.

"Jäger and beer all around!" Alexander said. "Eli's paying!"

"Ha! The hell I am!"

Ear Wax threw down a twenty dollar bill. "There's the first round, suckers," he said.

The shots and beers went down quickly. The second round went down even smoother. The jukebox blasted Whitesnake and Mötley Crüe. One of the metal girls, a dirty blonde with a strategically ripped Iron Maiden t-shirt, put her feet up and rested her boots on Alexander's knees. He grabbed her by the ankles and tipped her backwards, making her spill her beer and cry out in protest, but didn't let her fall.

The alcohol brought Marco out of himself. "You ready to see history? Come over to the warehouse afterwards. Hey Alex! How's it coming with those lyrics? For the dungeons and dragons song?"

Alexander rolled his eyes. "Pearls before swine," he sighed. He pulled out a tattered notebook, found the right page, and opened it on the table. Brandon picked it up, and Eli scooted over to read along. "It's about my love," Alexander said.

"Amelia?" Eli said.

"Seems like a great girl," said Brandon.

"Babylonia. The mother of my child."

"Oh," said Brandon and Eli in unison.

"Either that or an LSD sorceress who rules over the restless spirits in a forgotten cemetery," Alexander said. "One or the other, I can't remember which." Alexander flipped his shades up and down at the blonde, comically concealing and revealing his eyes. She swiped at the glasses, knocking them off his face.

"Your *love*, huh?" she said with distaste as she grabbed the notebook. Her painted lips moved silently with the words as she read to herself. After she'd digested it for a moment, she began to read aloud. "*My demon bride rides a darkened skyward tide,*" she recited. "*Following the devil through the night...into eternity.*"

Finally she looked up. Her mascara had more layers and shades of blue than a Colorado evening sky in June. "That must be the sweetest thing a guy ever wrote for a girl," said the dirty blonde. Her friend nodded. "How the fuck am I supposed to compete with that?" she said, dropping the notebook on the table in front of Alexander.

Chapter 9

CATNAP INSIDE A JET ENGINE

The warehouse space Marco rented was in the old industrial district, not far from *The Muddy River*. Semi-dilapidated buildings there housed artists, musicians, drifters and misfits of every description. Wild grass and weeds sprouted up through train tracks that hadn't been used for years. A Mexican ice-cream peddler pushed his cart down the block; his bell rang melancholy tones through the vacant streets. A weathered red brick clock tower on a World War II-era factory, five stories high, stood silent watch over the neighborhood; the skyscrapers and lights and action of downtown loomed in the distance.

A main central room in the band's warehouse flat served as their practice space, with a drum kit, guitars, amps and microphone arranged in a rough circle. An old 1950s cabinet TV set, plastered with band and skateboard stickers, had been turned into a planter; the branches of its ferns crept along the walls and up the ceiling. The walls were spray-painted with murals and graffiti tags. Candles were everywhere; wax dripped down the side of the amps and pooled on the worn-out old carpet. A cheap cotton tapestry of DaVinci's *The Last Supper* hung behind the drum kit in the practice area. Little side rooms had been turned into sleeping nooks, with milk crate shelves and trash bags full of clothes spilling out onto the floor. Eli found a couch and passed out, drunk from Jägermeister, as the band began warming up to rehearse.

He dreamed about Babylonia. He watched from above as she straddled him on the couch in the warehouse and woke him with a kiss on the lips. She wore dark wraparound shades just like Alexander's. They hid her eyes as her tongue forced its way into Eli's mouth. Her long dark hair and rich perfume engulfed his senses; pheromones activated and he felt electricity wherever their skin touched. Her full breasts pressed into his chest as they kissed deeply.

She stood up and beckoned for him to follow. A door in the warehouse he hadn't noticed before opened and they entered. The small room on the other side of the door seemed to have just been evacuated; a table was set with a plates and forks and half-cups of tea still steaming. Babylonia didn't pause; she pulled Eli along by the hand through another door into a room that looked as though it had been unused and untouched for a long time. The sparse furniture was dusty; a folded newspaper on a little side table was yellowed with age at the corners. "Come on," Babylonia said, opening yet another door. He followed, room to room. Each had less furniture and signs of habitation than the last, until they were passing through featureless, empty, whitewashed spaces lit only by hazy sunlight filtered through little windows with half-drawn shades.

"Where are we?" Eli asked.

"My labyrinth, darling," she said with a smile. The sunglasses were gone; she looked up at him with red-pupiled eyes surrounded by black mascara; her huge mass of black hair seemed to move with a life of its own, like Medusa's snakes. She placed another kiss on his lips, cupping his crotch in her hand. "Now come on," she said, tugging him firmly. He followed.

They passed through more empty rooms, walked down hallways, climbed and descended stairs, until Eli was sure they weren't in the warehouse any longer. He followed Babylonia down a spiral staircase. She led him by the hand, his fingers locked in hers, her long red nails digging into his skin. They exited the staircase into a kitchen, where a middle-aged woman in a pink bathrobe and hair-rollers was cooking bacon and eggs on the stove. She looked up at the two of them with a start. "Can I help you?" she asked. She stood frozen with fear, gripping her spatula as though it were a weapon.

"Where is the bedroom?" asked Babylonia.

The woman tisked and shook her head and turned back to her cooking, flipping over the sizzling bacon frying in the pan. "That way," she finally said, indicating a darkened hallway behind her with a tilt of the head. As Eli and Babylonia passed through the kitchen to the bedroom Eli looked back at the woman over his shoulder and saw that the bacon and fried eggs weren't real; they were plastic replicas. The stove was of cardboard, from a child's play kitchen set. She looked up to meet Eli's gaze as she pushed the plastic toy food around her toy frying pan with the spatula. Suddenly her face cracked open into a horrific grin full of rotten, broken teeth. Eli turned away.

He followed Babylonia down the dark hallway into the bedroom. A king-sized bed was the only furniture; red and purple candles placed around it on the floor gave off the only light in the room. A Sisters of Mercy poster hung above the bed in the indigo gloom.

Suddenly Eli was in the bed, naked on his back. Babylonia was mounting him. His face was between her breasts, which were barely contained by a black lace bra. He felt her sliding down warm and wet onto him. He tried to sit up but she put her hands on his shoulders and pushed him back into the soft blankets. She leaned down to kiss him; blood trickled out of the corner of her mouth, between her purple painted lips. It tasted salty and sweet. They rocked into each other to a steady beat. Her hair draped over their faces, obscuring sight. The room dropped away. Only touch and skin and smell and the rhythm remained. The rhythm turned into a drumbeat. It grew more complex; a shifting, snaking polyrhythm that accelerated, downshifted, galloped ahead again. Then: sheets of sound. Minor chords slashed above and below the rhythm, dissolving into a series of piercing, howling notes. A wall of sound crackled with electricity, throbbing and surging and rising up, building cathedrals of light above their joined bodies. Bass notes rumbled and rocked to the beat. Symphonic waves crashed, built up, crashed again. A great white light filled the dream as the cosmic orchestra climaxed.

Eli opened his eyes. Ear Wax was sitting next to him on the big thrift store couch, pulling notes from an electric bass guitar with his calloused thumb. Brandon played triplets on the bass drum with his foot pedal, pointing at Eli with his drum sticks and smiling, before crashing back into the song on the cymbals and tom-toms. Marco was down on one knee, his Les Paul guitar propped on the other, eyes closed deep in concentration, conjuring waves of feedback and echo that shattered against one another. Finally he ran his finger down the neck of the guitar, zipping the song up and putting it away. A descending bass line followed the guitar into silence; ringing cymbals vibrated to stillness.

Marco chuckled at Eli. "Good morning, sunshine! Somebody can't hold his liquor so well."

Eli rubbed his eyes. "Just a little catnap inside a jet engine," he said.

Marco plopped down next to him on the couch, guitar in hand, still fingering chords and licks up and down the fret board. "So whaddya think, Tiger?"

"Take the echo out," Eli said. "Just in that middle section. Play it the naked way. Because then, when you bring it back in on the chorus, it's like, whoah!" He looked around sheepishly. "Hey, I mean, it's just my opinion."

"What did you just say?" asked Alexander, emerging from an adjacent room with notebook and pen in hand.

"Just kill the flange effect in the bridge." He nodded to Marco. "If you want. Just play that riff dry."

"No, what did you say before? How did you say...?"

"Oh...the naked way. Play it the naked way. Without the reverb or echo or whatever."

"The Naked Way," repeated Alexander.

"So to speak."

"That's it," Alexander said. "That's the name of the band. Am I right or am I right? The Naked Way." He leapt onto the stage, grabbing his microphone from its stand and spinning around with a theatrical sweep of his long arms. "Ladies and gentlemen!" he intoned into the mic in a corny English accent. "Will you please make them feel at home...The Naaaked Waaaay!"

Ear Wax played a mock-burlesque riff on the bass. Brandon laughed and nodded; the featureless face of the Last Supper Jesus watched over his shoulder.

"The Naked Way, huh? That'll get the panties dropping fast, right?" said Marco, dry-humping the air.

Alexander slapped Eli on the back. "So, you named our band. What's next, you gonna fuck our women?"

Chapter 10
A GODDAMN GOLDEN TICKET

These were the days before Nirvana hit national critical mass and rearranged the radio dial. Big-hair corporate rock had ruled for years; clowns like Winger and Cinderella tried to convince a generation of kids that the saccharine dreck they marketed was "hard rock." Plastic pop princesses like Debbie Gibson and Tiffany ruled over shopping malls full of screaming girls. The sincerity of 70s singer-songwriters and the mysticism and musicianship of 60s rock had been driven underground, out of the marketplace, off of the radio. Punk burned itself out to a husk. MTV was a clown show. The upside of the lack of commercial attention to serious rock music was the freedom it gave to young artists. Kids with guitars who kept the flame of rock and roll alive mixed and matched styles as they pleased, made their own, or ignored genre altogether.

Nobody could say what kind of band The Naked Way was supposed to be. Ear Wax seemed to think he was in the Sex Pistols or the Ramones. Brandon spent hours studying Led Zeppelin's drummer John Bonham; he emulated Bonham's heavy, driving, complex sound. Alexander, of course, loved Jim Morrison and The Doors, but he saw himself as part of broader traditions too: the troubadour, the rock and roll front-man, and the radical rebel poet. Nobody was sure what band Marco thought he was in. As a guitar player, he sounded like The Edge or Johnny Marr on steroids. His riffs and song structures were simple, even simplistic, but they were delivered with overwhelming fire, passion and sonic force magnified by clever use of simple effects. His sound owed a lot to moody 80s bands like New Order and The Smiths, whose CDs were stacked next to the boom box in his bedroom - but heavier, more urgent and unpredictable.

When Marco wasn't playing with the band or writing music on his own, he prac-ticed martial arts in a courtyard behind the warehouse. Rain, shine or snow, he could be seen meditating, perched on one leg, long hair pulled back in a ponytail, brow furrowed in concentration, or executing dramatic flying kicks that covered twenty feet in a heartbeat.

The band's early practices were dominated by Marco and his axe. It was a paintbrush, making wide swaths of color with delay and feedback effects; a wrathful storm cloud, expelling sudden bursts of thunder and lightning; then a chainsaw, growling and snapping over Brandon's driving beats and cascading fills. Alexander was reserved and reflective in the early practices, writing in his notebook between takes, not pushing his singing. Unless there were women present. Then he became a firestorm, howling and jumping around, teasing Marco, glaring meaningfully at the women, seeking out Eli's eyes to see if he got the joke. Some of the songs were melancholic, some exultant, some apocalyptic. Each had a melody like a half-remembered dream. Now they were brought to full waking consciousness in all their primeval glory by Marco and his Les Paul guitar.

While the band worked out songs and rehearsed, Amelia got to work managing. This meant finding them shows to play locally, and building a buzz in the Denver rock scene. But she was already looking past the hometown to the big time. "This is the band that puts rock and roll back on the map," she'd tell anyone who would listen. "Alexander is more than a singer, he's a shaman, he's a poet. Reagan is gone and the 80s are over, thank god. America is ready for a new revolution!" Her vision for the band was limitless. She vowed not to stop until they were on the cover of *Rolling Stone* magazine and their CD was in every record store in the country.

Most days, she set up shop at *The Marketplace* coffee shop downtown as her business headquarters. The manager was in love with her and let her use the office phone, even rigging it up with a long extension cord so she could sit at her table in the café, chain-smoking and drinking her cappuccino behind shades and lipstick, working the phone for her boys. Eli was slightly in awe of her. She had experience managing clubs and bands in the Austin scene, and she was an impossibly mature and sophisticated twenty-five years old. Eli would sit with her at *The Marketplace* and read or write while she talked up the band to promoters and booking agents. She tapped her manicured nails impatiently on the wooden table as she tried to sell a band that didn't fit into the easily marketed niches of the day.

"Yes, they're called The Naked Way. No, they perform fully clothed. Well, mostly…Look, I know they don't fit into one of the little boxes the radio is pushing these days, but rock is going to make a comeback. Can't you feel it in the air? The kids want to rock! Come on, Barry, you remember rock and fucking roll! You should see the underground shows, they're getting huge! The energy is amazing! You need to get ahead of this thing!"

She kicked Eli under the table and mouthed *THAT Barry!* pointing at the phone. Eli strained to understand the barking voice half-audible on the other end. "No, they don't scream," Amelia said. "They *sing*. They're not *heavy metal*" — she made air quotes to match her facetious tone — "they're a classic rock band from the future! Moody but not really goth. Romantic. *Dangerous*. Jane's Addiction without the homoeroticism. Okay, maybe a little homoeroticism - but they rock ten times harder than all those haircut bands. No synthesizers, no fucking drum machine. Just guitar, bass, drums and vocals. Alexander is a classic front man. He writes great lyrics. They've got *soul*, Barry." She caught Eli's gaze and shook her head, pointing at the phone and rolling her eyes in exasperation. "What? No, they don't *rap*. No, not even a little. They don't dance. They aren't New Kids on the Block, for Christ's sake!"

Eli couldn't help checking out Amelia's legs as she crossed and re-crossed them in her tight black skirt. The café manager, a deferential little man who made no attempt to hide his adoration of Amelia, brought her another free cappuccino. She covered the phone and blew him a kiss. "Thank you Henderson, I'll get you back when my ship comes in, tenfold!" She turned back to the phone. "No, they're nothing like Bon Jovi. They don't do power ballads. Hell yes there are hits! I have it all mapped out, Barry. I..." She shook her head as the voice on the other end of the phone took over. "I know...I understand...I'll call you when I have a demo. Goodbye, Barry."

Amelia hung up the phone. She took off her shades and rubbed her eyes. "What am I going to do with these stupid bastards, Eli?" Her southern accent made Eli come out *E-lah*. "I'm trying to hand them a goddamn golden ticket and they won't take it from me!"

"Don't worry," Eli said. "Get them on stage and they'll sell themselves."

She nodded. "You see the same thing I do, don't you? You hear what I hear."

"They're incredible, Amelia. They can go all the way. Best band in the world right now."

She nodded solemnly. "Yes they are. So what's your story, Eli? You just sit around reading poetry and breaking hearts? You don't sing or play an instrument?"

He shrugged. "Never learned. I guess I want to be a writer. But I'm lucky if I can concentrate long enough to put two sentences together. Besides, sometimes

I think all the great books have already been written. I don't know what the hell I could write that would be interesting and original."

Amelia's face lit up and she slapped the table like she was throwing down a winning hand in a poker game. "Like hell you don't! I hereby declare you the official band historian of The Naked Way! When they make it big, you write the official behind-the-scenes story of their rise to fame." She put her finger to her temple. "It would take somebody like you to really understand Alexander, to get into his head. And to explain him to the world. He trusts you." She laughed and clapped her hands together, delighted by the newest wrinkle in her grand plan. "You're gonna write a best-seller, honey - what do you think about that?"

"Where do I sign?" he said.

Amelia lit a fresh cigarette and smiled at him. "Better start taking notes. I'm holding you to it, *E-lah*."

Chapter 11

THE IMPOSSIBLY BEAUTIFUL
SOUND

Amelia got The Naked Way their first gig as opening act for a reggae-punk-funk group called The Spixe. The show was set for an underground party in the basement of an old school building in Capitol Hill; the venue was known informally as *The Schoolhouse*. A defunct kitchen with peeling heart-pattern wallpaper served as the makeshift dressing room. A single flickering florescent bulb on the ceiling was the only light. Alexander and Marco sat on a musty old couch, getting their faces made up by a raven-haired girl in tight t-shirt and ripped stockings who had attached herself to Marco. She looked about sixteen. "Don't be alarmed, Eli," said Alexander. "Show business! Ritual transformation!"

"You make a lovely woman," Eli said.

Alexander batted his mascaraed eyelashes and blew him a kiss. Marco was stoned-face as the girl carefully applied white powder foundation and eyeliner. "Marco here is ugly as ever though, aren't you, you poor bastard?" said Alexander.

"Ha!" Marco said. He pinched the girl's nipples through her clingy mesh top. She squealed with laughter but continued her task with diligent concentration. "How ugly am I now?" Marco demanded. Amelia paced back and forth and smoked; Brandon and Ear Wax, their faces unpainted, chuckled at their band-mates getting made over. They unfurled the Last Supper tapestry, brought it out on stage and hung it behind the drum kit.

Eli joined the crowd of a few dozen milling around drinking beer from a keg; $5 bought admission and an all-you-can-drink red plastic cup. Candles and incense burned onstage. Marco completed his look with a solemn gray Japanese silk jacket.

He preened in a tinted, cracked old mirror, tossing his long hair to pull it back into a samurai ponytail. Brandon's freshly shaved head shone blue in the strange stage lights as he adjusted his drum kit and then retreated behind the curtain. Ear Wax mostly snapped his gum and stared at his shoes: checkerboard Vans. Marco peeked from behind the curtain. The crowd had thickened and the dingy, low-ceilinged basement room was filling with punks, hippies, rastas, goths, heavy metal head-bangers, street people. The three instrumentalists took the stage, followed by Alexander all in black, golden mane flowing, his pale painted face glowing with unearthly light.

"Fucking drag queen," snorted Camille, standing in the back with Eli. She'd dressed for the occasion in a blue 1950's house dress from the thrift store. Bethany stood with them in a tight black sweater, black skirt, and black knee-high boots, intently rubbing an AA sobriety medallion between her manicured fingers. Camille put an arm around Bethany and kissed her on the cheek. "Leave it to me to bring you to this crazy drunken bacchanalia!" she said. "I hope this wasn't a bad idea?"

Bethany didn't take her eyes off Alexander. He pranced and clowned onstage as the band tuned up. "It's okay," Bethany said, as a blast of guitar interrupted her. "It's okay," she shouted to Camille over the rumbling din from the stage. "I wanted to come."

Camille put her other arm around Eli. Alexander spotted them standing in back. He made a peace sign at them, then wagged his tongue obscenely between his fingers. "Look at him," sighed Camille. "The cheekbones. Son of a bitch is prettier than I am."

An excited murmur ran through the crowd. For a moment Alexander leaned on the microphone and stood alone at center stage, head bowed in a final moment of contemplation before the act of creation began. Then he tilted his head back, spread his arms wide, threw his body and soul open to the audience. In an instant the band ignited behind him and he roared into the microphone. The massive groove blasted like an energy wave from the stage; the crowd reeled as though it were on the deck of a ship at sea tossed by a great storm. Regaining its footing, the crowd surged toward the stage as one, instantly hooked by the aggressive beat and the slashing, searing guitar riffs.

Xavier appeared at the front of the throng, wearing a long black cape and urging on the madness of the crowd with bulging eyes, banshee screams and pumping fists. He clambered up onto the stage and dove back out onto the crowd, which caught him and passed him along overhead. His cape got tangled around his head and he flailed his arms and legs, crowd-surfing blind, until he tumbled in a heap to the floor.

A girl lunged at Alexander, wrapping herself around his thigh. He just kept singing, making love to the whole audience, seducing it, entrancing it, offering to do battle for it. "If the Devil was here right now, I'd kick his ass!" he boasted after the feedback of the first song faded away. No one doubted it. All roared loyalty to his banner. He was a wildeyed rock and roll prophet; overblown, obsessed, blessed. "If there wasn't a me, you'd have to invent me!" he claimed. "I love hype!"

As the band kicked into the next song, a weight hit Eli from behind – Bobby leaping onto his back. "*Carpe diem*, mother-fucker!" he yelled in Eli's ear. With his friend hanging around his neck, Eli charged into the crowd toward the impossibly beautiful sound.

Chapter 12

WHERE THE FUN IS

The Naked Way's debut was a success; the band left the stage to roars. The crowd only grew thicker as The Spixe set up. Body heat and smoke filled the little basement auditorium as The Naked Way loaded their equipment out. Alexander and Amelia stood silhouetted under a streetlamp in the parking lot, having an intense and animated conversation; from where he stood, Eli couldn't tell if they were arguing or professing their eternal love for each other. He felt a hand on his shoulder. He turned around to see Babylonia standing behind him.

She had lost her Egyptian goth style in favor of a 1950s pin-up girl look: long black hair pinned into buns, form-fitting blue dress that thrust forward her cleavage, and blood red lipstick. A single blue-green peacock feather in her hair pointed to the sky. "You're Eli," she said in a low, velvety voice, her hand still on his shoulder. "I saw you at the *Muddy River*."

"Yeah," he said. "You're Babylonia. How did you know? My name, I mean." Her ice blue eyes locked in on his.

"Oh, I know. I know what he does, who his friends are, who he loves and who he hates." She let her fingertips run slowly down his arm.

"Well, I must confess I heard a bit about you too," Eli said. "I didn't realize you guys still talked. I mean, he's with Amelia now and all."

"We talk." She fished around in her tiny purse for a pack of cigarettes. Eli pulled out a lighter from his pocket; she leaned in close to catch a spark. "We don't *talk*, talk," she said. But we talk." She tapped the side of her head. "Telepathically. Astral projection. I'm part of him, and he's part of me. I'm the mother of his child, for god's sake. Everything he writes, the ink comes out of my veins." She held out her forearm and tapped it with her fingers; Eli saw faint traces of track marks and scars in the dim midnight light. "His songs are about me...about us. Every one of them."

Eli looked over his shoulder to see Alexander and Amelia were still talking. The singer spun around in a mad pirouette under the streetlight while his lady stood watching, hands on hips. His laughter echoed across the parking lot. Marco called for him to help with the equipment but Alexander paid no mind, breaking out into drunken song in response. The streetlight glinted green on the Jägermeister bottle in his hand.

"So," Eli said, turning back to Babylonia. "Been astral projecting long?"

She laughed. "Goddamn it, you're precious. Not exactly. I've had spiritual visitations since I was a little girl. Alexander and I used to practice together, we learned to project together. We went some crazy places..." She shot an anxious glance in her ex's direction. "Come here, I don't want to get you in trouble," she said, taking his hand. She pulled him back into the building, maneuvering through the crowd; he felt her blood-red fingernails dig into his skin. She found an out-of-the-way alcove and pulled him to her, away from the flow of bodies.

"So," she said, looking up at him as he put a hand on her waist, "why do run around with these guys? They don't seem like your type. You're sweet...sensitive." He ignored the question and kissed her cheek, then her pale white neck. Her eyes closed and she sank back against the wall. She let out a sigh as her body began to yield. "Shouldn't you be in college or something?"

"College, no college," he said, lifting her fingers to his mouth and kissing her fingertips. "Sweet, sour. It doesn't matter. I don't belong anywhere anyway. May as well go where the fun is." He took her finger in his mouth. Babylonia grabbed his crotch and pushed him against the opposite wall, kissing him on the mouth; she tasted like blood. She purred and wrapped herself around him as they kissed. "I have an idea," he said. "Come with me." He led her to the makeshift dressing room and found it empty. She closed the door behind her, pushed him down on the couch and began unbuttoning his jeans.

Suddenly the door opened and Bobby and Brandon stood in the threshold. Eli's jeans and boxers were around his ankles. Bobby broke into laughter; Brandon's face screwed up in disgust. Eli saw a flash of Alexander's wavy blonde hair in the hall behind them as he hollered back at someone over his shoulder. Brandon slammed the door at the last second as Alexander turned around. Eli waited for the door to burst open, for the singer to come flying at him in a rage. But it didn't happen. Babylonia was oblivious. He stroked her hair and eased back into the couch, closing his eyes as the weak fluorescent light flickered above them and the massive, throbbing bass groove of the reggae band began vibrating through the walls, the floor, the furniture, their bodies.

Chapter 13

REBELLION, HEARTBREAK AND MURDER

The success of the opening gig with The Spixe led to more shows, at bigger venues and with bigger crowds. The Naked Way's name made its way around town. The guys in the band got a few dollars in their pockets and the alcohol flowed. The music sounded better and better; Alexander and Marco kept producing stunning new songs. Amelia brought a review from the local weekly arts and entertainment magazine, *WordsWest,* over to the warehouse. "Okay, now be brave, you guys!" she said. "It could be good or it could be bad, but we have to know what people are saying." The band gathered around reluctantly, snickering and shooting each other snarky looks.

"Can we have some milk and cookies before you read us the story?" said Marco, plopping down on the couch like a rambunctious kid.

"Marco!" Amelia's southern accent was too sweet and dainty to carry any menace. But the pout and the eyes got results. Marco settled back into the couch and took a pull from a bottle of beer. Alexander yawned and stretched his arms out, snagging Ear Wax in a first-date-at-the-movies embrace. Ear Wax elbowed him violently in the side. "Boys!" Amelia yelled. Alexander sat up perfectly stiff and straight, an exaggerated proper English schoolboy pose, before rubbing his sore ribs and turning pained eyes to Ear Wax. Amelia shook her head and sighed. Brandon sat away from the group behind his drum kit, white-knuckle gripping his sticks, anxiously awaiting the review.

She thumbed through the paper to the article and began to read aloud. "This is the biggest rock critic in town, guys! He's a big deal! Ok…" She read aloud:

A peculiar phrase has been burning my ears around town the past few weeks: "The Naked Way." Is it an adult film, I asked my informants? They said no. A check-out line romance novel? Apparently not. Perhaps The Naked Way is an escort service or a new bath house on the North Side? No, this preposterous name belongs to a rock band that has been demolishing house parties, basements, beer busts and small live music venues right here in our own fair city. A small cult of fanatics claims that this "Naked Way" is the second coming of rock and roll itself, and puts on such an urgent, compelling, balls-to-the-wall god-awful-important live show that they render everything else happening in music today irrelevant.

The Naked Way, I was indignantly informed, is not a punk band. Neither, a devoted fan told me, are they a "Goth" band. Even though they rock hard and some members of the group sport long hair, they aren't a mainstream heavy metal band either. They can rock every hairspray band from here to New Jersey right off the stage, their fans will have you know. I decided to investigate this curious phenomenon for myself.

I saw The Naked Way open a set for Liquid at The Deadbeat Club. The motley local crew of played-out old rockers, over-painted young girls with feathered hair and tight jeans, and non-descript sleazy suburban types on the prowl in skinny ties balanced out the influx of hip kids from downtown and gave the room the just the right feeling — just the balance of pheromones and drug-fueled desperation needed for a brilliant rock and roll show. The $2 extra-tall Long Island Iced Teas didn't hurt either.

Marco shook his head. "What the fuck, is he writing a book or something?"

Alexander was now on the edge of his seat, listening intently with a serious ear; the mischievous schoolboy was taking a break. He hushed Marco. "Go on, darling," he said, winking at Amelia, who blushed and continued reading aloud.

The Naked Way took the stage as a kind of walking rock 'n' roll cliché. The drummer strutted up to his kit with an exaggerated scowl, looking like an extra in a low-budget TV movie about kids getting in trouble after school on the wrong side of the tracks.

A chorus of laughs filled the room; Ear Wax tossed a crumpled up fast-food bag at Brandon. The drummer pouted, but finally gave up a forced, teeth-clenched grin. Amelia continued:

The guitarist and the bass player added to the Spinal Tap factor by bickering loudly about something I couldn't understand as they took the stage. The guitar player spent more time tuning his guitar and turning knobs on his amp than the Cape Canaveral techs do preparing for a Space Shuttle launch. Meanwhile, the crowd was subjected to the most powerful smoke machine known to concert-going man; I couldn't see a thing and my eyes watered and burned.

Finally the singer I'd heard so much about emerged from the fog. His name is Alexander, or "Alexander the Great" as a certain groupie I know calls him. I was told to expect the second coming of Jim Morrison. He looked more like a down-and-out David Coverdale on a three-day drunk, wearing a gray thrift-store suit with an open collar and a huge silver crucifix around his neck. When he shuffled up to the microphone through the smoke, I expected titty jokes or a belch. Instead I got Shakespearean diction and hilarious train-of-thought ramblings as if from a new Lenny Bruce. By the end of the night, I was completely sold on his unique persona: a post-apocalyptic, post-punk, post-modern rock and roll preacher, teasing and taunting the audience, promising heaven and threatening hell, preening like a beatnik Mick Jagger, calling for a Sunday gospel revival to drive away the bad spirits.

When the band kicked in behind him, I had a moment of total dislocation and vertigo. The impact of this three-piece band is visceral; I felt every beat of the kick-drum in my ribs. The drummer thinks he's John Bonham and he's not far off. He drives the songs with a complex, muscular, dynamic style that must cost him serious bucks in broken sticks and skins. The kid is all business. He grunted approvingly in my general direction when I made a Led Zeppelin reference after the show. When I told him I heard echoes of Billy Cobham and Elvin Jones in his playing as well, I got a blank look and a sneer; the perfect rock and roll drummer's response to a jazz reference.

The guitar player astonished with powerful slashing lead lines that were deceptively simple, fusing the power chords of classic guitar rock with more dissonant shadings of post-punk and new wave. Insert your own post-modern deconstruction of the phallic guitar solo here; it won't matter anymore after you hear him. The last time I was cajoled into going out to see an unknown "hard rock" band in this town, I left feeling beaten, bullied and bludgeoned by a night of corny and clichéd lead guitar antics. But The Naked Way's tightly-wound little axe man wrenched fantastic, frightening, shimmering sounds out of his Les Paul that sent kids in the audience into a literal frenzy. I've never heard anything like it. He may be an idiot-savant from the distant future, playing some kind of transcendent blues music from outer space.

The Naked Way pull off a magic trick. They renew and rediscover the power of classic rock without sounding like anyone else. In a rock music world evenly divided between closet-queen heavy-metal cock-rockers and dopey tree-huggers with no red blood in their veins, The Naked Way have created a combination of sound, image and words that makes rock seem dangerous, primitive, smart and sexy again. When the music starts, it's just too late to stop.

I didn't understand all the lyrics and the idea of "poetry" in rock music was ruined for me twenty years ago, but the singer's powerful pipes and sensitive phrasing make whatever he's say-ing sound awfully good. Some of the hard stuff seems to be about witches, fortune tellers, the

undead escaping their crypts and the like, with some general rock and roll themes of rebellion,
heartbreak and murder thrown in for good measure. As bloody as their rocking numbers are, The
Naked Way's quieter love songs are as sweet and tender as anything on "Rubber Soul." Hearing
this band effortlessly down-shift from earth-shattering hard rock to pretty, soulful pop ballads
was one of the most impressive parts of the show.

So embrace the cliché, accept the obvious metaphor - The Naked Way will leave you feeling
- naked. If you still give a damn about the music we call rock and roll, this band will leave you
feeling raw, exposed, ecstatic and hopeful.

Oh, and expect a fight or three when you go to see The Naked Way. If not between guys in
the mosh pit, between girls fighting over the guys in the band at the end of the show.

Amelia closed up the paper and put it down on the inverted wooden crate that
served as a table. Marco looked confused. "So…was it good?" he asked.

Ear Wax laughed. "The reviewer pretty much came all over us." He turned to
the lead singer. "Right, big Al?"

He nodded. "A mess of spunk everywhere," Alexander confirmed. He turned to
Amelia. "Get us a rag, love?"

She shot him a wry smile. "Guys, this is huge!" she said. "You know what I can
do with *this* in my hot little hands? Promoters will talk to us. Labels, studio time, a
real demo! Maybe an opening slot on a big summer tour!"

Ear Wax frowned. "He didn't say anything about me?"

Amelia thumbed backed to the article. "I must have passed over it, sugar. Oh
here it is. Something about how you're real enthusiastic and he likes how you chew
your gum while you play." She closed the paper back up in her lap. "See? Just real
nice." Ear Wax smiled. Amelia looked around with eyes wide for a response. "Well?
What do you think, boys?"

Marco sat stiffly, chest puffed out and a pouty expression on his face. "I'm pretty
sure that reviewer called me retarded," he said.

Amelia tried her most soothing, mothering voice: "No he didn't, honey!"

"He did too – you said it yourself, he said I'm an idiot savage. And it's in the
fucking newspaper? What kind of manager are you? You're supposed to get us *good*
press!" Exasperated, Amelia shook her head and buried her face in her hands.

Alexander put his hand on Marco's shoulder. "They loved you, brother! That
writer couldn't come up with the fucking words to describe how great and originally
you play, he had to compare it to fucking science fiction! You're the Luke Skywalker
of the guitar."

Marco shook him off. "Luke Skywalker is a pussy!" he shouted.

"Hey," Ear Wax protested. "That's sacrilege."

"This doesn't feel right," Marco said. He got up and retreated to his loft bedroom. Brandon tossed his drumsticks in the air in frustration; a gray tabby cat who'd been sleeping in an empty beer box in the corner panicked and ran for it when the sticks clattered to the floor too close.

Alexander reclined on the couch, grinning a Cheshire cat grin, unrattled by his partner's bizarre behavior. He blew Amelia a kiss. "It's a great review, darling. Tinkerbell will go and pray to his monkey god and everything will be all right."

She smiled. "You're right, baby. It's a great, great fucking review. Yes it is. The Naked Way is on its way."

Marco emerged from his room after a few minutes. The cloudy vibe of anxiety and suspicion had disappeared. So had his shirt. "I had a talk with God, everything is cool," he said on his way to the warehouse's rudimentary kitchen. Tattoos of dragons and exotic oriental characters writhed and pulsed across his muscular torso as he walked. He stood in front of the open refrigerator, perplexed. "Why is there no fucking beer in this place?" he demanded. He returned to the big room. Brandon found a flask in his jacket pocket and tossed it to Marco. Marco took a slug, and then another. He screwed the top back on the flask and tossed it back to Brandon. Then he put his hands together, bowed, and began an elaborate martial arts routine. Alexander rolled his eyes and reached out his hand for the flask as the bare-chested, grunting Marco throttled a legion of invisible enemies.

Chapter 14

WE'RE NOT TELLING BOBBY

Alexander stopped making it home to Amelia's apartment some nights. At first, Amelia made phone calls, visited likely bars, or waited at the warehouse when he went missing. But after a while she stopped looking. She wept instead. She tried to read herself to sleep, bringing armfuls of Alexander's books – French poetry, Henry Miller, rock biographies and studies of the occult – with her to bed. Sometimes he was there when she awoke bleary-eyed in the morning light. Sometimes he wasn't.

Those days, he would catch up with her in the afternoon at *The Marketplace*. Explanations and stories were necessary; sometimes there were fights and tears. But before long, Amelia was going into her purse to pay for Alexander's lunch and coffee. She lit his cigarettes and gave him "walking around money" from the "band fund." He relaxed, smoking and laughing and writing in his notebook, flirting and making eyes at girls passing by over Amelia's shoulder. His hands roamed over her thighs under the table as she worked the phone. He had too many muses, too many mistresses to please. No one knew who or what they all were but him.

Some nights Alexander drank with Bobby, Brandon and Eli; Marco and Ear Wax worked at restaurant jobs and saved their night-off requests for shows. The boys set up shop at dive bars, chatted up women, shot pool, and sometimes got kicked out for various forms of Alexander-inspired mayhem. One night they took over a corner of the bar at *El Chapultepec*, a run-down, hold-over 1940s joint at 20th and Market Streets, somewhere in between gentrifying downtown and the wild, overgrown train yards and abandoned structures of the Platte River Valley. The neon sign above the door hissed and flickered at the night. A jazz quartet broke down old show tunes and twelve-bar-blues on a tiny stage at the end of the bar. Framed 8x10's of the great musicians who had played there going back to Kerouac's day shared a wall with a sign that earnestly warned patrons: *No Dancing*.

Alexander howled when Eli pointed out the sign. "But we *have* to dance!" he shouted over the music, gripping Brandon and Bobby by the shoulders and shaking them on their barstools. "You schoolboys should see some of the dance parties I've been to over yonder in the valley. People who don't have anything to lose really know how to party. I'd like to take one of those debutantes you guys go out with to a big satanic sock-hop around the bonfire with the hobos and the train-jumpers." The guys laughed. "What about that Bethany, Bobby?" said Alexander. "What a looker! Are you going to close the deal already or what?"

Bobby smiled a tight smile that turned into a grimace and back into a smile again several times before he spoke. "Bethany and I were in rehab together, man," he said. "She pulled me back from the brink a lot of times. And the other way around too. Even though I'm drinking again, she's still there for me. Do you really fuck with that kind of friendship by bringing sex into it?"

Eli nodded his head. "Yes, you do," he said. "I'd like to bring sex into it, please. Into her, even. She's a freaking knock-out."

Alexander raised an eyebrow. "She's still sober, you say?"

Bobby nodded. "Yeah, she's on the straight and narrow, good grades, internships. She's going places."

Alexander smirked. "Damn right she is. But you aren't carrying a torch for her? Not even a little one?"

"Don't be a prick about it," said Brandon. "Of course he is."

Alexander patted Bobby on the back. "Don't worry, mate," he said. "Time is on your side." He drained his beer to the bottom in one long gulp, then sidled off of his barstool. "Nature calls, gents," he said, walking towards the cramped men's room in back.

Bobby smoldered. "Why's he gotta fuck with me like that? Is it not obvious I'm in love with her?"

"He's a professional asshole, that's why," Brandon said. "Don't let him get under your skin."

The jazz band finished their set to mild applause. Over Bobby's shoulder, Eli saw Alexander emerge from the men's room. A guy with a long black ponytail followed him out of the john. They shook hands for a beat too long; with their lefts, Alexander passed the guy a wad of bills. Ponytail guy slipped him a little plastic baggie in return, then exited out a back door. Alexander looked up and met Eli's gaze from across the room. For a moment he froze, then the twinkle returned to his eye and the self-assured smile spread over his handsome face. He fished around in his pocket and dropped a few coins into the slot of a battered old payphone. He blew Eli a kiss as he leaned against the wall with the phone to his ear. Eli turned back to Bobby and Brandon. "It's not like he has a chance with Bethany anyway," he said. "She almost clawed his eyes out of his head when they met, remember?"

"I'm actually kind of worried about her," Bobby said. "She hasn't answered her phone or called me back this week." He peeled the label off his beer bottle, scraping at its corners with his fingernails. "Just busy with all the reading and writing papers and stuff, I guess. She gives me half a mind to go back to school sometimes."

Brandon fidgeted and tapped his toe. "I'm sure she's fine," he said. "Eli, you still have the rest of that joint?"

Eli nodded and rose to his feet. He looked to the back of the bar but Alexander was gone. "You don't think Bethany's seeing some trust-fund grad student teaching assistant at school, do you?" said Bobby. "Like a tennis player, maybe? Dan Quayle type?"

Eli changed the subject. "Come smoke a joint with us. Mix it up a little."

Bobby shook his head and raised his hand for the bartender. "You know I hate that shit."

"Just freebase cocaine for you, then."

"That was just the once, Eli. Just to try it. An experience to check off the list. Another door of perception opened." He rapped on the polished wooden bar with his knuckles. "Shots when you get back."

Eli and Brandon crossed the street and huddled in the doorway of a boarded-up storefront to smoke, only half-hidden from the sickly pale orange light of an old streetlamp. A sleeping homeless man stirred under his blanket of newspapers in the next storefront but didn't wake. As Eli handed Brandon the lit joint, he chuckled at the sight of the jazz band burning down their own spliff in a little rectangle of light outside the bar's back door down the block. Suddenly Brandon's expression changed. "What the fuck is my singer doing?"

Eli turned and looked behind him. A block and a half away, a long, lean figure with long blonde hair and drainpipe jeans leaned against a wall, half-hidden in shadow. A brand-new silver SUV turned the corner down the abandoned street and cruised silently to a stop at the curb in front of him. The passenger door opened. Alexander tossed away a cigarette butt and climbed in. Eli and Brandon watched in silence as the car idled, brake lights glowing red, before it finally rolled off into the night.

"I've seen that car before," Eli said.

The jazz band started up again inside; Eli recognized the melody of *Take the A Train*. Brandon took another long drag on the joint and held it in. He released it with a long hacking cough, shaking his head. "We're not telling Bobby," he said when he finally recovered his voice.

Eli shook his head in agreement, hugging himself against the cold. "We're not telling Bobby."

Chapter 15

THIS IS MY MOVIE

Around this time Brandon began dating Kate. She was a whirlwind of energy — in her own way, as much a vortex of chaos and possibility as the band. Her father was a highly paid corporate lawyer for the regional Bell telephone company. He had come out as a homosexual when she was ten years old, a year after Kate's mother divorced him. To Kate, this made her into a figure of drama and tragedy unknown to most middle-class American high school kids. She wasn't wrong; kids are cruel and few gay parents were out in the 80s. Growing up, her cool older sister got her high and played her classic rock records in their unsupervised basement bedroom in their mother's rowhouse. Kate danced ballet, studied French, worshipped David Bowie, and wore berets to good effect — when berets weren't cool. She snuck out of both her parents' houses and partied until dawn on the weekend; they had both given up trying to stop her. But she got good grades and kept an eye on the future.

Kate met Brandon on the City College campus, where she was enrolled in an advanced placement program even though she was still in high school. She spotted him smoking outside of a classroom building and walked right up to ask for a cigarette. Her long hair was tied back under a beret and she had on a short skirt, knee-high socks and tennis shoes, and a denim jacket adorned with nostalgic New Wave band buttons. With effort, Brandon got his fingers to work well enough to get a cigarette out of the pack. Unable to speak, he tried to keep a cool poker face behind his aviator shades. She took the cigarette from his hand.

"You're all angles," she said, staring at him over the top of her red 1950s-style shades while sparking the cigarette with a lighter from her glittery little purse.

Brandon couldn't stop looking at the rouge lipstick pout of her lips wrapped around the cigarette. "What?" he said.

She titled her little pug nose and blew smoke to the sky. "Angles. Your face. Those cheek bones, wow." She took two full steps back, then framed him with her hands like a movie director. Her voice was sultry and full of innuendo, but a prominent lisp gave it a childlike Lolita quality. "And the arms and legs," she said. "So rigid and angular. Like a scarecrow. It's ok, I'm a photographer. Or I will be. I'm taking a photography class next semester. But I read books on art and design and stuff. And you should be some kind of male model. Maybe. Can you smile? It's ok if you can't, there are very successful models who never do."

Flattery put the blood back in Brandon's veins and gave him courage to speak. "I'm in a band," he proclaimed. The corner of his lip curled up into something between and smile and an Elvis Presley snarl.

"Of course you are," she said. "You're a rock and roll scarecrow! But not in a John Cougar Mellencamp way. I wouldn't do that to you!" She laughed out loud. His smile faded. "More like if David Bowie redid the Wizard of Oz," she continued. "With you as James Dean...as the Scarecrow. Will you take off those sunglasses, please?" He did. "Oh my!" she said looking him up and down. A little snort escaped at the end of her laugh; now his smile was easy. "Yes...you, as James Dean, as the Scarecrow. David Bowie is the art director. He'd probably play the Wizard too. And I can do all this" - she waved her cigarette imperiously – "because this is *my* movie." Brandon stared. She stared back. He nodded. It was her movie. He hadn't said a half dozen words since she'd walked up. "Now we *could* do the Prince version – like an updated *The Wiz*? But I think you're too white for that!" She exploded into laughter that resolved into a spasm of pretty little snorts.

"You have to come see us play." Brandon said.

"I'm going to do your band pictures. For your album cover and everything." It was a statement, not a question. "My daddy hasn't bought me a good camera yet so he's just going to have to let me use his. Are you guys free Saturday afternoon?"

"We have a practice," he said. "Maybe after."

She pulled a little notebook from the purse; bangles and bracelets jangled on her slender wrists. "Give me your number," she said grinning at him. "See, how easy that was?" Even though he didn't get a kiss for days, from that moment Kate was Brandon's girl.

Kate showed up at their Saturday practice as promised; the drummer beamed as his band mates' jaws hit the floor. She sat on the couch feet away from the band as they practiced their set. Each song blew her away more than the last. "Oh my god, you guys are going to be *famous!*" she lisped. Alexander sang to Kate. On one of the slow love songs, *'Til the End of Forever*, he got down on one knee and serenaded her. She fairly melted, turning red and giggling with delight. Brandon expressed his displeasure by stepping on Alexander's vocals with inappropriate drum fills and loud cymbal clashes. Amelia arrived in the middle of the serenade; she stood unnoticed in the doorway with her arms crossed until the song was over. When the practice ended, Alexander introduced the new girl to the woman of the house. Amelia gave Kate her biggest Southern smile; they exchanged air kisses and an awkward, one-arm embrace.

Kate announced that it was time for the photo shoot and herded the band into her father's silver BMW parked outside the warehouse. Amelia, who'd been in the bathroom, came running out as Kate was about to pull away. Kate reluctantly rolled down the tinted power window and looked up at the older woman from behind her dark shades; she blew a big pink bubble with her chewing gum as Amelia leaned in to talk. Brandon sat slumped and indifferent in the passenger seat; Alexander winked and blew Amelia a kiss from the back, where he sat with Marco and Ear Wax. "Oh no," Kate said to Amelia, popping her gum lazily. "I'm not sure there's room!"

Amelia straightened up. "Oh. Okay sweetheart. I'll follow? Give me a second, ok?" She scampered to her battered Toyota Camry, digging for her keys in her purse. She trailed Kate's BMW to a Gothic-style cathedral in an older residential neighborhood. As Amelia parked, the guys were already mugging for Kate in the tall arched doorways of the church. Kate snapped away with her father's camera, directing the band's poses. Amelia stood at her side and offered suggestions; Kate's only response was a wan smile. "Over here, guys," Kate ordered. "On those steps. Give me that look, Brandon." He pouted. She snapped the shutter. "Yes! Now by that cross." The guys stood around the base of a fifteen-foot high Celtic-style cross of smooth gray marble beneath an ornate stained glass window. Alexander leaned back against the cross, writhing and stretching his arms against it above his head.

"This is how Madonna does it, right?" he asked with a facetious leer.

"Oh my god! You boys are so beautiful!" Kate gushed, crouching low for a different angle. Amelia rolled her eyes.

After the photo shoot, the group went to a greasy spoon restaurant. "So guys, I have some big news," Amelia said, when the plates of eggs and bacon were almost empty and the ashtrays full. "Twice Jilted wants you guys to play a show with them. Second billing. The Disney Wizards will open. At the Gothic Theatre."

"Oh my god!" Kate almost screamed. "Twice Jilted is awesome! My big sister used to go out with their drummer. He got her pregnant — twice."

"I hear they suck," Marco said.

"They don't suck," said Ear Wax. "The bass player is my cousin. They're cool as hell."

"She had abortions both times," said Kate through a mouthful of scrambled eggs.

"What a waste of fine genetic material," said Alexander. He tried to meet Brandon's eyes to share the laugh, but Brandon coolly looked away and took a drag on his cigarette. Kate laughed and smiled coquettishly at Alexander's joke.

Amelia patted Kate's hand. "I'm sorry about your sister, honey," she said.

"Oh, it's ok," Kate said. "I didn't want to be an aunt anyway. Little brats running around crying and making shitty diapers — not for me!" She burst into unselfconscious laughter.

Amelia turned to Marco. "Twice Jilted does not suck," she told him. "They're the biggest band in the city. This is going to be great. It's their annual New Year's party, it's huge!" Amelia's Southern accent gave *huge* at least three syllables. "I have it from excellent sources that there will be agents there. You guys could get discovered!" Amelia looked around the table at the sullen faces of the band. She banged a fist down on the table. "Get excited, somebody!"

Alexander lifted his water glass in the air, clinking the rim with his spoon. "Hurrah!" he cried in mock delight. Ear Wax and Marco slow-clapped. Amelia gave Alexander frowning puppy-dog eyes. He leaned over and kissed her. "Well done, love," he told her.

"Oh my god," Kate said. "I'm having breakfast in the afternoon — with rock stars!"

Chapter 16
NEW YEAR'S EVE, 1991

Twice Jilted played a punchy, halting, moody style of music. Their bass-heavy sound and stop-start rhythmic dynamics invited comparisons to Primus. Brandon once said they were "like The Pixies, but even more depressed." Their lead singer was Justin, who fit nobody's idea of a rock star. He was a pudgy refrigerator repairman in his late twenties with a pregnant wife and a little bungalow house in a downscale suburb. His trademark was his hair: white boy dreadlocks, with a few thick strands dyed a deep, distinct blue at the ends. Sometimes he wore his hair on top of his head in a great unwieldy pile that tended to flop in front of his face and hide his eyes. When he sang, he stood stock still, eyes closed or looking at the floor, and bellowed from deep down in his gut. Only hardcore fans could understand what he was singing – but there were lots of those. Many girls found the combination of his oddly introverted stage presence and his booming, dramatic vocal style irresistible. His biggest female fans showed their devotion by dyeing the ends of their hair the same shade of electric blue.

The bass player was a busty, beautiful, dark-haired girl named Audrey – Ear Wax's cousin. Like him, she chewed gum while she plunked away at the electric bass hanging around her neck. Unlike Ear Wax, she had rings of male fans who gathered in front of her spot on stage every time Twice Jilted played. The lanky drummer had red curly hair and flailed away at his kit like "Animal" from the Muppets. The guitar player was a bookish-looking young man with glasses who sometimes looked embarrassed to on stage in front of people; he handled his electric guitar intimately but awkwardly, with long gangly fingers and strange facial expressions, like a pimply teenage boy trying to manipulate a woman's body for the first time. But the sounds he pulled from the guitar were like a David Lynch funhouse – atmospheric, spooky, full of bent and broken notes, with little deconstructed bits of Carl Perkins and The Clash. "Cubist twang," Camille called the band's sound.

The New Year's show was at the Gothic Theater just south of Denver, a crumbling 1930s movie palace recently restored and rebuilt into a concert venue. After helping The Naked Way unload gear, Eli and Bobby drank at the nostalgic art deco-style bar. "I think our boys are going to blow Twice Jilted away tonight," Eli said. "They just go further, deeper. I never really understood why people get so worked up over Twice Jilted, anyway."

"You wouldn't," said Bobby. "They're too workaday, too working class."

"Fuck you, they are," Eli said. "And fuck you generally."

Bobby didn't back down. He poked a fingertip into Eli's chest. "The way Twice Jilted does it, there's no fantasy, no sugar-coating, no easy mysticism. They aren't making some kind of esoteric occult ceremony or reaching for the stars – they're right *here*, in this fucking broken-down old cow town, right *now*. They just play their weird, gloomy little songs so people can get drunk and bob their heads and sing along on a Friday night. Then they sleep it off before they go back to their shitty lives the next day. Because that's what people *do*." Again he poked Eli hard in the ribs.

Eli swatted his arm away. "People can do better. Some people even *want* to do better."

"Come on, Eli. You know how things really are. More than most people." Bobby's big brown eyes were glassy and red. He was invoking the seldom-discussed bond between them: Unspeakably Bad Childhoods.

"So I'm supposed to like mediocre music?" Eli retorted.

Bobby exploded into laughter. More of their friends showed up. Kate came in the front door with Camille and Bethany just behind; Amelia and the band emerged from the backstage area where they'd stowed their equipment. Kate threw her arms around Brandon. He hugged her back stiffly with his scarecrow arms; public affection didn't come naturally to him. Kate grabbed his face by the chin and turned it toward Camille and Bethany. "Isn't he fucking hot?" she demanded. They laughed and agreed that he was. "So sullen, I love it!" Brandon's squished face smiled against his will.

Suddenly every head turned: Babylonia was standing in the entrance. She wore a tight-fitting black leather bodice with a floor-length black skirt and black boots. Her jet-black hair was straight and hung past her shoulders. In her hand she held the end of a leash. At the end of the leash was a collar around the neck of a boy with spiky black hair, pale white make-up caking his face, and black lipstick to match Babylonia's.

Babylonia stood there a moment, meeting Alexander's eyes only. Then she turned up her nose and paraded her pet over to the bar. Eli watched her order a whiskey sour for herself and a Sprite for her date. A ripple of nervous laughter went through the group. But Amelia wasn't laughing. "What the fuck is she doing here?" she hissed at Alexander. "*Again?*"

"Looks like she's walking her dog," he said. Amelia lunged at Alexander; Camille and Bethany held her back. "Darling, I didn't tell her to come!" the singer said. "She's stalking me across eternity for all I know...I can't control her! It's a free country, still, isn't it?" Amelia ripped herself away and stalked out of the bar. Eli saw a faint smile turn up the corner of Babylonia's mouth. She paid for her drinks and led her slave boy out of the bar into the performance hall, which was filling up with New Year's revelers. Eli mumbled something about finding a men's room and followed her out of the bar.

"Babylonia!" he called after her. She ignored his voice, strutting into the crowd at a leisurely pace, with her docile friend following close behind, eyes down. Eli caught up to her and put a hand on her bare ivory shoulder. She flinched and recoiled at his touch; her face was a mask. He withdrew his hand. The slave boy looked him up and down, batting his heavily painted eyes. "I'm sorry to – interrupt," Eli said, looking back and forth between them. He took a half-step closer to Babylonia and lowered his voice. "I just wanted to see you. I don't have your number. How can I..."

Babylonia put a finger to his lips to silence him. "You *can't*. It was a moment in time." She leaned in and gave him a kiss on the cheek – he felt the heat of her body, the smell of her skin, her cleavage brushing his arm, her moist lips pressing into his flesh. Her perfume and pheromones sent Eli's senses into a riot. But her eyes gave him nothing. "Goodbye, Eli," she said, removing the manicured finger from his lips. She turned her back and advanced into the crowd. Before the leash pulled him along, the slave boy wrinkled his nose and blew a kiss at Eli. Whether it was seductive or mocking, he couldn't tell. Eli spun around, almost colliding with someone on his way back to the bar.

Marco and Ear Wax had drifted off to a booth in the corner. Kate was raving breathlessly. "Boys on leashes?" she said. "This is like Andy Warhol's Factory or Studio 54 in the seventies or something! I can't wait to tell my Daddy!"

"The night is young, little lady," said Camille. "It could get even better than boys on leashes!"

"So anyway, like I was saying," Kate said, "meeting Brandon is the best thing that ever happened to me." The older friends shared bemused smiles but let her go on. Brandon stood next to her beaming, with his thumbs in the waistband of his jeans, cowboy style. "I mean, if you could do David Bowie before he was famous, wouldn't you?" Kate asked. Smiles slowly wilted. Kate looked from face to face. Alexander was the only one still smiling – his best big-bad-wolf grin. Kate looked at Brandon, who'd turned stone-faced, then back to Alexander.

Alexander raised his beer glass in a toast. "Here's to the time-machine Bowie fuck!" he proclaimed. Marco and Ear Wax snickered in the corner. "Wouldn't you indeed?" said the singer. "You absolutely would!" Bethany shot him a withering look. Bobby lit a cigarette and looked away.

Kate giggled. "I mean, like, David Bowie's *drummer*! You all know what I meant!" Brandon shuffled his feet. She squeezed his hand. "Hey sexy boy," she lisped in his ear. "Get me a drink, please? Bartenders usually think I'm like thirty years old but you never know!" Brandon brought back beers and shots, which were quickly emptied. Emboldened, Kate continued as the group shifted to Marco and Ear Wax's booth in the corner. "I mean it," she said. "This is my destiny! You guys are my ticket to immortality!"

Bethany shook her head. "*What* is your destiny, exactly?" asked Camille.

Alexander clapped his hands in delight. "Naked Ambition!" he said, looking at Kate. "Cosmic egotism! That's the real spirit of The Naked Way, right there!"

Another voice entered the conversation. It was downbeat, sarcastic, aw-shucks passive-aggressive. "Ambition, destiny, immortality – it could only be The Naked Way!" It was Justin. He shambled up in black denim jeans, white t-shirt and scuffed work boots. A large wool cap contained his dreads, but the blue-tipped ends stuck out. He stood at the outside of their little circle with his hands stuffed in his pockets, rocking back and forth on his heels, his one lazy eye pointing crazily at the ceiling while the good one bore into them, silently accusing them each in turn. "So, The Naked Way, in the flesh." he said. "I hear you guys really…*rock*." On the surface, it was a compliment and an affirmation; but it was also a question, a challenge, an insinuation, and a subtle mockery. In Justin's philosophy, "rocking" wasn't always the right thing for a rock band to do. If done wrong, his tone implied, rocking could be embarrassingly mundane, even hopelessly uncool. "I'm Justin, if you didn't know," he added with an awkward laugh. "Welcome to our humble shindig." He pulled off the wool cap and the blue-tipped dreadlocks tumbled down. "You guys really suck energy from a distance," he said.

"What the fuck is that supposed to mean?" Marco demanded.

"Easy Tiger," said Justin. "I mean it in a good way. Like your name is getting around. The *WordsWest* review and the good crowds and all."

Alexander lifted his glass good-naturedly; the rest of the table did the same. "We're just living out our fantasies on earth, brother," Alexander said. "Wine, women and song."

Justin lifted an imaginary toast in response. "I don't drink," he chuckled. "But thanks, guys. Welcome to the big leagues. You go on at eleven." He turned and walked away.

"I think he just challenged you guys to some kind of rock and roll showdown!" Kate lisped excitedly.

Ear Wax and Alexander burst out laughing. Marco wasn't amused. "We gotta get ready for sound check soon," he said, checking his watch.

"Not just yet, children," said Alexander. He pulled a plastic baggie from his pocket, spread out a napkin on the table, and dumped out the contents: at least an ounce of psychedelic mushrooms.

Marco bolted to his feet. "Mother fucker!" he shouted at Alexander. "You promised me no more fucking drugs!"

"Come on now," the singer said, "these aren't *drugs*. They're vegetables! They're a ritual *sacrament*. It's the New Year! We have to seek new visions, purge old demons. It's gonna be *1991*, man!"

Marco got in close, his finger in Alexander's face. "Enough with your bullshit!" He stalked out of the bar, brushing several people out of the way with his burly shoulders.

"Maybe he can go find Amelia out in the parking lot and give her a good hard fuck," the singer said.

"Hey!" Camille banged her beer bottle on the table, sending suds flying. She pointed at Alexander. "That's enough out of you!"

"Hey Gloria Steinem!" he said, pointing right back. "It's time for *you* to partake of this feast for the soul I've laid out before you." He waved his hand over the pile of strange gray-blue dried stems and caps on the table. Eli and Brandon were already slowly chewing their first bites.

Kate held a mushroom cap up to the light. "Oh my god, it looks like it's from outer space!"

"They taste like popcorn!" said Ear Wax. He popped one in his mouth. Gaining courage from the popcorn analogy, Kate followed suit.

Bobby sat staring across the table at Bethany. He'd tried to make conversation with her all night. She had gently but firmly brushed him off. He could see she'd lost weight - her cheeks looked hollow and her arms were nearly skeletal. When she finally turned her gaze to him, he flashed back in his mind to the first time they'd met in rehab. He saw again the flicker of passion and pain, the pure, no-filter, open-to-everything feeling that he'd seen in her glassy, red eyes the first moment they met. Now her eyes were clear, but the fire burned in them just as brightly. "So are we gonna do this?" he asked her, tilting his head to indicate the pile of mushrooms on the table.

Her glittery, painted eyelids fluttered. Bobby saw that Alexander was watching the moment unfold, bemused, over her shoulder. She focused on Bobby's eyes again. "It's New Year's," she said.

He nodded eagerly. "It's New Year's. We've made it this far!"

She stared deeply into his eyes. Unspoken words made the air crackle between them. "Fuck it," she said, lifting up a stem of psilocybin mushroom to her lips. "To 1991." Bobby poured them each a beer from a pitcher on the table. They popped the 'shrooms in their mouths, clinked glasses, and washed them down the hatch.

Ear Wax leaned back in his seat, fingers laced behind his head. "Just a matter of time now," he said. He let his eyes close and bobbed his head to the music in the bar. "Hey, wait a minute." He turned to Brandon. "Can you play on 'shrooms?"

Brandon was still chewing. He thought about it for minute. "I think so," he said. "Can you?" Ear Wax just laughed.

A frenzied Amelia appeared at the table. "Chop-chop, guys! Marco is setting up by himself! Give him a hand already!" Alexander and his rhythm section followed her backstage. The singer turned and blew big theatrical kisses to his friends over his shoulder. Bethany's face melted into a smile for the first time all night.

The Disney Wizards hit the stage first. They brought a motley collection of instruments: a 1970s home electric keyboard with fake wood paneling and built-in rhythm tracks; battery-powered toy saxophones, clarinets, and guitars; a child's drum kit from a Sears Christmas Catalogue of days gone by. The house lights suddenly went dark and a murmur went through the crowd. A kid in a football jersey put a record on a turntable with one headphone to his ear. Another, in a doctor's lab coat and fuzzy slippers with no pants, grabbed the microphone in one fist and began shouting incoherently at the top of his lungs. The band beeped, bleated and thumped behind him, like a school music room full of angry first-graders. The DJ played shiny, soulless, synthetic samples from The Thompson Twins and The Human League, while the frontman bounced across the front of the stage, shouting semi-coherent punk-rock vocalese into the mic like his life depended on it. A colored strobe flashing on and off and a spinning disco ball refracting its riot of color in a thousand directions compounded the sonic chaos. The lab coat guy ceased his shouting and took a solo: he grabbed a child's Speak 'N' Spell toy and frantically pounded its keys, holding its little speaker up to the microphone. A small knot of very young fans who had gathered in front of the stage went crazy with joy.

"That's a hell of a way to start a trip!" Bobby shouted over the racket. He turned his big brown happy-sad eyes to Bethany. She leaned against the wall, full breasts cupped by her tight top, one long leg pointed forward, the crazy kaleidoscope light playing over her body. Her face hardened into a mask even as the music and lights and drugs began dissolving her friends into puddles. She stared ahead at the stage and wouldn't look at Bobby.

Eli and Camille shook their heads in disgust at the Disney Wizards. "What the fuck is that?" said Camille after the first song ended. "Some kind of performance art disaster?"

But Kate saw and heard something different. "Oh my god, I think I just saw the future!" she blurted out, googly-eyed, alternately leaning on Eli and then Camille for support. Her pretty little knees could barely hold her up; she wobbled on her giant heels with the whiskey and the mushrooms turning her limbs to noodles. Eli and Camille steadied her on her feet, gave her water, stroked her hair and told her everything would be alright. Suddenly Kate was crying. "I love you guys!" she said, throwing her arms around their necks and pulling them to her in a tight three-way embrace. She didn't let go. Eli felt sobs run through Kate's body and Camille's strong, even breath through hers. He wanted to hold on, to hold on to them both and never let them go, but he knew he couldn't.

He opened his eyes and his lashes touched Camille's in an inadvertent butterfly kiss. The crazy blaring music started up again; the flashing psychedelic light projected shifting red and green and blue on their faces. Camille smiled and met Eli's eyes and understood everything. She pulled Kate close to her, whispered in her ear, and rocked her gently back and forth like a baby sister who woke up in the night from a bad dream.

The Naked Way hit the Gothic Theater stage at quarter to midnight on New Year's Eve. Marco stomped on stage with his guitar slung over his shoulder like a solider with his rifle going off to war. He pulled hard from a half-pint whiskey bottle before tuning his axe anxiously. Brandon and Ear Wax seemed to float onto the stage, grinning ear to ear. Brandon turned serious when he got behind his drum kit; he tested the heft of his sticks and warmed up with an improvised slow blues groove. Ear Wax joined in. The crowd cheered with excitement and surged forward towards the still-darkened stage. More than two thousand people filled the hall, by far the most they'd ever played to.

Marco struck a chord – a giant, electric chord, a master chord that seemed like it would never stop reverberating. It finally faded out to a waning feedback echo. Suddenly a singer emerged from the backstage darkness to center stage and grabbed the microphone – Justin. His female fans in the audience screamed. He wore an Abe Lincoln top hat and smiled his lazy eye smile out at the audience. He flipped the trademark dreads back over his shoulder before he spoke.

"Ladies and Gentlemen," said Justin into the mic, "these young men have come from nowhere – out of the unformed primal muck – and made some real noise in this town. Some people think they're going to pass us by pretty soon..." –he was interrupted by mixed boos and cheers from the crowd. Marco glared but Justin paid no attention. "That's right," he continued. "This band may be too big for our little town. But we won't worry about that tonight – tonight's New Year's Eve!" He thrust a fist in the air half-heartedly; the crowd roared. "Tonight," he continued, stepping to the side and indicating the three instrumentalists with a sweep of his arm, "tonight this group is beyond arrogance or humility. They're playing charades on a thunder cloud." Marco fingered a low, distorted, grumbling chord. "They're walking and chewing gum at the same time," said Justin, looking right at Marco, his voice booming and echoing through the hall over scattered laughter. "They're kissed by destiny and riding a state of grace – ladies and gentlemen – The Naked Way!"

The band kicked in and Alexander exploded from the darkness to center stage. Justin passed him the microphone and disappeared behind the curtains. The house lights flashed, momentarily blinding the audience, then gave way to a single spotlight on the singer. His golden hair shone like fire. The song was *Sister Sweet*. It began as a melancholy guitar lick that churned and built and swelled into a pulsing, rollicking rave-up. Eli and his friends were jostled as the crowd surged towards the band. Hands reached out for Alexander's boots as he prowled the stage. The music drove him mad; when Marco dug into a blistering solo, Alexander threw himself into the audience. They passed him above their heads out into the crowd and back again, just in time for him to clamber back on stage, spring to his feet, grab the mic and sing the next verse.

Eli felt hands on his shoulders and a body leaping onto his back — it was Kate, clinging to him, arms round his neck, saying "Put me up on your shoulders!" So he did; she rode him with devil-horn fingers pumping in the air as the band rode the biggest, wickedest groove imaginable, sending palpable waves of energy that swept up everybody in the hall in an enormous oceanic tide. Kate screamed with joy as the music carried them higher and higher, pounding wave after wave. Her hot, silky smooth thighs clamped tighter around Eli's neck as she held on for dear life in the surging, rocking sea of bodies.

On stage, Alexander danced a crazed dervish dance around Marco, who wrung a devastating climax out of his fretboard. Cymbals clashed; Ear Wax's floor-shaking bass line folded up upon itself; the universe of sound from Marco's guitar feedback slowly melted down into its most basic elements, which finally dissolved and trickled away into nothingness; Brandon sounded the song's death-rattle on his tom-tom drums.

The crowd roared. Alexander stalked the edge of the stage, shielding his eyes against bright stage lights to make out faces and see into souls. He dropped gingerly to one knee and put his hand to his brow, as if to pray. Instead he looked up and recited an improvised soliloquy into the microphone. "Last night I was out walking," he said, taking the hand of a beautiful girl in the front row. He turned and lowered his voice to a confessional tone, as if speaking only to her. "And I found this tiny flower, see." Her muffled giggle was audible through his mic. "And I picked it," said Alexander, pantomiming picking a flower, "and I thought of someone else, but then it reminded me of myself again." He tossed away the imaginary flower with disdain. "And I had to go..." He dropped the girl's hand unceremoniously, stood up and walked away.

The crowd shrieked with uncomprehending excitement. Alexander took center stage and preached as Brandon and Ear Wax improvised a shuffling blues riff. "Those who have become spiritual," the singer intoned, his eyes bugging ominously, "know that if they HUNGER...they cause MURDERS!"

"Oh my god!" yelled Kate into Eli's ear. "I just saw bats flying out of Alexander's cape!"

"Bats?" Eli shouted over the crowd. "He doesn't have a cape!" As the audience surged forward again, Eli felt Kate starting to panic. Her body convulsed, her legs tightened around him, she grabbed clumps of his hair in her hand for balance. He quickly stooped to one knee to let her down, but it was too late: a warm, chunky liquid splattered on his hair and his shirt and jeans. Kate was violently puking up her feast of mushrooms and whiskey.

Kate was inconsolable. She wanted to be taken home to her mother, despite the fact that she was tripping out of her mind and the clock had just struck midnight on New Year's Eve. "My mom parties, she'll understand," she told Eli in the lobby as she softly sobbed and tried to wipe the vomit off her shirt.

He drove Kate home in her car. She sat fuming and softly weeping in the passenger seat. The embarrassment factor took on epic proportions in her mind. She wouldn't hear anything of clean shirts and going back to the show – vomiting on oneself in public was a humorless catastrophe that required total withdrawal from the situation. Eli strained to focus on the task of driving, ignoring as best he could the streaks of light, elastic telephone poles, and other manifestations of the mushroom trip passing in the night outside the VW Bug's windshield. On the car radio, Melissa Etheridge kept demanding that somebody bring her some water; Eli turned the dial to the classical music station. "I can't believe I had to leave Brandon's show after one song!" Kate lisped through the tears. "I was having a genuine aesthetic experience!"

Chapter 17

THIS WIDE-WASTING PESTILENCE

Eli walked the sniffling, disheveled Kate up to her doorstep, where her mother gratefully shepherded her inside. Mom was around forty but looked like she could be Kate's big sister; Kate had her figure and good looks. She tried to get Eli to come inside; he could see that she could see that they were tripping their heads off, but it was okay. Mom had kindly eyes. Eli gave her the keys to Kate's car and insisted that he should get home, he'd be fine. He watched her lips – the same shape as her daughter's – wrap themselves around the words *thank you* as she closed the door.

It was way too far to walk back to the show, and getting a cab on New Year's Eve seemed hopeless. Eli walked home on old red flagstone sidewalks that breathed and pulsed and turned to mosaics of grinning skulls under his footsteps. Darkened canopies of tree limbs laced together above his head, their icy branches backlit by a cold, luminous full moon that watched his journey silently from on high. Sirens, music from open windows, drunken shouts and shattering beer bottles thrown from passing cars provided a chaotic soundtrack.

When he finally made it to his apartment, Eli cleaned himself up, lay down in the dark and felt the trip surge through him, taking him up and down like a roller coaster. Closing his eyes, he saw and heard The Naked Way in his mind almost as vividly as if he'd stayed at the concert. *Sister Sweet* played on a loop in his brain; he saw each giant chord as much as he heard it. Finally he resorted to music to clear his mind of music and to bring him back to rest in his body. He put on the John Coltrane Quartet - *After the Rain* - and drifted off to sleep.

The scream of the telephone smashed into his face, jolted his body, shocked his mind to attention. He reached out unseeing toward the piercing noise and found the receiver in time to silence it halfway through the second ring. "Hello?"

"Eli. Eli, are you there?" It was Brandon. A twisted, frantic, deranged version of Brandon he'd never heard before. "Do you have your ID with you?" he asked.

"Brandon! It's ok, Kate got sick, I took her home. Camille was supposed to tell you. She's fine."

Brandon gave no sign of knowing who Kate was. "Do you have your ID with you?" he asked again. "That proves who you are. You might be somebody! I don't know who I am right now. Does the ID make me real? Who *am* I, Eli? Who the fuck am *I*?"

"See now, wait," Eli interjected. He sat up in bed, rubbing his eyes in the darkness. "See what you're doing to yourself with semantics? You're you. You're still you, Brandon."

"Eli, will you check my ID? It says my name right here. And my age. We're so young...we're so goddamn young, Eli!"

Eli held his head and winced. He lay back and covered his face with a pillow. The clock read 5:12 AM. "Brandon, who's sober over there?" he asked. "Are you okay?"

The voice changed. "Eli?" It was Camille.

"Camille, talk to me," Eli said with relief. "What the hell is going on?"

"Shit, where do I start? It was a great fucking show. The best yet. They totally blew the room away, and half the crowd left before Twice Jilted went on. But then everything got screwed up. Amelia wanted a bigger cut on the door because The Naked Way pulled most of the crowd in. Justin and the Gothic manager didn't want to give it to her. Marco went nuts and threatened people...threw a bottle through a window. Ear Wax and Brandon finally got him out of there before the police came."

"Christ. Then what?"

"Then everyone started getting high. Higher. Again."

"What happened to the meet with the agents afterwards – the skinny tie guys? The tour opening for Afghan Whigs?"

"Critically fucked. Amelia left them standing there while she got into a pissing match with Justin. I watched the agents shake their heads at each other and go. Ear Wax followed them and tried to talk them out of leaving. They patted him on the head and kept going right out the door."

"Fucking shit."

He heard the sound of the receiver jostling on the other end. Alexander's voice came on the line. "Young master Eli! We'll be needing your services! Come over to Amelia's apartment, won't you, lad? You've got to lead your people out of Egypt.

Bobby spent his whole paycheck on coke and acid from a guy Bethany knows. Quite a fancy little bird, this Bethany! She might be the queen of *all* my dreams." Alexander laughed, and a woman's musical voice laughed with him. Bethany. Eli had never heard a happy sound come from her mouth before.

Eli gritted his teeth. "Rich college girls get all the best drugs. You know that, Pontiff."

"It's getting pretty heavy," Alexander said. "The coke is half gone and the acid is hitting hard. The trip is coming back…but this time it's synthetic. Plastic fantastic, you dig?"

"You fucking guys. Did you pitch in any money? How's Bobby going to pay rent? He just spent a shit ton on that fancy mountain bike."

"Money? You know that as high priest I can't concern myself with such matters. Please, Eli. Help us, Obi-wan Kenobi, you're our only hope. Your friend, young master Brandon, is on the brink. He needs his Rabbi already…what? Brandon says bring your ID!"

Eli arrived to a scene of total debauchery. Amelia's apartment was lit only with strings of Christmas lights and an eerie purple blacklight glowing from a desk lamp. Eli's eyes adjusted slowly. Bethany was sitting on Alexander's lap in an overstuffed chair, kissing him. Brandon and Bobby were sitting at Amelia's desk, examining their IDs under the blacklight. In front of Bobby was a crude but poignant ink sketch of a naked Christ hanging on the cross. Giant nails pierced his wrists; equally giant cock and balls hung between his legs. Bobby showed the drawing to Eli, who smiled approvingly. "I've always preferred my messiahs well-hung," he said.

Camille blew him a kiss from where she sat reclining on the couch. Next to her was Ear Wax, who smiled blissfully and held a twelve-pack of Milwaukee's Best beer on his lap. Hüsker Dü played low on Amelia's cheap boom box stereo. The tinny little speakers and the purple haze of psychedelic static in the room made their heavy rock songs sound cartoonish, even comical. Bobby tugged on Eli's sleeve. He used his ID to scrape together a line of cocaine on a mirror that lay flat on the desk. "Pull up a seat, big boy," he said.

Eli shook him off. "I've sworn off coke before breakfast," he deadpanned.

Brandon finally turned to look at Eli. His hair was a mess of blonde spikes and his eyes were big as saucers. "Did you bring your ID?" he asked in deadly earnest.

Eli patted him on the shoulder. "Yeah, buddy. Still me. You're still you too, far as I can tell." He turned to Alexander, who had gotten to his feet and loomed tall and shadowy in the half-dark, the Christmas lights like stars twinkling around his head. "What the fuck, you guys!" said Eli. "No more drugs for the drummer, you're gonna kill him!" Brandon shook Eli's hand off his shoulder and bent his head over the desk to snort another line through a chopped McDonald's straw.

Alexander put an arm around Eli. "Don't worry about us, mother superior," he said. There were agents at the show tonight...they left but they'll be back. They saw what they saw. They heard what they heard. Nothing can stop destiny. Amelia has meetings set up for next week. We might open for The Meat Puppets on their tour this summer. Fuck the Afghan Whigs anyway! The wheel of fate is turning, young master Eli. And now, we will celebrate in nature. You're taking us on a magical mystery tour to paradise. Back to Eden. We've got to get ourselves back to the garden!" Bethany came up from behind the singer, wrapping her arms around him. She undid the top button on his silk shirt as he spoke and ran her fingers over his taught, smooth chest. Her fingernails were painted a deep, royal purple.

Eli struggled to keep a smile on his face. "Amelia is a hell of a manager, isn't she?"

Alexander grinned an ironic grin. "She certainly is. Great job, darling!" he shouted toward the bedroom. "Keep up the good work!" Bethany cackled and kissed him on the cheek, neck, ears.

Eli went to the bedroom and found Amelia face down on the bed in panties and an open blouse. Her pert round bottom was highlighted by a shaft of light from the door. He smelled vomit. In the darkness he kicked a trashcan next to the bed; it turned out to be the puke receptacle. He checked to make sure her pulse and breathing were okay. Leaning in close, the scent of her perfume caught him up: lilacs, déjà vu, lost things. Then the smell was overpowered by the stench from the trashcan again, sickly sweet, and the moment was gone. He brushed the hair away from Amelia's face, pulled the blanket over her, and closed the door behind him as he returned to the party.

"She has a great ass, doesn't she?" said Alexander. Bethany slapped him full across the face, hard. Everyone turned to look. Alexander just stared at her, wry smile and laughing eyes. She laughed and pulled him to her by the back of the neck and kissed him.

Ear Wax handed Eli a beer and put on a Flaming Lips tape. Eli slumped into a chair next to Brandon and Bobby. "This acid is seriously kickin' in right now, hoo boy!" whooped the bass player. Bobby snorted and grinned and wiped his sleeve across his face, smearing white powder on his shirt.

Eli shook his head at the whole scene. "Crazy fuckers," he said. "Give me some of that." Without a word, Brandon cut two fat lines and slid the mirror to Eli. Their eyes met.

Brandon's gaze was distant, unfocused, vaguely terrified. Eli covered a nostril and snorted deep through the other. He let out a gasp and a howl as the coke hit his brain. A demented scarecrow smile slowly cracked open the tight façade of Brandon's face. Bobby laughed.

"Don't get too comfortable, Pablo Escobar," said Alexander. "I wasn't kidding about the road trip." He handed Eli a set of keys. "To Ear Wax's van. City Park, Captain," said Alexander. He executed a crisp salute; Eli had to laugh. "Your mission, if you accept it, is to drive this motley crew of rock stars, drug addicts and vagabonds to the park for a healing dawn ritual. A cleansing ceremony in nature..."

"Cleansing ceremony...I'll give you a cleansing ceremony right up your rear end," snorted Camille. She turned to Bethany, tilting her head towards Alexander and silently mouthing *what the fuck?* Bethany smiled coquettishly and shrugged *who, me?* Camille rolled her eyes and took a slug from Eli's beer.

"Alrighty then," said Eli. "Everybody in the van." The bathroom door opened slowly and a new face emerged. A pouty, pretty, pixie-faced girl with an almost boy-ishly petite figure and a bobbed brunette haircut drifted shyly across the floor.

"Eli, this is Tessa," said Camille. "She latched on to us during the show. I think she's tripping pretty hard. Tessa, honey? You want some water? Beer?" Tessa turned slowly in response to her name, as if in a dream. Bobby smiled and offered her a beer. Her face flushed red and she took the beer without a word. "I think she came with Ear Wax's cousin," Camille said. "Or that guy I had the cross-cultural psychology class with last year? I can't remember. Tessa, honey, do you remember? Who did you come to the show with?" Tessa just stood there silently looking at her shoes and sipping timidly on her beer. "Oh well," said Camille. "We're going on a little trip, come on darling." Tessa smiled and shuffled after Bobby as they all left the apartment for the van.

Alexander serenaded Bethany through the halls and down the echoing stairwell with an old Sinatra number: *Fly me to the moon, let me play up there with the stars...* "Quiet!" Camille hissed. "Amelia's neighbors are sleeping!"

A battered old pick-up truck crawled past along the street outside as they piled into the van. A bearded old man with a wool cap pulled down tight over his head threw newspapers at darkened doorways from the back of the pick-up; steam hissed from manhole covers in the street and drifted up through the glow of pink-orange streetlights into the blackness of infinite night. Bobby pulled out a little plastic baggy with tiny colorful LSD blotters and dangled it in front of Eli as he started the van. "No way, buddy," Eli said, waving it off. "How am I going to take care of you guys if I'm out there orbiting Jupiter with you?"

Camille handed Eli a cassette tape of Lou Reed's *New York* album for the van's stereo. "It takes a busload of faith to get by, baby!" she said, before kissing him on the cheek and piling into the back of the van.

Ear Wax, in the passenger seat, wrinkled his nose at the sound coming from the speakers. "Lou Reed? The Velvets were great but he's too old, he's over!"

"Lou Reed is never over!" Alexander roared from the back seat. "Your grandchildren's grandchildren ten times removed will all be dead and buried and forgotten, Lou fucking Reed will still be happening!"

"Ok, take it easy!" Ear Wax snorted. "I could really go for some Slayer right now is all I'm sayin'…"

"Oh *hell* no, not on my magical mystery tour you don't," said Eli.

"You guys are harshing my trip!" complained Brandon earnestly from the back. "Big time!"

"You guys are marshing my harshmallow!" retorted Eli.

They pulled up to a red traffic light along a commercial strip. Storefront neon danced for the trippers' eyes in the urban wasteland gloom of predawn. Ear Wax bobbed his head to the music in the passenger seat, despite his earlier protest. Eli looked in the rearview mirror and saw Bethany. Her glassy eyes shone with a spectral light. A passing headlight flashed in the rearview, momentarily blinding him. When the light receded, Eli and Bethany's eyes met in the mirror. She looked into him, and through him, like a cat would. Her thick black mascara and arched painted eyebrows amplified her coked-out glare. She was sitting in Alexander's lap, running her fingers through his long wavy hair. The singer leaned into view and grinned a wicked grin at Eli from behind his Wayfarer shades, which he wore un-ironically in the dead of night.

As the van straightened out onto Colfax Avenue, Eli caught sight of Bobby in the rearview: little Tessa sat on his lap grinning from ear to ear. Their faces were close together; Bobby laughed nervously and looked away, out the window into the night. "Pretty colors!" he said, pointing out the red riot of neon to Tessa as if she were a child. She laughed; passing crimson and blue light danced across her face with the movement of the van. Bobby laughed with her – until he got a mouthful of Bethany's hair. Alexander had bent her backwards in a deep kiss that pushed her back into Bobby and Tessa's space. Tessa just giggled; Bobby spat Bethany's blonde-and-black streaked hair out of his mouth. Eli watched his eyes narrow in anger and bulge in disbelief before he found center again and forced out a laugh. He put his hand on Tessa's back tentatively. Alexander pulled Bethany back up into his lap and reached a hand up her top. She let out a little moan.

"Jesus Christ, enough already!" screamed Camille from the far back seat. "Get a fucking room!"

The van rolled to a stop in an empty lot at City Park under barren looming trees and silent stars. Ear Wax got out of the passenger seat and opened the side door. Everyone tumbled out into the moonlit fantasy landscape. The park had a panoramic view of the city skyline: lights twinkled from empty office skyscrapers a few miles away and behind them, in the distance, the Rocky Mountains spanned the darkened horizon in mute meditation. Slowly, the mountains began to gather the blackness of night back into themselves. Intimations of first morning light turned the distant snowcaps a ghostly deep blue. A man-made cross of light on a mountainside, a thumbnail in the sky a hundred miles away, drew lost souls hovering in the ether to itself like an airport runway beckoning to lost pilots in the fog. Layers and shades and stripes of blue and black and indigo throbbed and melted and unfolded slowly into one another above the horizon.

"The mountains are breathing, man," said Brandon.

Alexander put his arm around the drummer. "They're sleeping. They're dreaming of us."

Ear Wax leaped up onto a park bench and held his beer high, toasting the horizon. "They're thinking, *how can we be as cool as The Naked fucking Way?*"

Tessa stood apart, staring up at a skeletal elm tree with childlike wonder. She wrapped her arms around its trunk and let out a little sigh of contentment.

"I thought 'tree-hugger' was a metaphor," Bobby said. "Like a mean stereotype made up by Republicans."

"Looks like you've got the real thing," Eli said. "She's cute, no?"

"Hell yeah," Bobby said, pulling out a cigarette from a pack in his pocket.

Tessa wandered away out of the clearing and into a thicket of bushes and trees. "Watch out, the raccoons will eat you!" Alexander hollered.

"Leave her be!" said Bobby. Sounds of rustling leaves and snapping twigs came from the darkness. Finally Tessa returned with a big self-satisfied smile, holding a large branch in her arms. The branch was of dead, cracked, graying wood and was nearly as long as she was tall. She cradled it awkwardly, holding it tenderly to her chest like a new-born even as its end dragged heavily on the ground. "What have you got there?" Bobby asked.

She frowned and pulled the branch closer to her bosom. "Mine!" she said. It was the first word Eli had heard her utter all night.

Bobby laughed but nodded approvingly. "A walking stick," he said. "I think she's on to something. There's not much we can latch onto in this world of bullshit and lies." He shot a pained expression at Bethany. "Hang on to the most basic thing you can find. A simple, sturdy walking stick. It's a good start." At this, Tessa smiled and sat down next to him on the picnic table bench, still clutching her prized find.

"This is brilliant," Eli said. "Give somebody a couple tabs of acid and you get to watch the whole development of the human race all over again. Consciousness starting over from square one. The invention of technology. First, the stick. Next, the stone age?"

"No, don't you see?" interjected Alexander. "You of all people, young Master Eli. This is metaphysics, not materialism. It's a totem. She's found her god! Worship is what separates us from the animals. She's like a walking illustration from one of your religious anthropology books."

"There are spirits in the trees and in the branches," said Camille, who stood apart with her back to the group, staring at the moon hanging over the horizon of darkened city and mountains. Her silhouette was still, except for the smoke from her cigarette that drifted up to the sky. "And there are spirits in the birds and the sun and the sky," she said.

"Okay Mother Earth, not you too! Jesus Christ!" exclaimed Bobby. "I'm surrounded by fucking ecstatic hippie Jesus-freak Jungians. But I don't accept it! I don't believe in what I can't see!"

"You can't see love, Bobby," Bethany said.

He sprung to his feet. "From *you*! That's rich. This" — he drew a frantic line in the air connecting Bethany and Alexander — "proves to me that there is no such *thing* as love. No such thing — we're just monkeys running around looking for anything hot-blooded with a pulse to grind on." He paced around the group in a little circle, making his case like a lawyer arguing before a jury. His eyes were bloodshot and his fingers twitched where they hung at his side. "I'm losing all faith in humanity right now!" he said. "Are we just apes? Armpit-scratching monkeys? Is this as good as it gets?"

Brandon snorted a bump of coke off of his apartment key. "This is pretty god-damn good, Bobby." As if to second Brandon's affirmation, just then the peaks of the surreal skyline over his shoulder — both man-made and natural — were touched by highlights of rose from the coming dawn in the east.

"I have to agree with Brandon, Bobby," nodded Eli. "Pretty goddamn good. Look at us. You can't say we aren't living the life now, can you?"

"We were born monkeys, Bobby," said Alexander, his voice taking on a theatrical tenor. "But we become gods. By our will, we become gods incarnate!" His blue eyes were wide, glowing with self-belief. "We walk the earth as supermen!" he shouted, leaping onto a creaky steel merry-go-round. Ear Wax gave the steel wheel a push, spinning Alexander around faster and faster. The singer stood in the rotating center, hair flying, laughing, fists raised defiantly to the sky. Bethany ran to him, leaping heedlessly onto the merry-go-round. Their limbs entangled in a blur and Bethany screamed; they went flying off the merry-go-round into the sand, thrown clear by the force of the spinning wheel. Their bodies lay in a heap, unmoving.

"Oh shit," said Ear Wax, frozen in place. The creaky merry-go-round spun on without its passengers; the cold metal glinted dull in the moonlight. At last the human pile stirred. Alexander leapt to his feet laughing. He picked up Bethany in his arms and carried her back to the group through the web of shadows under the haunted trees. "The gods die and are resurrected to new life!" he proclaimed. Bethany clung to him, arms around his neck. Alexander put her down on her feet; Camille handed her a fresh beer and brushed the sand out of her hair with her hands. Bethany straightened herself, tossed her hair and put her hands on her hips, as if she were posing on an invisible catwalk.

Eli could see Bobby wanted to fight. He stepped up to Alexander, shuffling his feet on the ground like a bull ready to charge, even though he looked half the other man's size. The singer smiled down at him indulgently. Bobby stared back, inarticulate rage spinning inside him, shaking his head back and forth, kicking the ground and spraying dirt at his antagonist's feet. Finally he poked a finger into Alexander's chest. "No more of this mytho-poetic psycho-babble," he said. Bobby's soft brown eyes were bugging out of his head, his pupils huge from the drugs and adrenaline. "That might work on stage, but not in the real world. You can't just..." His voice trailed off as he stared at Bethany. She circled away from him, keeping Alexander between herself and Bobby. "Just cut the fucking bullshit!" Bobby shouted. "I see a world of people struggling, fighting, suffering. But I can't see what it's all for. Love, god, spirits, fucking mysticism. Bullshit! Give me something real!" He was practically frothing at the mouth, straining to meet Bethany's eyes as she maneuvered to keep away. "Don't you remember the things we went through together, Bethany? What the fuck are you doing, doing coke and drinking all night? And since when do you fucking smoke?" A cigarette burned between his own two fingers as he pointed them accusingly at Bethany.

She turned indignant. "What am *I* doing?" she screamed at him from behind the towering singer. "This shit is going to *kill* you, Bobby!"

"Fucking hypocrite!" shouted Bobby. "Still using your Narcotics Anonymous key chain? Two years clean my ass! You've been on a bender of epic fucking proportions ever since you met this wanna-be rock star," he sneered, pointing at Alexander. "When's the last time you were at a meeting?"

Bethany started weeping. "Fuck you, Bobby! Fuck you and fuck every minute of every hour I spent with your stupid addict ass! Listening to you tear yourself down, over and over again. Never changing, never growing." Now Alexander was keeping her from getting at Bobby; he scooped her up in his long arms and lifted her away as she lunged at him. "You're a hopeless case!" she growled at Bobby through gritted teeth, straining to break through Alexander's arms. "When's the last time *you* were at a meeting?"

"August 28, 1989, that's when!" Bobby yelled at the top of his lungs. "But I don't pretend I'm something I'm not, and I'm never going back!" He dug through his pockets and found a coin, which he held out to her. "Here's a quarter," he said. "Call your sponsor!" Bethany surged at him again; Alexander held her back with evident effort but equal amusement. His eyes met Eli's; Alexander flashed a wicked, mirthful smile.

"Man, chill, you guys!" said Ear Wax. "The police gotta come through here once in a while, right?"

Bobby ignored him. "Oh, and you know what?" Bobby said, pointing his cigarette at Alexander but giving significant looks to Brandon and Ear Wax as well. "Your band *fucking sucks*." Brandon raised an eyebrow. "It's just another con, isn't it? Smoke, lights, noise. And you've got people who should know better" – he tilted his head at Camille and Eli, who responded with comic-surprised *who me?* shrugs – "convinced that you're some kind of witchdoctor alchemist about to turn lead into gold or some shit! Or fucking William Blake with a power trio! When what you're really doing is bouncing around, jerking yourself off all over the stage, getting everybody all lathered up until the girls' private parts are engorged like fucking orangutans!"

"Whoa!" Camille and Bethany yelled in unison. Bobby was the one who was all lathered up; he wiped spittle from his mouth.

"Actually, Bobby," piped up Ear Wax, "if I'm not mistaken, it's the Bonobo monkeys that are known for engorged sexual organs. I wrote a report about them in high school once. You see, when the female's monthly cycle…"

Bethany dismissed him with a wave. "Oh really, Bobby?" she screamed. "Who's the wanker? Some people talk about art and poetry and philosophy until they're blue in the face. But *some* people just *do* it. Some people stop and write it down and do the work and *make* something."

Bobby ran his hands through his sandy curls in exasperation. "Oh yeah? *Some* people have mommies and daddies and trust funds and brand new Jeeps and expensive educations." He circled around, trying to get closer to Bethany; she and Alexander maneuvered away, matching him step for step as if in a choreographed dance. "You know what I have? I have a library card!" bawled Bobby. "A library card, a job cutting meat and seafood for $7.25 an hour, and zero fucking days sober!"

"Fuck you, Bobby!" Bethany screamed. Her face was streaked with tears and running mascara and rage. "You're just pure pain! That's all you are," she hissed.

The three of them stood frozen in a pose of tragi-comic confrontation: Bobby was a scrappy, undersized mutt poised to attack. The moment extended, a beat too long. Bethany writhed in Alexander's arms between them; she grunted and sobbed and struggled as he whispered endearments and calm in her ear. It sounded to Eli like the unsynched audio track of a bad 70s porno flick.

Brandon stood up slowly and deliberately, not looking at anyone in particular, and took a slug from his beer. Finally he cocked his head to one side thoughtfully and asked, "Does anybody remember laughter?" The crisis of the trip had passed for Brandon; his sardonic, aloof cool returned.

They did remember laughter. Bobby laughed in spite of himself. "Brandon, you son of a bitch," he chuckled. Laughter washed over the group, except for Bethany, who glared holes through the back of Brandon's head. She turned and buried her face in Alexander's chest.

"No tears," Alexander said, stroking her hair as she wept softly. "There, there. *Listen* darling. I'm writing a *poem* for you." He spun away from her, gesturing like a high-school drama-club Shakespearean orator. "The world is a poem that we walk through together. A poem is a new world in miniature. And this" – he swept his arms, taking in the vast shrouded universe being born again around them – "is a new world. *Our* new world." He dropped to one knee before Bethany and took her hand. He looked up at her beseechingly. "True opener of my eyes, prime angel blessed!" She grinned weakly at him through the sobs. "Be glad of spirit, my love! Much better seems this vision, and more hope of peaceful days portends, than all the pains we've suffered. We leave it all behind and go forward into our own kingdom!"

He kissed her hand tenderly. Then he rose to his feet and bounded up onto a large boulder. From atop it he addressed his tribe like an acid-crazed Old Testament prophet. "And yet, even in the new dawn, there are demons tugging at our souls," he intoned solemnly. "Accuse not nature! She has done her part!" At this, a flight of geese took off from the park's man-made lake, which the creeping light had revealed in the middle distance. The geese honked and soared into the crumbling darkness of the sky; the surface of the lake rippled silently, with pixels of copper and gold and violet shifting like static on an old television set left on overnight.

Alexander smiled, gratified at nature's endorsement of his rant. "With obsequious majesty she approved my pleaded reason," he smirked knowingly. "By my love" – he looked meaningfully at Bethany – "by *our* love, my queen, this wide-wasting pestilence is transformed..."

He was interrupted by a volley of small missiles. One hit him in the chest. Another fell at his feet, bouncing off the boulder to the ground. Ear Wax was chucking pinecones at him. "Hey man, the show's over," Ear Wax said. "Save it for next time."

Alexander tisked at him. "Dear boy. Can't you see, your brutish vice disfigures your own likeness, not God's?"

Ear Wax chuckled and shook his head and opened another beer. "Whatever you say. You're the authority on brutish vice."

Bobby sat down on the picnic table bench next to Tessa and laughed. His rage had subsided. Eli watched as he tentatively put his hand on Tessa's. She giggled shyly and looked away but didn't move her hand; with her other hand she nervously stroked the totem-stick.

Bethany approached the boulder where Alexander stood. She trembled and hugged her chest with her folded arms and looked at the ground. He leapt down to meet her. "Please...shut up," she begged him. "I'm cold...I'm tripping too hard right now." She wrapped her arms around him and slid down to her knees. Her sobs redoubled as she clung to his waist. Dawn began boiling over just below the horizon; the growing light showed her eyes puffy and red, mascara running down her face. In the strange psychedelic morning she looked like a broken, defeated goddess, lovingly rendered in a Pre-Raphaelite painting. Or an impossibly beautiful supermodel in a debauched postmodern fashion shoot staged by a sadistic photographer. "No. More. Talking!" she cried on her knees, clinging to Alexander's long, lean body, her nails digging into his thigh.

Camille shook her head. "Get up, Bethany. You're embarrassing me."

"Don't speak!" Bethany growled. "*Don't anybody fucking talk any more...*" Alexander crouched down and brushed the hair back from her face and wiped the tears from her eyes. She sniffled and looked up at him. Eli could barely make out her hushed voice. "I have some pills," she whimpered. "In my purse. More coke...in the van." Alexander nodded. They rose and he took her hand and led her to the van, parked a hundred feet away.

An awkward silence descended on the rest of the group as the two climbed in the van and closed the door behind them. Bobby's face clouded over again; he pulled out a fifth of Jack Daniels from his back pocket and took an angry shot. Tessa frowned and hugged her branch.

At first Eli thought the squeaking sound was an animal. He looked around for a bird or a squirrel in the bushes. The sound was regular, rhythmic. Then he heard a muffled moan coming from the van. The squeaking sound was the sound of the van rocking. The group let out a collective groan, followed by snickers and hoots. Tessa stared at the van, wide-eyed, as it visibly rocked back and forth in place. She rose to her feet, turned to Bobby, and spoke her second word of the night. "Here," she said, handing her tree branch totem to him. He took it with a fragile smile.

Tessa turned and walked east towards the van just as the first rays of the sun came pouring over the horizon. She went straight into the honeyed light; the glare silhouetted her slender, girlish figure, surrounding her with pinwheels and streamers of pure radiance. The clouds drifting above her were pink and orange cotton candy. Dollops of hot caramel and butterscotch sunlight fell around her, splashing the parking lot and the van and the trees with color. She opened the door to the van, no hesitation, climbed in, and closed the door behind her. The rocking noise stopped abruptly.

"Oh shit!" said Ear Wax. "That girl has some stones!"

"Jesus Christ," said Camille, lighting a cigarette. "As if his ego isn't big enough already. One more notch in the belt."

Brandon whistled a dissonant melody and tapped out a nervous beat on his leg. Eli slowly got up and walked over to where Camille stood. He stretched his legs, then dug around in his pocket and handed her a joint. The van began rocking again. Bobby stood up. "Mother fucker," he muttered under his breath. With all his strength he threw the whiskey bottle at the boulder where Alexander had stood and preached. It shattered loudly into a thousand pieces.

Chapter 18

WAR

The Naked Way was broken up. Marco holed himself up in the warehouse, accusing Amelia and Alexander of botching their big chance to get noticed at the New Year's show. He jammed with Brandon now and then; they talked of starting another project with new guys. Brandon spent most of his time with Kate. She showed him off at high school parties as her "rock star boyfriend." "The band is on hiatus right now," she told people, whether they asked or not. Bobby and Eli teased him about getting back on the high school social circuit. Ear Wax jammed with his brother's group, a glorified Ramones cover band. Alexander and Amelia made themselves scarce. Amelia's usual table at *The Marketplace* was filled by tourists or sat empty. Buzzing her apartment, Eli got no answer.

Classes started up again at City College for the spring semester. The campus and the country were under the cloud of war. Saddam Hussein's Iraq had invaded Kuwait months before. Now, a huge international force led by the United States was arrayed across the desert to counter-attack. President Bush rallied the country for war. Men wore red, white and blue to show their war fervor; women, yellow ribbons. Whitney Houston led the country in a star-spangled military pep rally at the Super Bowl. The bombing started in mid-January.

Eli and most of his friends were revolted by the enthusiasm for war and the media cheerleading that made it seem like just a big patriotic video game. He tagged along with Camille and Bethany to peace rallies. The organizers were gentle, soft-spoken people, many of them Quakers, mostly middle-aged or older. Camille knew them all by name and greeted them with enthusiastic hugs and kisses; she'd been protesting with them against nuclear weapons and wars in Central America since before she was old enough to drive.

Eli admired the organizers but worried that they weren't getting their message across. Their rallies had a left-over feeling of Vietnam and the late 1960s, with gray-haired folk singers trying to fire up crowds with songs written for another generation. Eli knew they were playing right into the hands of the media, who dismissed questions about the war by portraying protestors as out-of-touch hippie hold-overs.

He got a phone call from Brandon on a February night. "Come by practice tomorrow night if you want. The band is back together," he said. "You won't fucking believe how it happened. Kate calls me last weekend and says this crazy punk rock street guy gave her two free passes to a preview of that new Oliver Stone movie about The Doors down at the Mayan Theater. So we go. While we're waiting in line to buy popcorn, in walks Ear Wax. Marco comes in right behind him with some girl he's seeing."

"And the Lizard King?"

"Right on time. Alexander and Amelia, arm in arm. They looked like a million bucks, too. In a thrift store kind of way. She had a feather boa and the little round Janis Joplin shades. He had a floor-length black leather jacket. We all just laughed. After the movie we stopped at the liquor store then all went back to the warehouse and played."

When Eli got to the warehouse the next night, the practice was almost over, but the party was just beginning. The Naked Way's circus had come back to town. A half dozen pretty young girls he'd never seen before were hanging around the practice space, along with a few guys from a new band called Wax Candies. Eli introduced himself around and opened up a beer. When the last song was over, Brandon and Ear Wax did a kind of slow-motion cartoon Indian dance, hopping from one foot to the other, in a circle around Alexander. He played along, mugging and posing with the microphone while Brandon and Ear Wax pantomimed. Eli shook his head. "What the fuck is that?" he asked. Marco snickered.

"You have to see The Doors movie," Ear Wax said. "Then it'll make sense."

"Ride the snake," Brandon said. "Kiss the snake on the lips!"

"I still think that's some hippie bullshit," Marco said. "But I have to admit" – he cracked a broad smile – "they were pretty good."

"Well, you guys have something in common with The Doors," said Eli. "You're playing in wartime, just like they did."

"I saw a bunch of civilians were killed by our bombs yesterday," said Ear Wax. "That's messed up."

"I've been going to some protests," Eli said. "You guys could really help. We need to get the message out to kids. You guys could play a benefit show a week from Saturday."

"Hell yeah!" said Ear Wax. "Fuck this war-for-oil shit."

Alexander cocked his head and smiled wryly at Eli. "Social responsibility! Make love not war! Fight the power and stick it to the man!" One of the girls floating around the warehouse, a curly-headed brunette with an angelic face and pouty red lips, tugged on his sleeve. Alexander kissed her on the cheek and pulled her close. "You see this diabolical man?" he asked her, tilting his head towards Eli. She laid her head against Alexander's broad chest and smiled up at Eli. "He could pull the devil's own heartstrings," Alexander said. "He knows it's the sworn duty of every rock god to lead the faithful in peace prayers."

"So you'll do it?" Eli asked.

"Hell yes, mother fucker!" the singer roared. Eli gave him a high five. The curly-haired girl laughed and dragged Alexander away to a more private corner of the warehouse.

Brandon was neutral. "I'll do it if everyone else wants to," he said with a shrug. He turned to Marco. "Did you get the phone turned back on? I'm supposed to call Kate."

Marco pointed Brandon to where the phone hung on the kitchen wall. He poured shots of Ouzo and handed them around. Some of the new girls had followed him and Eli into the kitchen. Marco pulled Eli away to talk more privately. "I don't know about this protest stuff," he said. "Isn't it just a bunch of druggies?"

They were interrupted by one of the guys from Wax Candies, a heavy-set kid in denim overalls with a Charlie Manson t-shirt. "Marco, we're making a liquor store run, need anything?"

Marco handed the guy a ten dollar bill. "*Mas tequila!*" he said. He guided Eli away from the growing spontaneous party into the doorway of a darkened bedroom where they could talk. "See, my grandpa fought in World War II..."

"Mine too," Eli interjected.

"My dad fought in Vietnam," Marco continued. "My uncle was in Korea. I have a cousin in Germany right now, he might have to go..."

"Don't worry, Eli," said Alexander's voice. "We'll be there!" Eli and Marco turned around; Alexander was shirtless and reclining in bed in the half-dark behind them. There was a rustling from a lump under the blankets between his legs. The curly brunette's head popped up from under the sheets. Looking sheepishly over her shoulder at Eli and Marco, she wiped her mouth and started fumbling behind her back to put her bra back on. Alexander stroked her hair. "No, sugar, you're doing a great job. Our friends were just leaving." He raised an eyebrow at Marco. "We're playing the peace show, and that's final!" Marco downed his shot and stalked out of the room. As Eli pulled the door shut behind him, the brunette flashed a smile and a peace sign at him before she pulled the covers back over her head. Alexander's toothy grin glinted in the darkness.

Chapter 19

FREE BIRD

The peace show was booked in an old fashioned dance hall above a hip hole-in-the-wall restaurant called *Horoscope*. The proprietress was a middle-aged hippie lady who hosted poetry slams and did astrological evaluations as part of her hiring process. The back of the ballroom began to fill with bodies grouping loosely into two camps: mostly older peace protestors who were there for political reasons, and a younger crowd drawn first and foremost by music. The Spixe – the reggae band that let The Naked Way play their first show as an opener - was now opening up for them.

Bobby stood in a little circle with his friends, shaking his head. "It's a good excuse for a night out and a drink, but it's a ritual of idealism. We all know the war isn't getting stopped. Eli thinks he's saving the world. It's an empty exercise. Nothing is certain except the viciousness and stupidity of human beings. Never bet against it."

Eli patted Bobby on the back. "I love it when you talk about me like I'm not even here," he said.

"It's not a bet, Bobby," said Camille. "It's a protest. It's saying *not in our name*. And even when you can't change the reality, you can mourn together. You can dream the world that you want together, even if that world doesn't exist. Yet."

"I think it's a waste and a goddamn shame," said Bethany. Her eyes scanned the crowd, looking past her friends. "The war, I mean," she added with a distracted air. Bobby kept trying to meet her gaze; her eyes darted here and there almost frantically to avoid his. "The invasion. The bombing. The war. Not the show."

"Of course it is," Bobby nodded. "A shame."

The *Horoscope*'s owner and a bartender rolled out an old television onto the stage. "King George is speaking," she said into the microphone. The bartender plugged in the extension cord while she fiddled with the rabbit ear antennae. Finally she got a decent signal. President Bush's face appeared on the screen. "My fellow Americans…" His voice was drowned out by a chorus of boos from all corners of the room. The owner held the microphone to the TV speaker, setting off a deafening peal of feedback. She hushed everyone until Bush could be heard again; the dual audio from the TV and the PA, a half-second out of synch, gave his shrill voice an eerie echo. "…I have therefore directed General Norman Schwarzkopf, in conjunction with coalition forces, to use all forces available including ground forces to eject the Iraqi army from Kuwait," he said; another, bigger round of boos drowned out the rest of the broadcast.

The TV was rolled off the stage. Everyone knew it meant that after weeks of intensive bombing, the land war would now begin. The older activists spoke in hushed tones with grim expressions. High school girls with peace-sign face-paint shed tears and leaned on one another for support; rocker boys stood alone with arms crossed and brows furrowed, waiting for the musical ritual to begin.

"There it is," said Bobby. "The tanks are rolling." Eli just shook his head. He scanned the room and saw Babylonia leaning against a doorway in the back of the hall. An organizer tapped Eli on the shoulder with a question and he turned away. When he looked back, Babylonia was gone.

The proprietress declared an open microphone. A few earnest, terrible poems were read to scattered applause. One of Eli's political science professors, an American Indian activist, delivered a scathing indictment of militarism and imperialism, complete with references to the Nuremburg trials. A meek, self-conscious young man followed, nervously asking the crowd to join him in a silent prayer. Suddenly there was Xavier the street punk, on his knees in the middle of the room, ostentatiously crossing himself, nodding and murmuring with eyes tightly shut. As The Naked Way set up their equipment behind her, the proprietress took the microphone, drink in hand. "You know who will suffer the most in this war, don't you? Just like every other war. Women! We'll be left alone to care for the children when the men go off to fight. We'll be forced to keep the family together while men play their war games in the desert. Bombs will fall on our heads. Soldiers will rape us: first one army, then the other. And when it's all over, we'll be expected to make babies, lots of babies to replace all the dead in your damned war!" Camille and Bethany hooted and stamped their feet in approval.

Eli slipped away in the applause and commotion to seek out Babylonia in the back halls of the theater. Despite the cold weather she wore a short black skirt; he caught sight of her long ivory legs as she ducked into a side room.

A radical priest who served on the peace committee stepped into his path. "Eli, great turn-out tonight!" he said. "You should be proud of yourself — using music to get the message out to kids was a great idea!"

Eli shrugged and smiled unevenly. "We all did it together. Sorry, I really have to find the men's room. Excuse me?" He patted the priest on the shoulder and slipped away down the hall. He turned into the room he'd seen the dark-haired beauty enter. "Babylonia?" he said, groping for a light switch. The lights revealed Babylonia face down on the dressing room couch, her skirt bunched up around her hips, and Alexander behind, mounting her. The singer looked up with a look of alarm that turned to glee as he saw Eli in the doorway. Babylonia covered her face against the light. She wore a black garter around the ivory skin of her upper thigh. Eli turned the switch back off and left the dressing room, closing the door behind him.

Walking back to the ballroom with his mind lost in thought, Eli physically ran into Amelia. She gave him a playful shove. "*E-lah*, always with your head in the clouds!" Her southern accent came out strongest when she was happy. "You did a great job, honey! We have a great crowd!" She kissed him on the cheek. "Darling, have you seen Alexander? Is he back here?" Eli shook his head. "Well I'm gonna look…" Eli stood in her way. She tried to go around him, but he put his hands on her shoulders and stepped in front of her, staying between her and the door to the dressing room.

"Don't," he said.

Just then, a female whimpering sound became audible from behind the door. Eli looked at the floor but kept his hands on Amelia's shoulders. Her face grew red. The whimpering became a moan, which turned into a series of short, sharp screams. A grunting male voice joined in; a call-and-response song. Finally Babylonia's screams leveled off and Alexander's laugh boomed through the closed door.

"Goddamn mother-fucking son of a bitch!" spat Amelia. She shoved Eli out of the way and violently yanked open the door. "I knew it!" she screamed as she saw Babylonia straightening her stockings and pulling up her skirt.

Alexander moved to intercept Amelia, keeping his towering lean frame between his two lovers. Amelia boiled over, shrieking and throwing punches at her man; he raised his hands against the blows and tried to grab her by the wrists. Babylonia was cool. She checked her look in the mirror before maneuvering past the grappling couple on her way out of the room. "No use crying over spilled milk, sweetie," she said to Amelia. "Toodles!" She blew Alexander a kiss. Her eyes met Eli's, but they were cold, showing him nothing. He caught a whiff of her perfume as she brushed past, skirt swaying; he was transported in his mind to the wild blazing nighttime when she'd been his.

Amelia lunged after Babylonia as she strolled away. Eli and Alexander grabbed Amelia and held her tight until her rival was gone. As soon as Eli loosed his grip, she flew out of his arms and threw another punch at Alexander. He tried to defend himself and talk Amelia down at the same time, no mean feat. "No darling…She doesn't mean anything to me…nothing at all!" Gaining control of her wrists, he leaned in close to whisper in her ear. The anger seeped out of her body; she went limp and slumped into his arms. He released her wrists and put an arm around her. He stroked her long brown hair and murmured reassurances as she began to sob. "The songs are about you, precious love. Every one of them." Alexander looked at Eli with a grin and a wink.

Amelia turned around, wiping tears from her eyes. Mascara ran down her face. "It's ok, E-lah. We're ok." Eli stood his ground. Alexander's smile at Eli phased through comradery, gloating, and territorial warning. Amelia gave Eli a shove. "Go!" she insisted. Eli shook his head and walked back down the dingy hall into the ballroom.

He ran into Marco, who pulled him into a big bear hug. "Hey, is everything ok?" Marco asked. "The vibe feels a little weird right now." He looked right and left, as if for an unseen threat lurking in the ballroom. "There's a lot of hippies here."

"The vibe is not so good. There's a war going on," Eli said.

Marco shook his head. "Eli, man, you're a deep cat. Maybe too deep for me. I don't understand why we aren't supposed to be kicking Iraq's ass. They invaded that little country, right?"

"Yes, but with the weapons we gave them. Can't you see, it's about oil and money, controlling the oil and…"

Marco put his hands up to stop the rant before it started. His muscles rippled as he gracefully drew his arms into a little bow. "You don't have to explain. Maybe this peace thing isn't so bad." He furrowed his unibrow and stared up into Eli's eyes with disconcerting intensity. "All my life I've walked the way of the warrior. Sometimes it's served me well. Sometimes…it's a challenging path. Maybe there's a different way." He poked his finger sharply into Eli's solar plexus, hitting some kind of pressure point. Eli controlled his breath and didn't let the pain show on his face. "Tell me we're doing the right thing playing this show," Marco said.

"You're doing the right thing playing this show," Eli said.

Marco wrapped him up in another tight embrace. "I love you, brother!" he said.

Eli grinned and hugged back hard, trying to give as good as he got. "Love you too, man."

Marco left him with a slap on the back as Kate walked up. "Oh my god, Marco looks hot tonight!" she purred. "Those arms!" She watched his rear as he strutted toward the dressing room. "He's sexy in, like, a Napoleon complex way!" She laughed at her own joke until she snorted. On stage, an older man with a long beard, a huge bushy head of curly gray hair and a vest made from an American flag pattern was bashing out old folk songs on an acoustic guitar covered with stickers and peace symbols. "Oh my god!" said Kate, bursting into laughter. "He's like that one Woodstock guy! My dad plays the movie over and over!"

"That man got his head caved in by the Chicago Police during the 1968 riots," Eli said. "You can still see where his skull is all dented in on his bald spot."

Brandon and Ear Wax approached; Kate leapt into Brandon's arms. "Look how sexy my rock star boyfriend is!" she gushed. She kissed him on the cheek theatrically, then flashed her big exaggerated Marilyn Monroe smile around the room. Ear Wax rolled his eyes. Brandon bent her backwards and gave her a dramatic World-War-II-is-over kiss. A few older peace organizers oohed and ahhed until Brandon lifted her back to her feet; the audience applauded. Brandon beamed, red-faced. Kate pouted, laughed and posed. Ear Wax slow-clapped sardonically at Brandon. "I didn't know you had it in you!" he said. They went back to the dressing room to get ready for the show.

When the band emerged from the dressing room, Eli could see something was wrong right away. Brandon's usual show-time game face was drawn even tighter than usual into an angry scowl. Ear Wax was shaking his head. Marco was yelling at Alexander. Alexander was wrapping his right hand up in what looked like a ripped-up white t-shirt. He grimaced in pain as he pulled the strips of cloth tight, straightened himself up, put on his dark sunglasses and stepped on stage. He grabbed the microphone with his other hand.

"Children!" his voice boomed through the speakers, which gave off a deafening peal of feedback that made everyone cover their ears. When the piercing sound faded out, Alexander had the room's full attention. "We're at war," he said, pacing the stage. "We're at war, and thousands will die so that we can drink Coca-Cola and eat Lucky Charms and the bomb-factories can make a million dollars. A million damn dollars a minute for those cruise missiles. Well I say…Fuck 'em! Fuck George Bush!" The crowd roared. He shook his bandaged fist and pivoted to provoke one section of the crowd and then another. "Fuck him for trying to ruin our Saturday night! But we've got something he doesn't have. We've got each other!" More applause. Bobby rolled his eyes and mimicked a jerk-off motion; Camille and Bethany scolded him. "We're here for peace," Alexander said, a peculiar grin coming over his lips. "And we're here because we have a friend with a heartache the size of the world. He believes in us, so we believe in him."

Kate shrieked with excitement. "Oh my god, Eli, he means you!"

Eli smiled weakly. Bobby stuck a finger down his throat. "Look what you've done, Eli," he said. "You turned him into Bono!" Brandon looked uncomfortable behind the drum kit; he made a nervous drum roll and cymbal crash to move the singer along.

"We still have sex, drugs and rock and roll, and we're going to enjoy them all tonight!" Alexander announced to cheers. The band launched into *'Til the End of Forever*, one of their most emotionally upbeat songs. The singer flashed a peace sign. The crowd palpably relaxed as shimmering major chords from Marco's guitar washed over them and Ear Wax and Brandon's buoyant bottom-end groove lifted them. The baby boomers smiled and bobbed their heads; maybe there was a little summer of love in the room after all. "*Open up your doors!*" Alexander implored the crowd. "*We're sailing to distant shores!*" The kids at the front were in ecstasy as the throbbing speakers physically rocked their bodies. Eli grinned to himself. Kate screamed with joy, bouncing up and down. More bodies surged to the front of the stage.

But when the song ended, Alexander deflated the crowd. "Well you heard it, kids," he hissed. "The Great White Father has spoken. You got to put on your helmet and carry the flag and load your rifle and go kill some rag-heads." The hall quieted. A few booed and hissed the slur, ironic or not. Alexander prowled the stage. "Johnny get your gun! Uncle Sam wants you to deep-throat a Scud missile for Jesus! Ready boys? Open wide! And you know why?" He stalked to and fro; the light reflected from his insectoid rock star sunglasses, which hid his eyes as he looked into the audience's soul. He got face to face now with a girl who looked about twelve, then a salt-and-pepper middle-aged man in glasses and a button-down shirt, who faced him silently with folded arms. The man's grim-faced wife clutched his arm nervously.

"Daddy doesn't love us!" Alexander shouted into the microphone, inches from the man's face. "Daddy wants to diddle us in the shower and then leave us on the street!" He stood up and confronted the whole crowd. "We live in a fatherless world! Did it ever occur to you that God the Father is the Demon? That the Great White Father is the father of lies?" There were cries of agreement, bewilderment, mockery from the audience. "It's a fatherless world," the singer insisted, stamping his boots on the stage. "Father is a liar. Father is a killer. Father is a rapist! Can't you see what he's done to our fair sister the earth?" He held up his bandaged hand. "He nailed me to a fucking cross! I just pulled the fucking spike out of my hand! Jesus, it hurts... waitress? Can I get a bottle of something hard up here?"

Just then a bottle sailed through the air, just missing the singer's head. It shattered against Marco's Fender amplifier. Marco glared at the back of the room where the projectile was launched. "Hey, what the fuck!" he shouted.

"Incoming!" yelled Ear Wax.

Amelia threw another bottle. This one would have hit Alexander square in the face if he hadn't ducked at the last second. With his bandaged hand he shielded his eyes against the glare of the spotlight, straining to see who was throwing bombs from the audience. "Son of a bitch!" Amelia screamed. "Come down here and fight me like a man with all these people watching, why don't you!" She was beyond drunk. The shoulder strap of her dress was out of place and her hair was mussed. Her make-up was smeared and she had a black eye. For the first time Eli noticed what had to be a baby bump at her middle. She grabbed a table lamp from a nearby booth, but a burly doorman got his arms around her and wrestled her towards the door. "I'll fucking kill you, Alexander!" she screamed as several employees struggled to haul her away. Eli caught sight of Babylonia watching from the wings of the stage.

Kate asked in Eli's ear: "What the fuck was that?" Eli just shook his head.

For a moment Alexander seemed chastened. He pushed his long blonde hair out of his face and laughed weakly into the microphone, but no one laughed with him. The crowd churned restlessly. The singer looked down at his feet, as if lost in thought, then faced the crowd again. "Maybe we're safe and blessed," he said. "Maybe God is a woman. Maybe God is a woman and she loves us. Maybe God is a woman and I've offended her so much that I'll burn in hell for a thousand lifetimes..."

"Rock and roll, mother-fuckers!" came an impatient voice from the crowd.

Alexander laughed and raised a fist in the air. "Yeah, rock and roll, mother-fuckers!" he echoed. Marco glared at the singer, fingering the fret board of his guitar impatiently. Alexander gave him a little nod and gathered himself as he moved to center stage. "This is...*Blasphemers!*" Marco spat out a searing-hot, rapid-fire riff; the band crashed into the fray right behind him. Bodies surged toward and away from the stage. Alexander belted out a litany of violence, deceit and crime: "*If you feel your fate sliding away, you know it was the hate of the day that made it this way...taught to kill! Taught to slaughter!*"

Eli felt a tap on his shoulder as he was jostled by the crowd and the sheer violence of the wall of sound coming from the stage. It was an elderly woman from the peace committee, a revered retired nun who had been arrested dozens of times for chaining herself to the gates of the Rocky Flats nuclear weapons plant. She strained on tippy-toes to shout in Eli's ear over the cacophony. "Eli, dear," she said, "did he just sing 'sacrifice your mother on the altar?'"

He buried his face in his hands and nodded slowly. What the fuck had he done? He'd brought a demon of chaos to the peace prayers; a pornographic vandal into the innermost sacred temple. A mosh pit began swirling violently in front of the stage.

Kate was thrilled. She jumped up and down and pumped her fist to the music. "Woo-hoo!" she screamed. "Oh my god, they're brilliant! Listen to Brandon, he's killing it!" She chanted along with the lyrics: "*Stone beginners, lonely winners — everybody's got to be a sinner!*" Marco's guitar snapped, growled and roared; Brandon and Ear Wax drove the song ahead remorselessly. Kate swooned theatrically, leaning heavily against Eli. "Oh my god, I'm so high right now!" She squeezed his arm. "That weed you had before was so good," she breathed into his ear. "Is there any more?" She let her lithe little body slump against his broad torso in the surging, swaying crowd.

He nodded distractedly and gave her a friendly, big-brother squeeze around the shoulders. "Later," he said. It didn't matter; she threw her head back and laughed in bleary-eyed delight. Eli felt a chill go through him. A few heavy metal kids joined the mass of younger bodies in front of the stage as the discontented protest veterans gravitated to the back of the hall. Eli spotted the leaders of the peace committee consulting with the old hippie lady who owned the place. She was agitated, gesticulating and shouting. Several of the older organizers glared at Eli; this wasn't the music of the revolution they knew. He began to think he'd done A Very Bad Thing.

The band finished *Blasphemers* with a dissonant flourish of guitar feedback and cymbals and rumbling bass noise. Applause climaxed, then slowly petered out, leaving only the derisive groans from the back to fill the taught silence. Alexander said nothing. The next song, *Blues*, brought renewed hope. Its majestic, rocking melancholy split the difference between the exuberance of *'Til the End of Forever* and the malice of *Blasphemers*. Ear Wax gave the song a soaring, melodic bass line; Alexander seemed genuinely reflective and pensive as he explored the higher registers of his voice in the song's romantic, cathartic refrain. Marco echoed him with abstract, emotive guitar pyrotechnics. The song's conclusion met with full-on rapture in front of the stage and tentative applause from the back.

Alexander seemed to relax for a moment. A smile crossed his face as the applause washed over him. He brushed the hair back with the bandaged hand, eliciting gasps: blood was seeping through. The white fabric had turned deep red, and blood trickled down his wrist and his sleeve. "Fucking hell," he said, looking at the hand in the carnival-color stage lights. He held it up to the crowd. "If I die for you tonight," he asked them, "will you die for me too?" The question was met by dozens of female screams in the affirmative.

"Fucking hypocrite!" someone shouted from the back of the crowd. It was Bethany. She stomped to the front of the stage. Her high-heeled boots clattered on the old wooden floor as the mosh pit parted for her like the Red Sea. Every eye was on her as she stood in front of Alexander, her face level with his worn brown cowboy boots. "Enough of your rock and roll messiah bullshit!" she screamed, pointing up at him. "You fucked up your hand when it you put it through a window trying to hit a woman!" A chorus of boos boomed through the hall. "Yeah, that's right, I just talked to Amelia outside. She found you fucking Babylonia backstage…"

"It was self-defense!" the singer pleaded. "She was trying to kill me!" He threw his arms wide open, appealing to the crowd. "Girls, don't fight over me, there's enough to go around! We're here for peace!"

Marco was infuriated at another interruption to the show. "Hey dipshit, keep your women under control!" he growled at Alexander.

Alexander shrugged and smiled. "Sour grapes?" he asked into the microphone, looking pointedly at Bethany. She scowled and stalked out of the ballroom.

The owner of the *Horoscope* approached the stage from the side. "What's this about people throwing punches at women in my building?" she demanded. Ear Wax intercepted her and tried to talk her down. The crowd churned with murmurs and boos. Brandon bashed his cymbals in frustration. Marco fingered the chords for the next song but Ear Wax and Brandon ignored the cue. Someone in the audience had passed Alexander a bottle; he took a slug and preened in the spotlight, laughing and mugging even harder when the boos redoubled. From where he was standing, Eli could only catch snippets of the conversation between Ear Wax and the hippie lady. "I will shut this show down so fast it will make your head spin!" he heard her say.

Kate looked dismayed. "They can't stop now!" she said to Eli, snapping her gum. "They haven't played *Sister Sweet* yet! Brandon said they were going to dedicate it to me!" Her moist lips glistened in the shifting light as she pouted.

A lone voice in the audience cut through the chaos. "Free Bird!"

Alexander tilted his shades up to look for the source of the voice. It was a twenty-something white guy in jeans and a black t-shirt. He seemed very pleased with himself, and very drunk. "Yeah, come on, Jesus!" he yelled. The room's attention was focused on him now. "Come on Jesus! Sing Freebird!" His buddies laughed and cheered him on.

Someone else in the crowd picked up the cry. "Free Bird!" A clique of young girls had never heard anything so funny. They took up the chant: "Free Bird! Free Bird! Free Bird!"

"Fucking bullshit!" said Bobby.

Alexander laughed. He surveyed the scene: a confused crowd slipping through his fingers; his drummer and guitarist both about to throttle him; his bass player trying to convince the venue owner to let them finish the show. He looked at the guy who'd begun the Free Bird calls, laughing and clinking beer bottles with his friends. Alexander tossed his pint bottle over his head; it shattered on the stage floor behind him. He flew off the stage, landing on the Free Bird guy in a rage, swinging wild punches with his one good hand.

Marco's eyes bulged. "Fucking shit...no!" He dove into the audience after the singer. A deafening buzz of feedback blasted from the stage as the guitar fell out of its stand in front of the amplifier. Brandon and Ear Wax followed Marco into the crowd. Marco wrestled Alexander off of the Free Bird guy; Alexander's sunglasses were smashed underfoot. Free Bird wiped blood from his mouth as Marco held the singer back. "Some peace concert!" he spat. A few of his friends had gathered at his side. "You guys fucking suck! You can't carry fucking Bon Jovi's jock strap!"

Marco's unibrow furrowed tight. His eyes narrowed. He released his grasp on Alexander and his hands clenched and unclenched at his sides. The veins in his forehead and neck popped out. His shoulders bunched up into a mountain of muscle and he bent his knees into a fighting stance. One of Free Bird's buddies laughed and slapped the heckler on the back. "Fucking *Bon Jovi?*" Marco growled. He suddenly leapt in through the air and executed a 360-degree roundhouse karate kick, connecting his boot with Free Bird's jaw. Chaos ensued.

It eventually took three cops to get Marco off the guy. Alexander slipped out the backdoor, evading the police. Brandon and Ear Wax were questioned but not detained. Marco was taken off in handcuffs. "This is your fault, Eli! This is fucking bullshit!" he yelled as he was shoved into the back of a waiting police car by several burly officers.

In the parking lot, Eli gave Amelia his coat as the crowd trickled away and the spinning lights atop the cop cars played over her tear-streaked face: red, blue, red. "I'm going," she stammered between sniffles. "I never should have come here. I'm getting a ticket back to Texas tomorrow. I'm giving up the baby for adoption." Her hand moved to her belly, swelling under the dark dress. "He won't be able to hurt me anymore. He won't be able to hurt my baby." She fell into Eli's arms, sobbing and trembling. "I love him, Eli. God, I love him."

Chapter 20
A BIG COSMIC JOKE

The Naked Way was done. The war went on.

Alexander disappeared from Denver. Some people said he'd gone to Seattle to form a new band. Others heard he went up to Alaska to make a stake on the fishing boats. Another story had him following his twisted muse to Mexico. Marco had outstanding warrants and stayed in jail. Brandon and Ear Wax visited him once. When they returned to see him a second time, he'd been transferred out of state. They retrieved their things from the warehouse rented in his name and never returned.

Brandon and Kate took refuge in their own wartime bunker, a gloomy one bedroom apartment they seemed to light only with candles, lava lamps and blacklights, as though Denver itself was threatened by air raids. Brandon kept the shades drawn and smoked ungodly amounts of pot, which he bought in nickel and dime bags from kids in the park. Eli came by some nights to hang out and smoke. They sat in the purple gloom under the Last Supper tapestry, which Brandon had rescued from the final show and hung on his wall. He'd added little glow-in-the-dark star stickers, putting them over the eyes of the disciples and making a halo around Christ's head. "I'm glad the band is dead," Brandon said unconvincingly. His swagger seemed forced; he was the shy nervous gangly kid Eli had met in high school all over again.

Kate made a disbelieving face. "What do you mean?"

Eli didn't understand either. "What are you talking about? You were brilliant. You guys could have hit it big. *Would* have hit it big. We all knew it."

"I know," Brandon said. "But he screwed us. He fucked as all royally." Kate and Eli knew Alexander was the royal fucker Brandon meant. "We all believed in him. But he didn't give a fuck. It was all just a big cosmic joke to him." Brandon took a drag off a cigarette and peeked out the window through the blinds at the wintry blackness of night. "So fuck The Naked Way and fuck his songs. I've got my own songs." Kate caught Eli's gaze. The care-free exuberance in her eyes was gone, replaced by a crestfallen look of sadness.

Brandon took out his acoustic guitar and played for his friends, just like he used to in high school. "This is a new one," he said, sitting cross-legged on the floor, hunched over the guitar in his lap, eyes shut tight, rocking gently back and forth. He creaked and croaked through the first few notes, like a baby bird pecking out of its own shell and trying to find its voice, before he found the range. The song was small and delicate, a private Aquarian melody, the opposite of Alexander's grandiose anthems. Brandon sang it like a mournful old lullaby.

Chapter 21
THE MIRROR CRACKS

Eli snapped out of his daydream as the bus screeched to a halt. "End of the line!" the driver said, as the small handful of other passengers began trickling out. Had he dozed and dreamed about the band? He looked out the window but found nothing in the bleak, windswept terrain to orient himself. For a moment he wondered if The Naked Way itself was a dream. He looked out the other side of the bus at the Denver City and County Jail, and he knew The Naked Way was real. Or had been. Alexander was locked up inside.

The roar of a jet plane coming in low for a landing overhead blasted the cobwebs out of Eli's head as he stepped off the bus. The jail was a nondescript institutional building isolated on the far outskirts of the city, next to the runways of Stapleton Airport. Inside, Eli asked for Alexander, using his full legal name. He was told he could see him during the next visitation period, in twenty minutes. A television suspended on the wall in the waiting room blared above the heads of the wives, girlfriends and mothers waiting to see their men. Children played, laughing and climbing over dirty plastic benches and chairs. Eli thought about Gwen. Why had he come here? Alexander couldn't wait another day? He felt like he was waking up from a dream within a dream.

How to explain Gwen to Alexander? Him to her?

A guard told announced they could begin check-in for the visitation room. Eli shuffled down the hall along with the others, waiting in line to pass through a metal detector. He took off his coat and turned out his pockets at the security check with the other visitors. He watched as corrections officers peered into the mouths of little kids with flashlights, looking for contraband.

In a big open room with walls painted a sickly pale yellow, Eli took a seat at a long U-shaped counter separating the realm of the jailed from the land of the free. After a few minutes, prisoners in green or orange jumpsuits began to enter from a door on the far wall. Most leaned over the barrier to kiss girlfriends and hug toddlers. A few spoke in serious, somber tones to their visitors; most strutted in full of cocky bravado and defiance. *"They ain't got nothin' on me." "I ain't said shit 'bout nothin' to nobody." "Don't worry baby, I'm workin' this place like a motherfucker..."*

Finally, the last prisoner entered the room: Alexander, fashionably late as usual. He was the only prisoner out of dozens who didn't get a green or orange jail uniform; his was snow white. He held a sly guarded grin as he scanned the visitor counter, finally finding Eli. His eyes flashed relief, then apprehension, before settling on pleased bemusement.

He sat down face to face with Eli, smiling broadly. "Eli! You're a prince among men, a gentleman and a scholar. You're the only fucking visitor I've had." Memories flashed through Eli's mind as he looked into his friend's face: Amelia's black eye; the music and the good times; fucking Babylonia in the dressing room with Alexander on the other side of the door. With effort, he refrained from returning Alexander's smile.

"White is your color," he said. "Been worried about you, man. What the fuck?"

Alexander tugged on the sleeve of the white jumpsuit. "I died and went to heaven. I'm a desolation angel, baby! What the fuck did you think?"

Now Eli had to laugh in spite of himself. "Where are your wings?" He looked Alexander over. His hair was unkempt and his skin looked oily, almost reptilian, under the institutional florescent lights, but otherwise he seemed ok. "How'd they nab you?"

Alexander shook his head. "I was drinking with Justin from Twice Jilted down at the Ballerina Club. First time I set foot in this fucking city since your so-called peace concert. I was trying to close the deal with this beautiful little babydoll. We drank more than we could pay for, so we ran out on the tab and got cornered by the pigs in an alley. I had a warrant from the fight. So here I am."

"After the show, after the fight...where did you go?"

"I had a girl. Another girl, you guys didn't know about her, up in Boulder. Got her to pick me up in lower downtown after I slipped out the back door. I bled the whole way over there." He held up his hand and wiggled his fingers, then balled them up into a fist. "She paid for the doctor who sewed the tendon back together. I could have lost the use of the hand." He looked at Eli and laughed. "Fucking peace concert? Eli, you created your own little Altamont! Congratulations. You're going down in rock and roll history as the man who ended the greatest band that never was. You destroyed my world, asshole!" He pointed a finger in Eli's face, getting the attention of a guard. "And you didn't stop the fucking war."

"That's rich," Eli said. "I didn't put your hand through the fucking window." They faced off for a long moment. Finally Eli asked, "Have you talked to Amelia? She was pregnant."

Alexander snorted. "I know she was pregnant, Sherlock. I never want to see her face again. She couldn't manage a band out of a wet paper bag."

"Did you hit her?"

Alexander laughed. Eli's face was stone. Alexander shook his head. "Eli, you saw how it was. Those girls were trying to rip each other's eyes out! I was just defending myself, trying to break them up."

"Trying to defend yourself from a window?"

"Eli, you don't know that woman. You don't know her witchcraft. You don't know…"

"Witchcraft? You gonna burn her at the stake too?" Now it was Alexander's face that turned to stone. Finally Eli changed the subject. "I met a girl. I'm hopelessly in love. I'm a goner."

Alexander's eyes widened. "When did you meet her?"

"Twenty four hours ago. Rich girl, from the East Coast. She's at my place right now."

"My lad, what the fuck are you doing here?"

Eli shrugged.

"And she's the one?"

"I can't explain. We imprinted on each other like baby animals on National Geographic or something."

"What's her name?"

"Gwen."

"Ah yes. Gwen." He relished the sound of the name passing his own lips, like fingertips running up and down a bare thigh. "Gwen and Eli. Eli and Gwen. Guinevere! A mythic name, a name from legend and fairy tales! That fits for you, Eli. So does this make you Lancelot, the conquering stud muffin?" he asked archly, with a single eyebrow raised, "or Arthur, the cuckold?" He leaned in as close as the barrier would allow. "Does she give good head?" he asked in a stage whisper.

Eli replied with two raised middle fingers. "Fuck you, asshole."

The singer laughed out loud. "Oh come on, now. She's a great beauty, I have no doubt. My super-psychic powers of deduction tell me that her tits are perfect." Eli chuckled but didn't take the bait. Alexander became animated and his hands and face moved with his words. His stage persona emerged; the trickster poet saw all and told all. "Never-ending love is a very strange subject," he pronounced in a clipped and deliberate cadence. "Broken hearts. Endless lies!" He stuck a finger in his mouth, made it pop out loud from his cheek like a champagne cork. "The mirror cracks!" A guard looked over, alerted by the singer's strange sound effects and gesticulations. Eli wiped a bit of Alexander's spittle from his cheek. Alexander winked at the guard. "Hearts are not to be depended on!" he told Eli in an earnest, conspiratorial tone. "They fail – like beauty and love, until oblivion gathers up the lot for good, to start all over again!"

"Impressive, you should write that down," said Eli. "This girl is different some-how. She's been…hurt. She's a bird with a broken wing. Needs someone to take her in and mend her."

"How fucking precious is that?" Alexander sneered. "I forgot, Eli always turns the girls into little flowers!"

"At least my girls don't get black eyes," Eli said.

Alexander shook his head. "You think Amelia doesn't have a fierce right cross?" His knowing smile turned into a defensive sneer. "So tender-hearted, so full of com-passion for all the sufferers in the world, aren't you Eli? Especially if they have perfect tits. Such noble idealism! Your little heart really broke for all those brown people in the desert, didn't it? Oh me too, my dear. Me too. But you know what the difference between us is? I knew they were going to die no matter what we did. But you won't accept that. Life is cruel, life is wicked, it's a kill-or-be-killed world. Get it through your head! You think Gwen is hurting and you can fix her. She *is* hurting. Just like everyone hurts. And you know what's going to make her feel better? Cutting your heart out and eating it on a fucking shish-ka-bob, Eli. That's what."

Before Eli could respond, a shrill institutional buzzer rang overhead, signaling the end of the visiting period. The two friends rose from their seats on either side of the barrier.

"How long you in for?" Eli asked.

"Six months," Alexander said. "Getting the fuck out of this cow town when I get out." He stuck his thumb out like a hitchhiker. "Back to Portland or Seattle, maybe. I don't know." A guard put a hand on his arm, herding him back towards the cell blocks. "Maybe Hollywood," he said over his shoulder with a sly grin. "Where an erotic politician can make an honest living!"

Riding home on the bus, Eli thought about Alexander back in his cell. He'd been close to fulfilling his dreams. The Naked Way was headed for bigger things. They should have been preening on posters hanging in teenagers' bedrooms and touring for their first album by now. But they'd pissed it all away. Now the singer had four walls and a white jumpsuit and not much else. The same primal, mystic energy that brought The Naked Way into the world made it tear itself apart. They kissed the snake on the lips – and it bit, hard.

An old woman, shriveled and beat by time, got on the bus and sat a few seats away from Eli, cursing quietly to herself with little twitches and spasms. Somebody got on the bus, she cursed. The bus stopped at a red light, she cursed. To her the world was one big ongoing profanity, a damnable abomination she couldn't escape. What had happened to her? Who had hurt her, betrayed her, disappointed her?

Eli was overcome by a dark fantasy: he was on a prison bus, rumbling toward the huge iron gates of a concentration camp. There, bodies would be destroyed and personalities blotted out. Oblivion would gather up the lot for good, to start all over again. Dejected smokers waiting at bus stops played their parts in Eli's grim scenario, shuffling aboard the bus lifeless and resigned as though they knew they were headed to their doom. "Fuck it," hissed the old woman, tugging her ragged winter hat down over her brow. "Damn it all."

Eli's life replayed in his mind like a movie. The happy times were clipped, fuzzy, blurred. The hard times were in sharp focus. He didn't know who he was in the world, and he didn't know who he was supposed to be. He didn't know why he was alive or what he was supposed to do. But he believed there were cracks in the wall, miracles, signs that pointed the way to fate and destiny. He knew Gwen was waiting for him in his little apartment. He knew right then and there that he would love her with his whole heart and soul, no matter what it cost him.

Chapter 22
OLD JAZZ RECORDS

As he walked up to the building, Eli spotted Camille standing outside, smoking a cigarette. She had changed outwardly in the months since the spectacular demise of The Naked Way. She was dating a prominent lawyer who'd been knocked out by her beauty at *Rock Island Line*, the coolest downtown nightclub. She'd changed for him, to Eli's surprise. She grew out her hair into a respectable bob and wore business suits from Anne Taylor. She got a job as a bank teller and tried to straighten out her act. She had begun to utter shocking words and phrases like "mini-van" and "a little house with a backyard — for a dog." But Eli had his doubts that it would last. She was no Stepford Wife in the making. Nobody was going to turn her into June Cleaver overnight.

"Here's an upstanding pillar of the community," he said, giving her a little hug. "Guess who I just saw in jail? Your boy." She shrugged and blew a puff of smoke to the sky. "The Lizard King," Eli said.

Camille's eyes bulged. "Alexander is in town? In jail? What the hell..?"

"Xavier told me."

"Fucking Xavier?"

"Yeah, and don't say his name again or he'll show up. You know how that works."

Camille dropped her cigarette on the ground. She fumbled in her stylish little purse for a replacement and a lighter. She got one lit; Eli saw her fingers tremble. She kept an outward façade of calm. "What is he doing in there?"

"There was a warrant from the fight. He ran out on a bar tab on Santa Fe Boulevard. He got caught, like the genius you know he is," Eli said.

Camille bowed her head and rubbed her eyes with her fingers. "Fuck," she said. "David can never know about him and me. Is he ok?"

"His hand was healing up. From punching the glass…or whatever. He's still Alexander. With the poetry coming out of his ass and everything. He had a girl up in Boulder who took care of him after the fight. Said he's leaving town when he gets out. That's all I got."

Camille dragged anxiously on her smoke. "Fuck me. I don't know if I should see him or not. Guess I can't do anything about it tonight anyway." She stabbed out the cigarette and hid the butt in her pocket. "Bobby and Bethany are here, we're going to see a movie. Come with? Bobby wants to see *Fried Green Tomatoes*, Bethany wants to see *Terminator 2*."

Eli shuffled his feet. "Can't." He couldn't help grinning. "I have a girl upstairs."

"*Well*! Isn't that fancy! Bring her!"

"Bad timing," Eli said. "Next time."

"Hmm, what's up Eli? What kind of treasure are you hiding up there?"

"I love her."

Camille tapped the side of his head as though it were a broken appliance. "You *what* her? Who are you and what have you done with Eli, carefree bohemian seducer of multiple maidens?"

"Beg pardon? Who are you, and what have you done with my friend Camille, hippie-punk-anarchist-feminist-revolutionary? And does David know you're still smoking?"

"Ugh," Camille groaned. "There are too many things David doesn't know. I brought a boy home from the club the other night. Remember Devon? The dancer who used to wait tables at *The Muddy River*?"

"Yeah…I thought he was gay."

"Yeah, well, so did he." Camille blushed and stabbed out her cigarette on the concrete steps of the apartment building. "We're…experimenting. What David doesn't know won't hurt him. Poor David. He's taking me to the opera tomorrow night, can you believe that shit?"

Eli held open the door into the lobby for her. "Not really," he said. "Tell Bobby and Bethany hi for me." He tilted his head to indicate his apartment upstairs. "Wish me luck," he said.

She shook her head as he started up the stairs. "Eli in love? I've gotta see this girl."

When Eli opened the door to his apartment, he found Gwen sitting on the floor with his most private and personal belongings spread out on the floor around her. The door to the closet was open, as were the drawers on his desk.

Gwen had pulled out old pictures, notebooks, letters, school papers, awards, and childhood mementos. Boxes of dusty treasures were emptied and their contents spread out for her inspection. In her hand was a picture of Eli's mother as a young woman; her clothes and the style of her long, dark hair dated the picture to the mid-70s. Gwen wore only panties and one of Eli's t-shirts, but as he stood there in the doorway, looking at Gwen with his whole life spread across the floor, he was the one who felt naked.

She leapt to her feet and threw her arms around him. All the words he'd planned to say on the bus ride home fell to the floor with a silent clatter. The swirl of emotions produced by finding Gwen exploring his things was stilled by her kiss on his lips. She pressed her body into his and pushed her tongue into his mouth. He felt her full breasts, heavy against his ribs. The kiss lasted and lasted. Finally she pulled back and looked into his eyes. "Don't be mad, I wasn't spying," she said. "I just want to know you better." She held his face between her hands and kissed his cheeks. "I want to know everything about you," she whispered in his ear.

He sat on the couch; she sat on his lap. She held the picture of his mom, smiling at it. "She's so beautiful," Gwen said. "I can see the resemblance!" She put the picture down on the coffee table and brushed the mop of brown hair back from Eli's face. "She's dead, isn't she?"

Since the moment he'd re-entered the apartment, Eli's world had collapsed back into the tiny space between himself and Gwen. Now her face was the whole circumference of the world. "When I was ten," he said.

"She's dead and there was no one to really take care of you after that, isn't that right?" Eli could only nod, looking down mutely at the artifacts of his life spread out over the worn hardwood floor. Gwen's tone grew warm, indulgent — motherly. She pulled him to her and stroked his hair. "That's why you live like this, isn't it?"

"Live like what?" Eli asked.

She brushed the hair away from his face gently. "Like…" She made a gesture with her hand that encompassed Eli's apartment, his neighborhood, his whole life in the dusty backstreets of his obscure little city. "Like…you're still finding yourself. Because you're smart, Eli. I've read your papers and your stories," she tilted her head towards his notebooks, open and strewn across the floor. "And you're a smart little fucker. Smarter than those boarding school boys I grew up with — they're all Ivy League now. You can do whatever you want. You know that, right?"

"I can do whatever I want, huh?" He wrapped a strand of her golden hair tentatively between his fingers. "Does that include keeping you forever?"

She smiled and silenced him with a warm kiss. "So," she asked. "Was your friend okay?"

He shook his head. "Can I just say, I don't know why I left you here. I felt terrible about it once I was there. What the hell was I doing? He'll still be there tomorrow or the next day or whenever you're gone. It made no fucking sense for me to go to a freaking jail today instead of being here with you."

"It made perfect fucking sense. I was proud of you," Gwen said.

"Proud of me?"

"You're a loyal friend. You showed good character. You put your friend ahead of your own wishes and desires. Because I *know*" – she raised a single perfect eyebrow imperiously and poked him in the chest – "you'd rather be with me. Than with… what was his name?"

"Alexander."

"Alexander? So formal. Kind of pompous?"

Eli laughed. "Yeah, pretty pompous. He's a singer. A poet, kind of."

She nodded. "You admire him," she said.

"No. Yes. He's very talented. But no. He's not really the best guy. You can't bring him home to mom," Eli said.

"Like I could bring you home either!" Gwen said.

Eli's face dropped. "Is that right?"

She grabbed his hands. "No! I mean, come on, you know how parents are. I mean…maybe if we just took out your earring…" She tugged playfully on the silver hoop in his left earlobe.

"Come on," he said, pulling away from her. "It's in the hetero ear and everything."

"Well never mind," said Gwen with a wave of her hands, as if to clear the air. "Your friend, Alexander. A singer. He's in a band?"

"He was. They don't exist anymore."

"They had a name?"

"The Naked Way."

"Excuse me?"

"I know. The Naked Way."

"Did they play…?"

Eli shook his head. "No, fully clothed."

Gwen laughed. "Okay. Were they good?"

"Better than that. They should have been huge."

"You're biased. They're your friends."

"Decide for yourself," Eli said. He gave her a pat on the bottom to get her off his lap; she smacked his butt harder as he bent over digging through a stack of tapes and CD's on his stereo. He cued up the band's demo CD to *Blues* and pressed play.

He sat back down on the couch; she lay down with her head in his lap. "They had a CD?" she asked.

"They made it in a basement or something. Sold like a dozen copies at the neighborhood record store."

She lay on her back looking up at the ceiling. Eli ran his fingertips along her bare legs; she brushed them away when they got too far up her thigh. The sound washed over them and filled the room. Eli watched the expression on her face as she listened to the lyrics. A smile touched her lips here, her little pug nose wrinkled there. By the time the guitar solo had run its course she'd heard enough. "I feel like this has nothing to do with my life," she said with a sweetly dismissive smile. "But it's kind of brilliant, I admit. Does your record player work? You should play me some of your old jazz records."

"You like jazz?"

"Not really. But it seems romantic."

"We could go out somewhere," Eli suggested.

"No! I mean, let's not. I like it here. It feels like home."

"It does?" he asked. She smiled and nodded. "I can go and get us a bottle of wine," he said. "We'll stay in."

"We drink so much every night on the mountain. You have no idea. Last weekend somebody threw up in a punchbowl. Nobody wanted to clean it up, so we just pushed the bowl behind a chair. It was still there when I left. Out of sight, out of mind." She shrugged off the digression. "You think I'm crazy now. But I feel so high when I'm with you, I don't want to numb my feelings. For once. I just want to feel everything with you." She squeezed his arm. "So go pick me out a jazz record, please?"

Chapter 23

SHE BOP

Gwen woke Eli up in the middle of the night. "Eli? I think it's my time."

"Your time?" he mumbled groggily. "Like your time to shine?"

She shoved him. "My period, silly. It came early. I need a tampon."

"I'll go to 7-11."

"Is it far?"

"Five or six blocks."

She pulled him close. "I don't want you to go that far away. What about your neighbors? You said your friend Camille lives downstairs?"

He pulled on his jeans and gave Gwen sweat pants and a t-shirt to wear. He was groggy and disheveled, but happy for the chance to show off his new love nonetheless.

Cyndi Lauper's *She Bop* blasted from behind Camille's closed door as they descended the stairs. Eli gave Gwen's ass a squeeze. "The extended remix, if I'm not mistaken."

Gwen playfully smacked his hand away and smiled. "I guess she's home, then?"

"Must be," said Eli, knocking on the door.

Gwen rubbed up against him. "You know what that song is about, don't you?"

By way of answering, he cupped her bottom in his hand again and lip-synched along with the lyrics: "*They say I better get a chaperone / because I can't stop messin' with the danger zone*." She giggled. They made out in the hallway until a neighbor came by, taking her clothes to the laundry room. Gwen blushed and gave Eli a little shove. "Ok, Romeo. Hurry up before I'm bleeding down my leg!"

He knocked harder on the door; there was still no answer. "Sometimes she paints with the music up loud," he said. "Or smokes a joint and cleans the toilet or whatever.

I'll try the door." He turned the knob; the door opened and he stepped through. "Camille?"

As he entered the apartment, Eli was greeted with the sight of a male rear end in a diaper, high in the air. An astonished face with a pacifier in its mouth looked back at him: it was Javon, the handsome waiter from *The Muddy River*, now all but naked and on all fours on Camille's bed. Camille stood in the middle of the room with her back to Eli and Gwen, who'd entered the apartment behind him. She was wearing a Nazi officer's cap, black pumps, thigh-high fishnet stockings, a lacy black bra and panties, and holding a long black riding crop in her hand. "You know what happens to bad little boys, don't you?" she shouted over the pounding music. Javon slowly lifted a finger and pointed behind her; Camille turned to see the unexpected visitors just as the stereo shifted gears into Joy Division's *Love Will Tear Us Apart*. She turned down the music as Javon sat up on the bed, covering himself with the sheets and twiddling with his pacifier self-consciously.

Gwen tried to make light of the moment. "Oh, I miss those," she said, pointing to his pacifier. "So soothing."

Eli stepped forward. "Camille...I'm sorry. This is Gwen. Javon, meet Gwen. Gwen, Camille and Javon."

The two women shook hands, smiling awkwardly. Gwen looked Camille up and down. "Eli said I shouldn't be jealous of his friend who lives downstairs," she said with a nervous giggle. "He didn't tell me you were so...interesting."

Camille laughed graciously. "And he didn't tell me that you were the most beautiful woman ever to walk the earth!" Gwen laughed.

"The hell I didn't, you just didn't believe me!" said Eli.

"You sure know how to pick, 'em, Eli," said Javon, relaxing a bit.

"I'm sorry to barge in on you guys," Eli said. "Camille, Gwen really needs a tampon if you can spare one."

"Oh of course," Camille said, tossing the riding crop onto the bed and smiling warmly at Gwen. "Hold on, doll." She went to the bathroom and returned momentarily with a handful of tampons, which she handed to Gwen. Eli and Gwen thanked her profusely and turned to go.

Gwen gave Camille a little hug and waved an awkward goodbye to Javon. Camille stepped out into the hallway and Eli whispered into her ear. "I thought he was gay?" he said with a discrete tilt of his head toward Javon.

"We're experimenting," she said with a wink. "And you just ruined the fun by parading the most gorgeous girl in the world under my nose. Now I gotta go get it up for him instead?" She blew Eli a kiss as he headed upstairs after Gwen. "Good luck," she said.

Chapter 24

JUST US

In the morning, Gwen packed her bag and they headed back downtown. They had breakfast at *The Marketplace*; the baristas behind the counter winked at Eli on the sly. Afterwards they walked to the bus station.

"You've already changed my life forever," he told her as they waited. "Even if I never see you again, God forbid."

Gwen's eyes shone as she soaked in his words of love. "Don't be ridiculous," she said. "You'll see me again as soon as I can get time off work to come down."

"Maybe I could come up and visit you in Vail?"

Gwen looked at her feet and shook her head. "No, I have idiot roommates. It's obnoxious, like a college dorm or something. I love being at your place, it's just us there."

———

They talked on the phone most every night. Gwen said he'd see her soon, but wouldn't say when. "Wouldn't you rather be surprised? Think how excited you'll be when all of a sudden you see my smiling face out of the blue?" she said.

———

As Eli let himself into the lobby of the apartment building one afternoon, Camille's door opened. Out came Gwen. Camille stood in the door. Their faces were flushed. Gwen's lipstick was slightly smeared and she was buttoning the top button on her jeans. "Eli!" she exclaimed, throwing her arms around him in a big hug. Eli's eyes met Camille's over her shoulder as Gwen clung to his shoulders.

"I found this beautiful waif waiting for you on the doorstep, Eli," Camille said. "You should be more careful with your treasures."

"She doesn't belong to me," Eli said, holding Gwen around the waist with one hand and stroking her hair back from her face with the other. "She's an angel who fell out of the sky. Comes and goes as she pleases. Maybe if I'm lucky she'll belong to me one day."

Gwen laughed and kissed him. "I decided to show up and surprise you but you weren't home. Camille let me use her bathroom."

"She's gracious and hospitable like that," Eli said, as Camille closed her door with a wry smile.

Gwen made herself at home at Eli's place and announced that they'd be ordering pizza. After dinner she asked Eli to turn off the lights — candles only. The happiness of love's reunion made them feel weightless.

Chapter 25

MOTHER NIGHT

Someday is far, the future is far. The past is a dead stone. In the night, there are only these two bodies, these two faces, two lives, and they become close, very close, almost indistinguishable: two hearts beating as one. Only the moment is real. Only love is real. Everything else is conjecture, fantasy. But the night is long, and there's time for every fantasy and conjecture.

What is the strength of two children against the ocean? Of two fragile human bodies against the flood? The dark water of night crashed in around them, as if rushing into the hull of a wrecked ship, sweeping their tiny forms away, out to sea, into her vast body – the embrace of mother night. There is plentitude in her grief. In her sorrow there is love abundant. She knows, so they can forget. She is sleep. She is peace.

When we're together, asked the boy, *do you ever forget which one you are? You or me?*

Yes! said the girl. She put his hand on her belly and held it there with hers. Her eyes rolled back into her head. *When you touch me, I forget.*

But the night is long. Gwen's demons returned. She cried, lost to herself and the world in a private hell where Eli couldn't reach her. "When you live a lie your whole life, you forget what's real," she sniffled. "When you live in a hall of mirrors you can forget which image is the real you."

"Gwen," Eli said, "pretend I'm him. Hit me."

She stopped crying. A strange blank look came over her face, revealed in eerie strips of streetlight through the blinds of his darkened apartment. Slowly, vengeance curled her eyebrows, ever so slightly; something fierce flashed across her eyes. Then it was gone again, giving way to helpless confusion. "Pretend you're who?"

"Pretend I'm him and just punch me once as hard as you can."

"Eli, I don't want to hit you. I love you."

"I love you too. Just…just pretend. Pop me one. Let me have it. It'll be good for you."

She crossed her arms and hugged herself. "I don't know what you're talking about."

"You won't hurt me," he said. "What's the worst thing that could happen - you'd break my nose? Big deal." He dropped his arms at his side and presented his bare shoulder to her as a target. "Come on." She just stared at him with wild eyes, quivering. "You treat me like I'm him half the time anyway," he blurted out in frustration.

She began to cry again. "Maybe you should hit *me*, at least I'd understand that," she said through the tears.

He pulled her gently to him and softly stroked her hair, regretting his attempt at therapeutic psychodrama. Silent squares of light from passing headlights drifted and collided on the wall behind them as her sobs gradually quieted to sniffles. Then he felt it: her hand balled up into a fist, delivering tiny little punches to his forearm. They were timid at first, soft and testing, then grew firmer, exaggeratedly slow, pushing her knuckles into his skin. He smiled broadly in the darkness.

Chapter
I MADE IT ALL UP

The morning light was strange in the apartment, ashen and gray with an otherworldly tint of red. Eli lay propped up on one elbow watching Gwen sleep, her skin gold-green in the strange light, her dreaming head floating on a sea of pillows and quilts. She opened her eyes to see Eli looking into hers. Silent and unsmiling, she sat up and pulled on a thick flannel shirt over the tshirt of Eli's she'd slept in. "I think I'm crazy," she said, sighing and staring at nothing, anything but Eli. He made coffee and eggs, but hers grew cold. "I think I made it all up. About the rape, I mean. I definitely made it up." She tossed her hair, a practiced gesture that seemed to give her confidence. She nodded slowly, with determination. "It couldn't have happened. I made it all up."

Gwen got out of bed, wrapping herself in a blanket and crossing the room to the window, where she stood with her back to Eli and watched the city go by. He stood with her and put his arm around her. "I love you and believe in you no matter what," he said.

Finally she turned and faced him. She met his warm kisses with tiny little slow-motion pecks. Her eyes were giant pools of blue that saw into him from a place deep within the agreed-upon mystery of herself. She spoke his name, as though from a cloud.

"Eli," she said, "I don't think we should see each other anymore."

Chapter 27
ASTRONOMER

Yet after she returned to Vail, his phone still rang late each night. *I had to hear your voice*, she'd say. *What are you listening to? What are you wearing? I just wanted to see how you're doing. I just wanted to say I love you.* Sometimes they would stay on the line for hours, just listening to each other breathe when they'd exhausted words. *Are you in bed yet?* she'd ask. *You should get in bed.*

In the daytime, Eli's apartment felt like a lonely tomb. The empty space in his bed where she had slept mocked him. Dust motes, dancing above him in morning sunbeams as he peered out from beneath the covers, mocked him. So he covered his face with a pillow and slept late, finally rolling out of bed and making his way downtown to *The Marketplace* as morning turned to afternoon.

He'd set up shop at a well-positioned table with his notebook and something to read while the café filled up with bodies retreating from the cold outside. Coffee refills were free. Minutes turned to hours. Voices rose and fell gently, blending into a soothing murmur like running water, spiked here and there by loud laughter. Eli held court as three or four sets of people cycled through his table over the course of an afternoon; the person he'd sat down to visit originally would be long gone. Talk moved easily from one topic to the next: god, poetry, politics, music, love. Classical music played in the background: a great cascade of piano notes tumbled into the silence between words; low, brooding strings underlined the main points of conversation. Empty coffee cups and crushed cigarette packs piled up on the little round wooden tables.

And there were women. Eli's radar still worked. A certain brunette with short hair sat in a back corner almost every day, doing her homework. She wore scarves — every day a different color. She always looked up when he came in. A pretty petite redhead who waited tables at a bar down the street smiled and made conversation in line for coffee. He wanted to run his fingers through her fiery red curls.

Instead he thought about Gwen. The irony of spending his empty hours in the place where they'd met was not lost on him. Sometimes he'd take the table where he first sat down to join her, letting the melancholy memory replay in his head over and over. He wrote poems to and about her, pouring out his love and pain, and petitioning her to see things his way.

I'm not an astronomer
and you are not a comet
to be regarded from great distance
mapped and charted in the vast blue-black sky
not isolated by light years
but by fear colder than empty space
I'm not an astronomer I'm a man
I'm a midwife - I brought you into the world
in my bed (you can't go back)

Chapter 28

DON'T TRY TO TELL US THAT WAS YOUR GRANDMOTHER

He sat on the floor in the darkened kitchen, knees bent to his chest, cradling the telephone to his ear. "Explain this to me," said Gwen on the other end of the line. "You say you love me so much, you'd do anything for me - how can you even think of sleeping with someone else?"

Eli shook his head in silent exasperation. "Because you just come and go when you want, that's how. I'm not your boyfriend - you've never given me that kind of status. I'm just supposed to eat shit alone until you happen to feel like showing up?"

Gwen let out something between a sigh and a hiss. "You know it's more complicated than that." A double peal of laughter rang out from Eli's living room. Female laughter. "What was that?" Gwen asked. "Is somebody there?"

"No," he said, stretching the word out with scorn for her suspicion. "Just the TV." He got up and went to the living room doorway, covering the receiver and putting a finger to his lips. The two girls on the couch stifled their giggles and looked at him with anxious smiles.

Hurry up! mouthed the short-haired brunette. She had introduced herself at the coffee shop that afternoon, and they went to the bar to shoot pool. After a few drinks, she convinced the waitress – the stunning girl with pale white skin and long, curly, red hair who was now sitting in her lap on Eli's couch — to come home with them. The brunette's blue silk scarf was wrapped playfully around both their necks; she idly fingered the redhead's curls. *I'm trying!* Eli replied silently. He went to the stereo and turned it up to mask the sound of his new friends making out while he got Gwen off the line.

"Look," he said, back in the relative privacy of the kitchen. "I didn't say I'd been with someone else. You asked if I would if I had the chance. Maybe I would. I'm a warm-blooded mammal and I'm lonely. Sue me."

"But you don't want to. Do you?"

"No, beautiful. All I want is you. You know that."

"Good."

He could hear the smile in her voice. Music from the living room filled the silence. He allowed himself a hopeful tone. "Can you come down next weekend?" he asked. "May as well put a face to the voice if you're going to call me every night."

She laughed. "Maybe. I love you."

"I love you so much. I'm going to go to sleep now. It's almost two."

She sighed. "Okay. Call me tomorrow?"

He said he would and hung up the phone, then returned to the living room. "Must have been a very important call!" said the redhead.

The brunette laughed. "Eli, get over here!" she slurred. She took a slug from the tequila bottle the redhead had taken from the bar.

"And don't try to tell us that was your grandmother!" said the redhead, grabbing Eli by the waist of his jeans and pulling him on top of them.

Chapter 29

THE LIGHTNING BOLT

School started again after the holidays. Eli dragged himself to class, feeling like a ghost in the long hallways full of living, breathing people. He signed up for a psychology class. The professor's introductory lecture made him regret it. It painted a soulless, mechanistic picture of the human psyche that Eli instinctively rejected.

"Psychology is like any other science," the professor declared in a pinched voice. He was relatively young, but clammy and lifeless looking; his hair was thinning and his cheap necktie was so tight around his throat it seemed on the verge of strangling him. "We observe input and output," he continued. "Behavior can be studied — *must* be studied - in a systematic and observable manner with no consideration of internal mental states." Eventually Eli couldn't contain himself any longer and raised his hand. "I wasn't planning on taking questions today," sighed the visibly irritated professor. "But go ahead, what is it?"

Eli cleared his throat and raised his voice to be heard in the large lecture hall. "What about the subconscious?" he asked. Snickers and groans could be heard from the back rows. A cheerleader sitting in front of Eli writing giant doodles in her notebook with an oversized pink pen snapped her gum and rolled her eyes.

"The subconscious?" the professor repeated incredulously. "Where am I, Vienna in 1905?" A kid in the front row who got the reference laughed rather too hard and too long, making sure the professor knew he was in on the joke.

Eli gathered his courage and continued. "I mean there is such a thing, right? We're all driven by thoughts and feelings we don't understand, at least sometimes. Repressed memories. Dreams. Love?"

"Love is beyond my pay grade," said the professor with a dismissive wave of his hand. The class laughed. "The latest research says there is no subconscious - or if there is, it is beyond our area of interest in this class. Only observable behaviors can be studied, since internal states such as thoughts, emotions and moods are too subjective. Freud and Jung are dead. If you're looking for God, join a church or a temple. If you're depressed, there's a pill for that. If you're in love, draft a good prenuptial agreement."

The class laughed again; Eli slunk down into his seat and the lecture continued. The cheerleader looked back over her shoulder and smiled at Eli. When she turned back to face the front of the class, she traced a big heart in red marker next to her scant lecture notes, big enough for Eli to see.

The psych class emptied out into a long three-story atrium with high ceilings, glass walls and students lounging on chairs and benches grouped around kiosks with mute TV sets. As Eli paused to watch the cheerleader walk away and disappear into the crowd, he felt a firm hand on his shoulder. He turned around to see Dr. Russell, his political science professor from the year before.

Russell, a few inches shorter than Eli, was staring keenly up at him through his thick glasses, wearing his usual uniform of jeans, cowboy boots and a black leather motorcycle jacket with a pin that said *Indian Liberation*. His long straight black hair hung down his back past his burly shoulders. He stood with arms crossed at his chest, rocking slightly back and forth on his boot heels. "Eli," he said, "I've been looking for you, man. I've been wanting to talk to you since I saw you in the newspaper when you got hit by lightning." Eli chuckled; he hadn't thought about the lightning strike since Gwen found the newspaper article and breathlessly questioned him about it. Dr. Russell smiled and gave him a friendly pat on the shoulder. "You okay, man?" he asked. "You look hale and hearty, sturdy and strong."

"I'm okay," Eli said. "Just trying to find my way."

"You got a minute?" Dr. Russell asked. "Come up to my office and talk for a bit."

Eli followed him up the stairs to the political science department offices. Russell had changed the way Eli saw politics and history forever. In addition to teaching, the professor was an activist – not just a letter-writer or a petition-signer, but a down-in-the-trenches fighter. He limped noticeably as they climbed the stairs. One rumor was that he was wounded in a shoot-out with the FBI at a standoff on a reservation some years ago. Another said he took a bullet fighting in the jungles of Nicaragua with the Miskito Indians against forced collectivization by the Sandinista government. In class, he wouldn't confirm or deny specifics. But he told stories. "Those Miskitos don't even have shoes, some of them," he'd once said. "They were fighting against guys equipped and trained by the Red Army. They had old rifles, some of them left over from World War II. That's all they could get. You know what their slogan was? They carved it into the stocks of those old rifles: *Only Indians help Indians*." They had been fighting to survive in the middle of a Cold War chess game not of their making. Russell taught that the whole left-versus-right dynamic hid the truth: both capitalism and communism were materialistic philosophies, twin demons who thrived on the extraction of resources from the ecosystem and the exploitation of people. Between them they threatened to bleed Mother Earth dry.

Russell's office was a glorified closet: a windowless, airless little room crammed to the ceiling full of bookshelves and stacks of papers. A poster on his door showed a cartoon of Columbus's three tall ships sailing off the edge of a flat world. "Five hundred year anniversary." the professor said. "We're gonna stir things up around here. No Columbus Day parade in Denver, you can bet on it." Eli would have. He sat on a chair surrounded by piles of books. Russell sat at his cluttered desk; an art print hanging behind him framed his head with blue southwestern sky over a stylized desert landscape.

"I saw you got involved with the war protests," Russell said, leaning back in his chair. "I was impressed when you got up to speak. You have a real way with words."

"Thanks," Eli said shrugging, mildly embarrassed.

"Even that thing with the rock and roll show," Russell continued. "I was there that night. I saw you took that hard but it wasn't your fault. You tried, but it went bad." He laughed. "Those boys had the real spirit in them, didn't they?"

"You could call it that," Eli nodded.

"Have you decided on a major yet?"

Eli fidgeted and looked at the floor. "I was thinking of doing psychology, just because I liked it from my own reading. But then I actually started a psychology class. I don't know any more."

"You'll find your way," Russell said. "What I really wanted to talk to you about… is this." He reached into a desk drawer and pulled out a folder from beneath a pile of documents. Inside the folder was a crumpled newspaper article, the same one that had transfixed Gwen. Russell it put on his desk between them. "I bet nobody has talked to you about what this means, have they?" Eli shook his head. "Tell me what happened," Russell said.

"I was working for this environmental group on a clean water campaign, getting signatures to ban toxic waste dumping, that kind of thing. I had a crew of canvassers.

The obnoxious kids who knock on your front door - that was us. On the way out to the neighborhood we were working, we stopped in a park for lunch. We sat under a tree and practiced role plays with the new kids, handed out everyone's turf assignments, and so on. A weather front rolled in but we didn't notice, we were still in the sunshine. We got a bolt from the leading edge of the storm, before a drop of rain even fell. It wasn't a direct strike - it hit the tree we were sitting under and scattered us like little toy soldiers. I got the worst of it because I was leaning against the tree; I was knocked out for a few minutes. But everyone was okay. You can still see the burn down the bark of the tree where the lightning hit."

Dr. Russell sat back in his chair, arms folded contemplatively, his glasses obscuring his eyes. "Do you feel any different since this happened?" he asked.

"Not really," Eli said. "I fell in love, if that counts."

The professor didn't acknowledge the awkward joke. "Do you remember what kind of tree you were sitting under?" Eli shrugged. "What about during the time you were knocked out? Do you remember anything?"

"Yes. It was only a few seconds, but...I saw memories. A lot of them, hundreds or thousands it seemed like, very quickly." He snapped his fingers rapidly - *snap snap snap*. "Kind of a life flashing before your eyes kind of thing, I guess. And I had a feeling like...like a déjà vu. Like I'd dreamed it all before."

Russell nodded a little nod to himself again, as he had when he found Eli in the hallway. "You're a very special person, Eli. Very special. Being hit by lightning is a big deal in my culture." He took his feet off the desk and leaned forward. "You know what happened, don't you Eli?" He didn't wait for an answer. "God tapped you on the shoulder." He looked at Eli for a long while through those big glasses. "How much do you know about Native religions?"

Eli shrugged. "A little – not that much. I've done some reading."

"Then you know that we believe God – the Great Spirit - is everywhere. You know that there are spirits in the land. Powers. That tree you were sitting under when you were hit – that's a very sacred place for you now. Trees, animals, rivers, mountains, the wind - they all have great spiritual powers that we have to learn to understand." He raised a single eyebrow and his voice with it. "And I mean *real* power. Not just symbols."

"For my people," he continued, "being hit by lightning is a very special thing. It's one of the ways that the spirits choose someone to fulfill a special role. Priests. Shamans. Visionaries. Artists. Healers. It's their job to communicate with the spirits, and tell the people the news. Not everyone can see what might be obvious to you, Eli."

He cleared his throat. "Now, if you were an Indian" - both men shifted uneasily in their seats — "I would tell you to go back to that tree. Go back there and think about what happened. Your spirit and the spirit of that tree are linked now, because the gods used it to reach you. Thank them. Thank the tree: thank the leaves, the branches, the bark, the roots. Say a prayer: whatever's in your heart. Take a piece of that tree and keep it with you. That's your medicine. My medicine is always with me, always." He reached into his shirt to clutch at something; Eli saw only a flash of color hanging on a necklace before he let it drop out of sight again. "There have been times I thought I'd die," Russell said. "When we were running from the Sandinistas through those swamps, boy…I just held onto my medicine and prayed. If I had been killed, it would have been okay. It wouldn't have mattered. It was all up to the spirits."

"There's a vision for you," Russell said, peering intently at Eli over the rims of his thick glasses. He tapped the side of his head. "Keep listening to the spirits."

Eli rose to leave. He wanted to hug the professor, but just shook his hand and thanked him instead.

He descended back into the teeming hallways, his head swimming. Was it true? Was he chosen? The backpack-toting daytime students were trickling out of the giant steel and glass building against the steady stream of night students coming in. Eli made his way out a side door just as a gust of wind blew up: clean, sweet, fresh air, promising the distant spring. He lifted his head and looked past the treeless interstate and the empty lots of gravel and past the dead grass, beyond the endlessly circling rush hour traffic and smog. With one hand he shaded his eyes against the intense rays of the sun, crimson and all-powerful, sinking down into the distant silhouette of the Rocky Mountains, beneath which all was the cool purple dark of the earth. The sky above the horizon burned in strips of magenta, pink and orange, singeing and devouring the long thin clouds that drifted too close to the sun's fiery flames. The light shimmered and danced through the haze of pollution and the mist in his eyes.

Chapter 30

THE TREE

The city changed as they drove south in the sporty little car Gwen borrowed from her roommate. The concrete desolation of Colfax Avenue gave way to quaint bungalows with green manicured lawns; legions of raggedy panhandlers were replaced by squadrons of robust joggers. "Keep going straight for a while, please," Eli said. "You'll turn left eventually."

"You don't have to say please," Gwen mumbled from behind her sunglasses. She had applied a fresh coat of lipstick in the women's room at the restaurant and it glistened in the sun as she sat low in the coupe seat, steering and shifting smoothly with her right hand, her left dangled out the open window, playing with the wind. The Red Hot Chili Peppers played on the stereo; she mouthed the words silently. "Where are we going, anyway?"

"Turn left here," Eli said. "And then right, through that yellow gate." She turned into the lot of a large, green city park, which was built around a small artificial lake with dirt running trails winding under sturdy old oak and willow trees. Mild spring-like weather filled the park with athletes and picnickers and dog-walkers.

Eli and Gwen got out of the car and Gwen wandered across the grass to the lake. Canadian geese were splashing around the shore, flapping their huge wings and chasing each other in circles. Eli came up behind Gwen and put his arms around her as she watched, mesmerized. "I like the geese," she said. They stood like that for a while, just watching the geese and the sun rippling across the water's surface.

"So are you going to tell me why we came here?" she finally asked. Eli smiled and took her hand. He led her away from the water, straight to a certain tree. Tall, sturdy and solemn, the tree was quite alike all the others in its row between the parking lot and a paved bike path. "Can we have a tree-climbing contest?" Gwen asked. "I might win." Eli said nothing but smiled and kissed her on the cheek. He walked around the tree once and then again while Gwen stood at a distance, hands in her pockets, glancing at a family picnicking ten yards away. Eli put his hand on the tree trunk. With his finger he traced a scar in the bark, slightly faded and healed by time, but plainly visible running from the crown down to where the trunk meet the earth.

Gwen appeared at his side. "What is it?" she asked.

"A burn mark," he said. "Remember the article you found about me getting hit by lightning?"

She let out a little gasp. He took her hand from where it hung at her side and put it on the tree, on the burned place. He looked at their fingers laced together there; she looked up, tracing the lightning's path with her eyes, up the trunk, through the web of branches and green spring leaves, into the blue sky. "Pray with me?" he said.

"I thought you didn't believe in God?" she said. He just smiled and closed his eyes and started speaking under his breath.

Gwen looked around at joggers padding past just a few feet away. A couple guys tossing a football were staring at her and smiling. "I think I'm embarrassed," she said. "I'm definitely embarrassed." A group about their age walked by, carrying a volleyball net and laughing amongst themselves. Gwen's eyes followed them, almost longingly, as if she might go join them. "People are watching," she whispered.

"No they're not," Eli said. "And what if they were?" They sat under the tree. He reached across and took her sunglasses from her face; she squinted against the sun. She fidgeted and turned so she was sitting at a slight angle to him.

"I can't face you," she said.

"I know," Eli said. He reached into his jacket pocket and pulled out three items: two small leather pouches, each hung on a necklace of string, and a pocketknife. He placed the leather pouches on his thigh, then opened the blade and carefully cut an inch of bark from the scar that ran down the side of the sturdy old tree. Then he snapped the piece of bark in two and put one piece in each pouch. He slipped one of the amulets over her head and the other over his own.

Gwen accepted the gesture wordlessly. She held the little pouch in her hand, feeling the leather and the chip of wood inside. Still she wouldn't look Eli in the eye. A breeze blew up from the west, cleansing the silence between them. Suddenly noise and movement nearby made them both turn their heads; the geese, as if of all one mind, took to the sky in unison and with a great commotion of honking and splashing flew off north, into the sun, leaving a dozen silent ripples to spread over the placid surface of the lake.

Chapter 31
ARE YOU SLEEPING?

Are you sleeping? Don't wake up. I'll talk. You don't have to say anything. Just keep the phone by you, so I can hear you breathing. Were you dreaming? I thought maybe you were dreaming about me. About us. I was just sitting here, it's very quiet, and I thought I could feel you. In fact I'm sure I did. I could feel you just like you were sitting right here with me. Isn't that strange?

It's snowing here. I'm right by the window and there are no lights on, except the streetlight way down the road, and the snow is falling. Big fluffy flakes. I can see the six points on each one. Are your snowflakes bigger out here? Or was I just blind all my life? God it's pretty, Eli. I wish you could see it.

Is it snowing there? Never mind, you don't know. You're asleep.

Thank you for today. I'm sorry I acted like such a geek. I don't know what's wrong with me. It was really beautiful. I mean the park and the geese were really pretty and all, but what you did was beautiful. I'm wearing my necklace thingy. I don't think I can like, wear it, wear it. Not all the time. But I'm going to wear it to bed every night.

I think what we did might count as a wedding ceremony in some states. Just so we're on the same page, you weren't trying to, like, secretly marry me today, right?

I had the best drive back. You know how I love that car. Well, I really love it on the highway. I'm lucky I didn't get pulled over for speeding. Not that I would have gotten a ticket if I did. I don't get tickets. Except one time I got pulled over by a lady cop. It was the worst.

Anyway. I think I cried on the way home. I did cry. You must think I'm the biggest cry baby in the world, I've hardly stopped crying since I met you. I swear I'm not usually like this. But I wasn't even sad. It was more like, I felt I was coming home to myself. Like I was really in my body for the first time, with all my feelings, good and bad. Like I'd just been watching myself from a distance all these years and now it was suddenly really me in my mind, in my body, in control of my life. Or that's what it felt like, at least. And that corny Pearl Jam song came on the radio, and all of a sudden I'm crying like a baby. Not the creepy song about the kid who kills himself. The other one. The happy one.

When I got to the top of the pass, it was so beautiful, with all the white mountains all around me. Like three hundred and sixty degrees of sky and sun and I turned the music up so fucking loud I probably damaged my ears forever. I took the car out of gear and just let it roll down the pass. I was going so fast. It was like flying. And I felt so free…

Chapter 32

COCA-COLA

When Eli showed up at *The Marketplace* he found Camille and Bobby at a sidewalk table out front in the sunshine. "Well hello, stranger!" Camille said, giving him a squeeze. "You missed the show the other night. Bobby was just doing his blow-by-blow replay of the world debut of the Love Renegades."

Eli grimaced. "Shit, Brandon's going to kill me. How did it go?"

Bobby and Camille smiled at each other. "We had fun. It's not The Naked Way, exactly." Camille finally offered.

"Brandon was doing great but he kinda freaked out and stopped playing his new stuff halfway through," Bobby said. "Switched to R.E.M. covers. I wanted to go up and hug him."

"Was it a good crowd?" Eli asked.

Camille shrugged. "Kate got half of her high school drama club in the back door somehow."

"Turns out they all knew the words to *Don't Go Back to Rockville*," said Bobby, unable to suppress his laughter.

"They were the opening act," said Camille. "People didn't really start showing up until later."

"It'll get better," said Eli.

"Speaking of music," said Bobby, "I have a very important question." He got up and crouched on top of his chair, hunched over a lit cigarette with his brakeman's cap pulled down over his brow, in manic monologue mode. "Are we supposed to like Pearl Jam? I can't decide if they're cool or not." He jabbed at the air with the cigarette. "Think carefully before you answer. They're all over the radio. Follow up question: is it just me or is their name super fucking dirty?"

Camille spread her legs with a mock-seductive look on her face. "I got your Pearl Jam right here," she purred, running her hands up and down her jeans. "And your Mudhoney too."

"Exactly!" Bobby exclaimed.

"Get a room, pervs," said Eli. "Better yet, take your coffee to go and come smoke a joint with me." They walked to a bench by the creek that ran through downtown. Eli sparked a spliff and tried to pass it to Bobby, but he refused. Eli snorted. "God forbid you take a puff," he said. "You drink a case of Milwaukee's Best to wash down your pint of Jack every night and now you're fucking around with that hard stuff. It just winds you up tighter. Have a hit and relax for once in your life."

Bobby shrugged and his face twitched. "Relaxing isn't my thing. You know that, Eli. I'm committed to staying alienated and pissed off."

Eli shrugged and took another drag before offering the joint to Camille. "Tempting," she said, waving it off. "But I've been trying to clean up. David's very spiritual, it's so inspiring. He likes it better when I'm not stoned out all the time."

Bobby rolled his eyes. "Oh, here we go…"

She playfully slapped his knee. "Come on, Doctor Doom. We're going to try a chant. It's very peaceful and centering. David taught me this one, it's from a book he's reading about Tibet…"

"Oh, *hell* no!" said Bobby, pulling down his hat over his ears as if it were the only way to keep his head from exploding with outrage. "Try something from your own culture – chant *Coca-cola, Coca-cola*, maybe!"

Eli pulled Bobby into a playful headlock and gave him a noogie. "Would it kill you to feel something you can't understand intellectually just once in your whole natural-born life?" Eli demanded. "Something holy, even?"

Bobby wriggled out of his gasp. "But that's just it – just wishing for holiness doesn't make it real. Saying the world is holy doesn't solve the problem of living! You still gotta get up in the morning and go to work, you gotta do the laundry, you get a mortgage and do everything you're supposed to do and say 'glory hallelujah' and make a new generation of little consumers to buy more VCR's and condos and Big Macs. What's it all for? What the fuck does it all mean?"

"It's for love, dummy!" Eli said. "Best I can figure. The love you take is equal to the love you make, and so on." He turned to Camille in a mock aside – "There were no Beatles records in his home growing up, you see – deprived childhood."

"So why aren't *you* up on stage singing about it?" said Bobby. "Let us hear what's in that little notebook you carry around all the time now. You know we all noticed it's the same kind Alexander had, right?"

Eli snorted. "A notebook is a notebook. He's got a copyright on using Walgreen's notebooks now?"

Bobby fired up a fresh cigarette. "It's one thing to talk about it, it's one thing to write it down, but it's something else again to put on your big boy pants and get up there and say it to the world."

"Like you have any place to talk, Bobby," interjected Camille.

"No, but at least I'm there for my friends when they put their ass on the line," he said, looking at Eli with a frown. "Brandon was hurt you weren't there the other night."

"That's the first show of his I've missed since I met the kid. I think I can get a little slack. Did he say something?"

"No!" sighed Bobby, gesticulating with his hands in exasperation. "It's Brandon! Everything is *unspoken*! But of course he was hurt."

Eli took along drag on his joint, then hid it behind his back and smiled as an elderly couple walked by. After they were past he leaned his head back and blew the hit up to the sky. "I'll be at the next show," he said. "I was going to go. But Gwen showed up that night."

"So why didn't you bring her out?" Bobby said. "Show her off? If she's as beautiful as you say she is, you should be parading her all over town. You're getting close to imaginary friend territory here, buddy."

"Oh no," said Camille, nodding with eyebrows raised for emphasis. "She's real."

"She won't go out," Eli said. "We always stay in. She shows up when she wants, usually announced. She cries. She holds on to me like it's for dear life. Then she screams at me and accuses me of horrible things, and cowers on the other side of the apartment and acts like she's deathly afraid of me. She speaks in tongues. Relives childhood traumas but can't tell me what she's seeing and feeling and remembering. I'm trying to get her to trust me so she'll let me in...I mean...no, you pig!" He punched Bobby in the arm.

"Ow!" said Bobby, rubbing his shoulder where Eli socked him. "I didn't even say anything! All kidding aside, it sounds like a crazy situation. What do you think happened to her?"

Eli shook his head. "I don't know. Something bad. Rape, abuse. In her family, maybe. She said she was raped. Then she says she made it up. Next thing you know, she's a puddle again." He slumped back into the bench with a sigh. "And I'm completely in love with her. Like, nothing else will ever matter again in love. It's fucking agony."

Camille squeezed Eli's knee and frowned. "Be careful, honey," she said.

"Careful?" Bobby said incredulously. "Eli's in love! That's the highest possible condition of life known to the human organism!" He turned to Eli. "You should dive in with both feet! You could be dead tomorrow, man. Go for it. *Carpe diem*, bro."

Camille laughed sardonically. "Dead Poets Society?"

"I'm serious!" Bobby said. "Robin-Williams-standing-on-a-desk-shouting serious!"

"She's been working and skiing in Vail for the winter," Eli said. "She comes down when she can. Or when she wants to, I guess."

"Has she had you up there?" asked Camille, already knowing the answer.

Eli shrugged. "She says she likes our privacy."

"So let me get this straight," said Bobby. "She lives on a mountain. She can come down and see you whenever she likes. You can't go up there to see her. Isn't that, like, a metaphor for a really fucked up relationship or something?"

"It's not a metaphor," interjected Camille. "It's an actual fucked up relationship."

"I'm trying to give her time," Eli said, thumbing his lighter to restart the joint. It was futile; the lighter was dead. "If she could just unlock her voice once and talk!"

Camille pulled a lighter from her purse and reached out for the joint. "Give that over here, baby. David can never tell when I'm high anyway." She took a long drag and let it go with the wind. "I'll probably go to hell for this," she said. "But I don't know if I believe her, Eli. Something about it feels weird."

Eli shrugged. Bobby's eyes bugged out of his head at Camille. "Whoa! You're shattering thirty years of feminist theory here! Last year, all you and Bethany talked about was repressed memories. You said they were the key to overthrowing patriarchy and creating new consciousness...or something."

"I know," Camille sighed. "And I meant that. Something bad must have happened to her. Maybe it's true. I'm just trying to look out for our boy here." She turned to Eli. "I hate to tell you, but you are whipped, son. Like a rented mule."

Bobby patted Eli on the back and briskly rubbed his shoulders like a trainer getting a prize fighter ready for the next round. "So what are you *gonna* do about it?"

Eli threw his hands in the air. "Do about it? I've told her I love her and I'll do anything to be with her a thousand times. What else is there to do?"

"What happens at the end of ski season?" Bobby said. "She just goes back East and it's over? That's bullshit."

"The truth is, women like dramatic gestures," said Camille. "You have to change the dynamic somehow."

"There's only one more thing I can do" Eli said. "I'll go to her. I'll go up the mountain."

Bobby slapped him on the back, a little too hard. "That's what I'm talking about!" he said. "No more passive meditation. This is action! This is some real will-to-power shit we're talking now."

"It's just a couple hours by bus," Eli said.

"Oh no, honey," said Camille. "We'll get you a ride somehow. I can't steal David's Beemer, though. Not again. Who do we know with a car that's free?"

"Alright!" said Bobby, clapping his hands and rocking back and forth with excitement. "This is real life happening!" He pumped his fist in the air and began chanting earnestly: "*Coca-cola, Coca-cola, Coca-cola!*"

Chapter 33

CAN WE GET SOME PIZZA?

"It's so beautiful up here," said Camille, leaning forward in the back seat to look out the window. "Look at these mountains, the trees, the fresh air…I'm glad we got out of the city for the day."

Ear Wax frowned and adjusted his cheap plastic shades against the bright sunshine glare as he shifted gears. "All I can see is fucking yuppies in their fucking yuppie four-wheel-drives as far as the eye can see," he grumbled.

Eli shifted restlessly in the front passenger seat. "You're a sport for taking me, Ear Wax. All of you guys, thanks for coming with." He looked at the van's improvised hood ornament through the windshield: a battered old Ken doll dressed up in a chef's white coat and hat and a miniature pizza box held high in one hand, racing forward into tomorrow like winged Mercury, stuck to the hood with an excessive amount of duct tape. The Romano Family Pizza Shop delivery van labored up the highway overpass, spewing dark exhaust from the tailpipe. Cars and SUV's twenty years newer sped past, most too fast to read the slogan painted in big white letters on the side of the old black van: *Sausage or Cheese, We Aim to Please!*

Eli began to shake his head. "Maybe I didn't think this through, guys." He turned to his friends in the backseat. "Is this a terrible idea?"

Bobby grinned from ear to ear and lifted his pint of whiskey as if to make a toast. "Would I be here if it wasn't?"

Eli laughed. "I guess not." He shook his head. "Ear Wax, don't take this the wrong way, but the van kind of stands out up here. Maybe we shouldn't park right in front of the lodge."

Ear Wax shrugged and turned his New York Mets cap backwards on his head. "What can I do? The Klingons destroyed my cloaking device, okay? And hey, I have to get this thing back to town by 4:30 for dinner rush deliveries." He fiddled with the knob on the van's radio. "Can't get a rock and roll station up here!" he complained. "This girl better be worth it."

"Oh, she's worth it," Camille said. Bobby and Ear Wax looked at her quizzically. "I mean, we met, just for a minute," she added quickly. "Smart girl, very beautiful." Eli thought he saw her blush, but it could have just been the booze. "And Eli," she said, smiling indulgently at him, "don't worry about the pizza truck. It sends a good message. Food is warmth, food is caring…"

"Food is love!" Bobby said. He and Camille exploded in laughter.

Eli smiled weakly. "Fuck you guys," he said. "I love you. But fuck you very much."

The van turned into the parking lot of the ski lodge where Gwen worked. Ear Wax found a parking spot for the Romano Family Pizza Shop delivery van. As the van came to a stop there was a knock on the passenger side window. A couple of boys who looked about fourteen with blonde surfer hair and expensive ski jackets were standing outside. Eli rolled down the window. The kids smiled at each other sheepishly, then one of them spoke up. "Hey, um, we were wondering if we could get some pizza?" Not even waiting for a response, the kids cracked up laughing and ran away towards the lodge.

Bobby opened the side door and yelled after them: "Punks!" Camille cackled and took another swig from the bottle before yanking Bobby back inside.

Eli held his face in his hands. "What am I doing? What am I even going to say to her?"

Bobby leaned forward to rub his shoulders. "It's okay, baby, if she says no I'm still here for you." Eli chuckled and shook off his friend.

"Just tell her you love her, that's all you can do," said Camille.

"Hey," said Ear Wax. He flipped his shades up and turned his baseball cap back around facing forward. "I read somewhere that a man who will humble himself for love can overcome any obstacle." He cleared his throat and continued in a voice like a nervous but solemn kid reading a report aloud in school. "If you ask for something with an absolutely pure heart, no one can refuse your wish," he said.

Camille let out a little gasp. "Ear Wax, that's very profound – that's really beautiful!"

He brightened at her praise. "You think?" He flipped his shades down and turned the hat backwards again. "Ah, it's bullshit - I just made it up," he said, his head turning on a swivel to watch two attractive girls walk past out the window. "Maybe I heard it in a song somewhere."

"Fuck," said Eli. "Pass me that bottle, you guys." He took a slug and passed it back to Bobby. "I'll try to make this quick," he said, opening the door and climbing out.

"I gotta be back on the road in an hour, max!" Ear Wax shouted after him.

"Good luck!" said Camille.

Eli walked up to the stately lodge building with hands in his pockets and shoulders hunched against the cold. He looked out of place with his mussed hair, scuffed black leather jacket from the thrift shop, plain t-shirt, Levi's with ripped knees, and Chuck Taylors; families passing by with matching gortex jackets and salon tans shot him suspicious looks.

He saw her right away when he entered the foyer. She was standing behind the reception desk about a hundred feet away, wearing a gold-colored blazer and a form-fitting white blouse, framed in a rectangle of light from the skylights in the roof high above. Her hair, worn up, seemed to sparkle and glow around her face. She didn't see him. He stepped into a phone booth where he could watch her without being seen. She sipped at a tall to-go coffee drink, leaving red lipstick on the rim. A family of customers approached the desk, and she turned on her thousand-watt smile. Eli felt his heart flip over in his chest. He watched while Gwen chatted with the family, ran their credit card and handed over their keys. The wife tugged at the arm of the husband, who was mesmerized by Gwen's smile. Finally they headed for the elevator, and Eli gathered himself to approach her.

As he opened the door of the phone booth, a guy in a gold blazer like Gwen's stepped out from a back office and joined her behind the counter. She turned and smiled up at him – a different smile, not the big cheerleader's grin like she gave the customers – but a small, sly, private smile full of familiarity. Eli felt his heart drop into his stomach. The guy was tall and vaguely good-looking, in a smug frat boy sort of way. He stood close to Gwen, too close. He leaned on the desk and his hand brushed against hers. Eli's heart pounded. The guy leaned in even closer and whispered in Gwen's ear. She laughed. Eli couldn't stand any more. He stepped out of the phone booth and walked to the desk. Gwen's back was to him and she didn't see him approaching; his footsteps echoed through the foyer and her laughter rang out like birdsong.

Eli stood at the desk. Gwen giggled low and ran her fingertip over the lip of her coffee cup as the gold jacket guy talked. His name tag said *Connor*. The smell of Gwen's perfume sent a wave of mixed elation and anger through Eli's body; his legs quivered with adrenaline as he stood there for a beat, then another, and another. Finally Connor acknowledged his presence with the slightest twitch of an eyebrow to Gwen, who turned.

"Welcome to the Laughing Bear Lodge!" she said as she spun around. Then she saw Eli. "Oh." Her face turned a dozen shades of red. "Oh. Hi."

Eli nodded. "Hi. Am I interrupting?"

Gwen brushed her hair back from her face and tried to regain her composure. "I, um…no." She leaned closer and lowered her voice. "What are you doing here?"

Connor raised an eyebrow and folded his arms. "Is there a problem here?" he asked.

"No," Gwen said to Connor without breaking Eli's stare. "But seriously, what are you doing here, Eli?"

Eli straightened up to his full height. "I love you," he said. "And I'm here to take you home."

Connor burst out laughing. Gwen turned around and shoved him away. "Shut up!" she hissed. "Go! I can handle this." Connor looked Eli up and down, snickering. Gwen pushed him toward a door to the back offices; he laughed and grinned a self-satisfied grin as he left them alone.

She turned back to Eli. "Seriously?" she asked, exasperated. "What the fuck?"

"I'm happy to see you too," he deadpanned. "Listen to me, I love you and I need you. And I…"

"Eli," she cut him off, "have you been drinking?"

"Would it matter?" He dropped down to one knee in front of the reception desk. "Gwen, I…"

"*No!*" she shouted. Everyone in the lobby stopped and turned to look. She lowered her voice to a whisper-hiss. "Eli, get up. We'll talk outside. Give me a minute…please."

Eli rose to his feet and stalked out. Bemused faces watched him on every side; he stared straight ahead and he marched through the automatic doors back into the chill mountain air.

Fifty yards away, Eli's people stood around outside the pizza van, smoking. They looked up as he emerged from the lodge. Camille lifted her hands and made a quizzical face, as if to say *so..?* Eli shrugged and mirrored the gesture back to her. He shoved his hands in his pockets and turned around to see through the glass doors that

Gwen was still inside, talking to Connor in the middle of the lobby. He was animated; she stood impassively.

Eli fumed and paced. The sun had gone behind a cloud and he could feel the temperature dropping rapidly. Finally Gwen turned away from Connor, and came outside looking composed and unruffled. She wore a gold skirt and tights with heels to match the corporate blazer.

"You came," she said.

"I came."

"No kneeling! Even if your shoe is untied!"

He nodded. "No kneeling."

She looked past him, over his shoulder. "You brought friends."

"More like they brought me. I needed a ride."

Gwen cocked her head hopefully to one side. "Can we get some pizza?" she asked. Eli shook his head. Gwen shrugged. She smiled and waved at Camille.

"I came up here to tell you this has to stop," Eli said. "I'm going to take you home and take care of you. You're going through something terrible. You don't have to flirt with middle-aged tourists and deal with shitty roommates. Let me take care of you. Jesus Christ, I'm in love with you, let's be together, for god's sake."

"Eli, I'm not *going through* anything. I'm skiing, I'm working, I'm twenty years old. I'm having fun! You can barely take care of yourself anyway."

"Are you or are you not the same woman who sobs uncontrollably in my arms for hours at a time in a trance where you hardly know your name? Who told me ten different scenarios where you might have been raped, by ten different relatives and friend's fathers and neighbors? Who said without my love you'd never get out of the black hole nightmare you're in?"

She looked up at him, the pale blue saucers of her eyes translucent and silent like deep waters. She bit her lip and her eyes burned into him. "Has it occurred to you that this is real life, not a storybook starring you as the handsome prince who saves sleeping beauty?"

"Yeah, it's real life, alright." Eli huffed and shuffled his feet. Finally he tilted his head toward the door. "Are you with that guy?" he asked.

"Oh my god, you're paranoid, Eli! He's my boss. Like, my supervisor. I had to get permission, I can't just walk out the door at work whenever I want!"

"He seemed to stand pretty goddamn close for a boss if you ask me."

"He's just...my friend. He flirts, what can I do?"

"Flirting is pretty much your job here, huh?"

"That's my job," Gwen said, crossing her arms and nodding defiantly. "Here, there and everywhere."

"You told me you wanted to have my baby," Eli stammered, red-faced and flustered. "You told me…a thousand crazy things I'll never be able to forget." His words grew thick, heavy, hard to get his mouth around. He struggled to keep his breathing even. "Just tell me…tell me we'll make it work out somehow."

A frigid wind rose up, making Gwen shiver and hug herself. "Don't you think I would if I could?" she sniffled.

Eli stuffed his hands deep in his pockets; his shoulders were hunched up around his ears. "I thought I did. Now I guess I don't know. I don't know anything for sure anymore."

Gwen looked past him to the black Romano Family Pizza van in the parking lot. "Those are some pretty good friends you have there," she said. "They brought you all the way up here just to talk to me?" Eli nodded. She smiled a funny little smile. "You really just don't care what anyone thinks, do you?"

"No, I don't," he said. He put his hand on her waist and leaned in to kiss her.

She held him at bay with a trembling hand on his chest. "No," she whispered. "I can't. Not here. Not now." She spread her fingers over his chest like a fan and stared at his lips. "You shouldn't have come here. You have more balls than I thought, I'll admit that. But you shouldn't have come." She wouldn't look up to meet his eyes anymore.

Ear Wax honked the pizza van's horn. The cold wind gusted again, cutting through their exposed bodies and blowing Gwen's hair into her face. She spat the hair from her mouth and pushed it back out of her eyes. "I have to go back to work," she said. She planted a single kiss on Eli's cheek, then turned and went back inside the lodge. Eli watched her bottom sway to and fro like a bell in the tight golden skirt as she walked away.

Chapter 34

LEAVE MY SOCKS ON

"You know that huge pile of clothes on the floor in your closet?"

"I know, I'm a slob. I'll pick it up."

"No, leave it. We could do it in there. Wouldn't that be great?" She drew a sharp breath that he could almost feel over the phone. "Mmm, think about it. We could just roll around in there for twenty four hours straight." Her voice dropped to a husky whisper. "No food. No phone. Just you and me."

"I'm really liking this side of you," he laughed. "If you were here right now…"

"What? What would you do if I was there?"

"I'd kiss you all over. I would run my tongue down your neck…I'd start undressing you, very slowly…"

"That sounds nice. Can you leave my socks on, though? My feet get cold."

"Of course."

"And you can't go so hard. Even though I love it."

"Why not? Did I hurt you?"

"No…" Gwen's voice trailed off into silence. "I'm pregnant."

Eli snorted. "That kind of joke is a good way to ruin a perfectly good phone sex session."

She sighed. "I'm late, Eli. Really late. Almost three weeks."

Eli got up and paced the floor with the phone. "But that might not mean anything, right? Besides, how is that even possible? We always used rubbers. Except…"

"Except the one time," Gwen said tersely.

"Except the one time," he echoed, smacking himself on the forehead. "Are you going to get a test? To be sure?"

"Eli, I'm a woman. We know these things."

"Jesus Christ, Gwen. What are we going to do?"

"There's nothing *to* do," she said. "And don't even think about the A-word. Don't even say it because it's out of the question." Her voice turned tender. "It's a boy. I can feel him. He *trusts* me."

Eli shook his head and tried to catch his breath. "Jesus. We'll do whatever we have to do. I'll stand by you no matter what." There was silence on the line. "I mean, it is mine, right?"

"Of course it's yours, don't be an asshole," Gwen said sharply. "You know how hard it was for me to even let you touch me…and I love you with all my heart."

"Ok, I'm sorry. What are we going to do? I'll…I'll go back to work. Get a better job."

"Eli," she sighed, "I'm going home in two weeks. Ski season is over. I have school to consider. You don't know what my parents are like. They're very…conservative." There was another long pause on the line. "In a perfect world, we'd be together. But we both know the world isn't perfect," she said.

"Who said anything about perfect? I just want to be with you."

"You know I want that more than anything," Gwen said.

Eli blew his top. "Enough with the fucking double-talk already! I think you were sent to ruin me. To break my heart and drive me out of my fucking mind." He knew he sounded crazy but he didn't care. "Well you can't do it! You hear me?" Gwen was still talking but he couldn't hear her; he shouted over her, holding the phone away from his face and yelling into the receiver. "I won't let you destroy me! You can't kill me! You can't kill my heart!" He threw the phone against the wall with all his strength.

Chapter 35

SMELLS LIKE TEEN SPIRIT

That night Eli went alone to a neighborhood bar. He fed money into the jukebox and bought women shots and knocked the balls around the pool table. *Smells Like Teen Spirit* rattled the speakers every twenty minutes. A leggy, pretty businesswoman fifteen years older got Eli talking and raced him to the bottom of pint glass after pint glass. She closed the bar with him and took him home, but he was too drunk to get it up. Instead he threw up in her toilet.

He awoke late in the morning face down in her expensive linens in her elegant apartment on the fifth floor of a high rise in the Governor's Park neighborhood. She wasn't there. He pulled on his ripped jeans and tried to tamp down his bed-head with a splash of water from her bathroom sink, to no avail. He let himself out of the apartment, emerging from the elevator into the sleek lobby and stumbling out into the stark, pale daylight. As he walked towards home he passed a clock in the window of a drug store and realized he had a psychology final to take in half an hour.

The psychology professor walked up and down the aisle of his classroom, placing a copy of the final exam on each desk. Eli's desk was empty as the bell rang to signify the start of the testing period. Eli was lying on a bench near some trees outside the big steel and glass building. The morning sun had disappeared; the sky was a perfect gray lid over the earth. Eli covered his eyes with a forearm and dozed.

A hand on his shoulder woke him. He opened his eyes to see Camille's face looking down at him. Kate's face popped up next to hers.

"Well, look what we found," Camille said to Kate. "Shall we take him home?"

Kate giggled. "Can we, mom? I promise to feed him and walk him and everything!"

Camille put a hand on Eli's forehead. "Are you okay?" she asked. "You've never been the sleep-on-a-bench type."

"I'm hung over - I feel like I have gutter water in my veins. What are you guys doing?"

"I ran into this little goddess on my way out of a test so we went to coffee," said Camille, playfully stroking Kate's hair. "How are your finals going?"

Eli sat up and shook his head. "I don't know," he said. "My psychology final is going on inside right now. I can't concentrate on anything. Gwen says she's pregnant. What the fuck am I going to do?"

Camille sat down on one side of him, Kate on the other. "About Gwen, you mean?" Camille asked. "Or about school?"

"About my *life*!" Eli said. "What the hell am I going to do? I'm not good at anything except *feeling*, and look at where that's gotten me. The pay isn't too good either. What am I going to do now, have a kid? Be a dad? Jesus Christ."

"Fuck that bitch!" said Kate. She covered her mouth after she said it, as if shocked at her own outburst. Camille giggled in spite of herself. "Seriously," the younger girl lisped. "Eli, you need to get out of town and clear your head. You're coming with us to Italy. That's final."

"Beg pardon?" Eli said.

"Italy. You know, over in Europe, the one shaped like a boot?" She snorted at her own joke. "It's an art history class for four weeks this summer. You like art, right? You like history. You're a smart boy. European girls are beautiful. Brandon and I just put down our deposits. I know he'd love it if you went."

"Might be just what the doctor ordered," said Camille as she tried to smooth Eli's hair into place. "Damn, son! You look a fright."

"Worst hangover of my life," he said. He let his body sink down on the bench and put his head on Camille's lap, like a toddler who needs a nap. "She was the right flavor, at least," he sighed.

Camille nodded and smiled and stroked his hair. "Yes she was."

Kate giggled and snorted. "Oh my god, you guys!"

Camille raised an eyebrow at her. "Inside joke," she said.

Chapter 36
SOMEONE IS SINGING YOUR NAME

Eli wasn't expecting company when he heard the buzzer. Maybe Camille locked herself out again. He pulled on a t-shirt and went downstairs in his bare feet to answer the door. It was Gwen, waiting on his stoop with several suitcases. She grinned a beautiful lip-sticked grin as he opened the door. "Did you miss me?" she asked. Eli was speechless. "Help me with my bags?" Eli let her in and carried her bags upstairs.

She took off her coat and handed it to Eli, who tossed it unceremoniously on a chair. "I missed you," Gwen said, kissing him warmly on the lips. Eli's arms hung at his side as she embraced him. She went around the room pulling the blinds closed. Then she sat down on the couch and began to take off her boots.

"What are you doing?" he said, still standing as Gwen made herself at home. "I figured you'd be getting ready to have our baby in the backroom of some secluded nunnery for rich girls gone bad back East somewhere by now."

"Very funny," she said, pulling the boot off of her left foot. "I got my period like ten minutes after I got off the phone with you."

His eyes fairly bulged out of his head. "That was almost two weeks ago! You just left me hanging thinking you were pregnant? You couldn't pick up the phone and tell me the news?"

"Relax!" she said, yanking off the other boot. "You were too mad to talk like a grown-up. Besides, all's well that ends well, right?"

Eli let out a sigh of mixed exasperation and relief. He sat down on the couch next to her. "I have some news too. I'm going to Italy."

Gwen unbuttoned her top. "Italy?" she repeated. "What the hell? That's kind of a random plot twist, isn't it?"

He shrugged. "It's a school trip for a few weeks. I'll use the last of my mom's money. What can I say, you ruined the Western Hemisphere for me."

Gwen pulled her t-shirt off over her head. She'd been slowly, steadily stripping since she walked in the door. She gave Eli another warm kiss, a longer one this time, then reached behind her back to undo her bra. It dropped to the floor, exposing her full, round breasts. "Let me make it all better," she whispered in his ear as she climbed into his lap.

———

"Eli?" Gwen was gently shaking him. "Eli, someone is singing your name." He opened his eyes but thought he was still dreaming. He pulled Gwen's hand to him and kissed her fingers.

"Go back to sleep, beautiful," he murmured. "It's the middle of the night."

Gwen knelt on the futon next him, peering out the window between the blinds. "He's dancing too," she said.

Eli rolled over and pulled a pillow over his head. Then he heard the voice. It was a male voice, rich and soulful and tinged with mischief. "*Eli,*" the voice sang, to a melody that seemed familiar but beyond recognition. "Eli, can you come out and play?" - stretching out *plaaay* like a trite horror movie villain. Suddenly Eli recognized the voice, and knew he wasn't dreaming.

He sat up and peered through the blinds with Gwen. Out on the street below his window Alexander sang and danced under the lurid coppery streetlight. He wore a long black leather coat, jeans and cowboy boots; an oversized silver cross gleamed around his neck. He held a bottle in one hand and hopped on one foot in a drunken little jig. "Are you there, Eli?" Alexander slurred at the top of his lungs. "Babylonia sent me with a message for you!"

Gwen turned to Eli. "Who is Babylonia?" she asked.

Eli shook his head. "Nobody. I don't know." He began pulling some clothes on. "I'll explain later." He tied his tennis shoes and kissed Gwen on the forehead and went outside.

"Hey good-lookin'!" Eli shouted in as friendly a tone as he could manage as he emerged from the apartment building and walked towards the tall, long-haired man in the street. "Bad timing for me right now. What are you up to?"

"Young master Eli!" Alexander said, raising his bottle in a facetious toast. "I hope your studies are going well? You're looking fit and trim. Keeping the rooster greased, I trust?" A crooked grin spread from ear to ear. "Fucking your buddies' girls much?"

Out of the corner of his eye, Eli saw a few neighbors looking out their windows; Alexander's roar cut through the night air. "Chill out, man," Eli said, stepping closer to the circle of light under the streetlamp where Alexander stood in the middle of the side-street intersection. "When did you get out?"

"Just a few hours ago, little brother," Alexander said. His face was twisted by a cold, wry smile; his mouth was a sneer on the verge of a snarl. He gripped Eli's shoulder in his large hand and took a deep pull from his bottle of whiskey. He wiped his mouth with the back of his sleeve and offered the bottle to Eli. Eli reached out for it but instead of handing it over, Alexander lifted the bottle high over his head and then threw it down with all his strength against the pavement, where it exploded like a starburst under the eerie streetlight. "Stupid motherfucker!" Alexander shouted. He stepped into Eli, shoving him with both hands to the chest. Eli tumbled to the pavement but rolled and sprang back onto his feet. He squared up to Alexander with raised fists.

Alexander raised his own fists but laughed instead of attacking. "Eli the pacifist, putting up his dukes! That's a pretty sight! Well you should, you little punk." He bobbed and weaved and feigned a punch, barking at Eli to throw him off balance.

Eli kicked a piece of broken bottle from the pavement between them. "What the fuck is wrong with you, man?"

Alexander snorted. "Babylonia came to see me in jail, Eli. She told me everything. That's what the fuck is wrong with me!"

"You were with *Amelia*!" Eli shouted. "Babylonia hit on *me*! It was just...I didn't think..."

"You didn't think I would find out? You thought you could keep it secret? You're messing with powers you don't understand, kid." Alexander stepped closer; Eli circled to his left, trying to stay out of range of Alexander's long arms. "Babylonia is my wife for a thousand fucking lifetimes. We've traveled through dimensions of time and space together that you can't even begin to understand. Across the fucking astral planes! That's not just another piece of ass, Eli. That's where my son came from!"

Alexander suddenly lunged forward and threw a haymaker right hand at Eli. Eli staggered backwards, just barely dodging the punch aimed at his skull. He hopped back onto the curb in front of his apartment building. "Father of the fucking year," he spat.

Alexander bent his knees in a combat stance and launched himself like a big cat, tackling Eli to the ground. They tumbled over the dead grass, grunting and cursing and wrestling for advantage. Eli took a knee to the ribs. Alexander's jacket ripped loudly. Alexander got on top of Eli and straddled his chest. He tried to hold Eli down with his bad hand and rain down punches at his face with the good one. Eli covered up as best he could and wriggled violently to get out from under the bigger man. Suddenly Eli's black Chuck Taylor basketball shoes were around Alexander's throat; with his legs he forced the singer's head back and down to the turf with a thud, escaping from the pin. His shoelaces tangled in Alexander's hair as he scrambled to his feet; the singer howled in pain as Eli kicked his feet free, ripping out a clump of hair.

Eli wiped blood from his lip. Alexander struggled to his feet, coughing and holding his throat. "Good God, man," he gasped. "Those are some strong legs and big feet you've got there." He grinned impishly as he struggled to catch his breath. "You know what they say about a man with big feet."

"Size twelve, bro," said Eli, brushing dirt from his sleeves. "Come see about me." Alexander laughed. A couple of skater kids who'd been watching the fight got on their boards and rode away. "Listen," Eli said. "I didn't mean to disrespect you with Babylonia. It just happened. She threw herself at me. You know how women are, man. She played to my ego but it was just to hurt you. Can't you see she did it to make you jealous? She never gave two shits in a paper bag about me."

Alexander listened to all this stoically, panting with his hands on his knees. "That's very poetic, Eli. Very literary. *Two shits in a paper bag* - a symbolic image that advances the plot, defines character, and invokes unexplainable emotions in a single elegant stroke of the pen. Bravo."

"Serious, man," said Eli. "You're like a brother to me. I didn't mean to hurt you." He put his hand on Alexander's shoulder. "I'd tell you to come in and crash at my place, but I've got a girl here." He patted him on the back. "You're the real poet around here. Go write a song about it instead of kicking my ass in the street, will ya?" Alexander smiled tenderly. In a flash, he swung his shoulders and drove his left fist – his good hand - up under Eli's ribcage into his gut. All the air went out of Eli's lungs, his knees buckled, and he collapsed onto all fours.

Everything went dark. Then he was blinded by stars. He tried desperately to fill his lungs with air, but instead vomited violently, uncontrollably. As Alexander stood over him, Eli puked his guts out. It all came out. Love and loss. Mystery rapists. The Naked Way. He puked up Rodney King and Desert Storm and Only Indians Help Indians, all over the sidewalk. He threw up lightning bolts and destiny in tart chunks that clung to his chin. He puked and puked, gasping for breath in between the involuntary convulsions that were wrenching his stomach dry.

Finally Eli put together two, three, four deep inhalations in a row before choking on one last spasm of vomit. He coughed and spat chunks and wiped at the mess on his face. He turned to look at the building and saw Gwen watching at the darkened window. Her pale face and long blonde hair glowed blue against the blackness of the darkened apartment behind her. She was still, transfixed, framed in the eerie gloom like a picture by the window pane. Her face was expressionless, featureless, spectral, ghostly; a luminous, occult symbol of uncertain meaning.

"Ah, it's Guinnevere, then, is it?" said Alexander with a theatrical flourish. "Fear not, darling, Lancelot is here!" He offered Eli a hand. Eli looked back to the window; Gwen was gone. He took Alexander's hand, and the singer helped hoist him to his unsteady feet. "That's enough of the rough stuff now, right little brother?" said Alexander, putting his arm around Eli in an embrace that was at once consoling and menacing. "Here's the deal," he said. He nodded towards Eli's apartment. "Give me the keys. I'll let myself in and introduce myself to the Mrs. You just go take a walk. Go to the bar, clean yourself up and have a shot and a beer. I'll be gone in a half hour, and we'll be even-steven. Okay?" He slapped Eli on the back, hard. "I'll leave a mint on the pillow for you when I'm done. And I won't even leave any marks on her," he sneered. "At least nothing permanent."

Eli stared at the empty apartment window. Then he looked up at Alexander. The singer's eyes were solid black lenses. The corner of his mouth turned up like a wolf snarling at its prey. Blood dripped from a cut on his cheek. Eli felt Alexander's strong fingers digging into his shoulder. He lifted up his foot and stomped as hard as he could on the top of Alexander's boot. He heard a snap and felt bone give way.

"Son of a bitch!" Alexander screamed. "Oh shit!" he hopped away from Eli on one cowboy boot-clad foot in a frantic replication of his Indian war dance under the street light earlier. "Son of a bitch, Eli! I think you broke it. Jesus fucking Christ it hurts!" Eli stepped closer, as if to offer help. Instead he wound up, aimed, and punched Alexander in the nose with all his might. Alexander's long wiry frame went sprawling; he landed on his back on the sidewalk with blood spurting from his nose.

A window opened on a second-floor apartment across the street and an older woman in hair curlers leaned out. "You boys stop it now, or I'm calling the police!" she shouted.

Alexander staggered to his feet, grimacing in pain. Blood covered his hands and ran down his face and matted the ends of his long hair; the sleeve of his jacket dangled uselessly by a handful of threads. He stood and pointed an accusing bloody finger at Eli. "*I will haunt you*," he growled. "You better watch your fucking back, Eli. In this lifetime and in twelve times twelve more, by everything unholy and deathless, I curse you!" He gripped the big silver cross hanging around his neck. It was slick with blood, dulling its reflection of the pale streetlight above. "And when I can walk" - he tried to lift up his broken foot but immediately grimaced and gasped in pain - "When I can walk right, I will find you, and I will send you on to the next life. Where I will *also* find you and fuck you up yet *again*." Eli stood silently, rubbing his sore knuckles in his hand. Alexander spat at him; Eli sprang back out of range.

Finally Alexander turned and hobbled down the street, favoring his wounded left foot. The sound of his boot scraping over the broken glass of the smashed whiskey bottle along the pavement was like fingernails on a chalkboard. Eli watched him shuffle along, wincing with every step, until he turned the corner out of sight.

No sooner had Eli opened the door to the apartment than Gwen threw her arms around him. "Honey, I'm a mess," he said, squeezing her tight anyway.

"It's ok," she said. "I'm going to take care of everything." She took him into the bathroom and made him give her his stained shirt and jeans. He sat on the toilet seat while she tenderly wiped his face clean. She hummed a soothing little melody as she washed his cuts with soap and water and rubbing alcohol and kissed them softly. She ran a hot bath. "Can we have bubbles?" she asked. He added shampoo to the steaming water pouring from the faucet of the old clawfoot tub to make a bubble bath. She helped pull off his socks and boxer shorts and he climbed into the hot water. She turned the stereo on and the lights off, then knelt by the tub in the semi-darkness, washing him with a washcloth like a baby, until he finally convinced her to get in the tub with him.

She sat between his legs, back to his chest, and leaned back against him. He cupped a full, heavy breast in one hand and stroked her silky blonde hair with the other. She sighed and let her weight melt into him, sinking under the water. They dozed. Eli opened an eye and saw a hint of dawn glowing in the bathroom's dingy little window. They hadn't been asleep too long; the water was still warm. He gently kneaded Gwen's tit, pausing to softly pinch and stroke her nipple with his fingers. *Remember this*, he told himself. *Remember this when you're old and gray and nobody wants you anymore.* He felt Gwen's nipple grow hard at his touch even though she gently snored, her head resting on his shoulder. *Remember this when you're old and gray and nobody loves you.*

They dozed again and awoke in lukewarm water with gray pale morning light in the window. Eli gently coerced Gwen out of the tub. She leaned her body weight against him as he dried them both off with a towel before carrying her to bed. They slept a few fitful hours, awaking again in the late morning.

Eli climbed out of bed and went to the bathroom to pee. "Was last night a dream?" she asked him from bed. He looked at the bruise over his eye and his scabby split lip in the bathroom mirror.

"Mirror says no," he replied. "So do the aches and pains and the puke-stained clothes in the corner." He returned to the bedroom and leaned against the wall brushing his teeth, naked as the day he was born, looking down at Gwen.

She looked up at him with her still, silent blue eyes. "Today is our last day. I have to be on the bus in four hours." She patted the tattered old Midwestern quilt that covered the futon. "You should come back to bed," she said.

Afterwards they lay spent. Beams of afternoon sun through the windows painted their naked intertwined bodies. Gwen cried. She wept so violently Eli worried passersby under the half-open window would think she was getting beaten within an inch of her life. He held her and stroked her hair and whispered comfort to her.

"I don't want to go," she said, sitting up and wiping her bleary eyes.

"Stay then."

"I can't," she sniffled.

"You can. You're making a mistake."

She touched a cut on his brow from the fight. He winced. "You have to put something on this," she said.

"It's fine," he said. "I'll be fine."

She turned her eyes away. "You have to call me a taxi," she sighed. "I won't be able to do it." He watched her impossibly beautiful lips move as she said the words. There was nothing else to do. He pulled on a pair of jeans and went to the phone. As the line rang to the taxi company he looked out the window. A neighborhood cat was lapping at Eli's vomit on the lawn from the night before. The sound of a passing car startled the scruffy orange tomcat; it looked now this way, now that way before it resumed the feast.

Gwen got dressed in the bathroom. She emerged looking magazine-cover beautiful, with her hair in a braid and her make-up simple but just-so. Without a word, he helped her put on her coat. They walked out of the building, Eli carrying Gwen's suitcases, just as the cab was pulling up to the curb. The skittish orange cat ran away. Eli dropped the bags and hugged Gwen to him as the cab idled. "Don't let me go," she whispered into his ear. She clung to him as the cabbie honked. Finally she released her arms from around his neck. "Here," she said fumbling in her purse. "This is my ski pass. I don't need it any more. It's a pretty good picture. Something to remember me by." He looked at it and then put it in his pocket without a word.

She stepped back, took her sunglasses from her pocket, and looked up at him through the cold, opaque lenses that reflected the pale sun. There was nothing more to say. He lifted her bags and walked her down the stairs to the curb. He opened the cab door and put her bags inside. "Don't let me go," she said, but with wavering conviction. The driver began to mumble and complain in a foreign language. Gwen kissed Eli and then got in the cab. She rolled down the window as the cab pulled away, watching him from behind her dark shades as the glare and dust and smog and distance and time began to pile up between them.

Chapter 37
GRACE

She was nearly as tall as Eli, statuesque, with long brown legs and wavy black hair halfway down her back. She was silent and aloof, efficient and indifferent, as she glided between the tables of the ancient dining hall in running shorts and a cropped top that flattered her curves and showed off her lean stomach. In an idle moment, her posture never slumped and her gaze never fell to the floor; she stared straight ahead, clear-eyed, over the heads of the noisy diners, out past the ancient stone courtyard splashed with evening summer sun, beyond the gently rolling wine country hills, to some great and humbling abstraction in the distance upon which her thoughts were fixed. Eli was determined to get inside her.

In Italy, Kate, Brandon, Eli and their group stayed in a renovated six-hundred-year-old convent tucked away on a narrow cobblestone street in an ancient walled town overlooking the green countryside of Tuscany. The dormitory was owned by an American university, which rented accommodations to groups like Kate's class. The mystery brunette worked in the kitchen. Eli used her athletic wear as a pretext to introduce himself. One night about a week into their stay, he contrived to cross her path in the hall after dinner.

"Excuse me," he said. "I noticed you must be a runner. Those are nice shoes. I'm Eli, by the way."

She turned to face him. "I'm Grace," she said. He smiled; her expression was blank and unreadable. Her long sleek legs tensed like a deer surprised in a quiet meadow.

"I was wondering if you knew any good routes to run around here," Eli asked. "I brought my running shoes too."

Grace relaxed slightly and gathered up her hair into a pony tail as she answered. "Sure…just head left out the front door until you get to the little chapel and fork to the right. Follow that road until it turns to dirt. Turn left at the corner with the chickens in the yard. That road loops through the valley and back into town. About eight kilometers, if you can handle that."

"I'll do my best," he said with a laugh. "Thanks…I'll let you know how it goes. If I can handle it." She nodded and went on her way without another word.

He ran the route she described the next day. Acclimated to oxygen-poor high altitude, Eli felt like the sea-level summer air of the Tuscan countryside gave him superpowers, and he galloped through the hills. The endless replay of the split with Gwen receded from heavy rotation in his mind for the first time.

That night, Eli sat at the table with Kate and Brandon finishing their dinners and knocking back glasses of red table wine bottled right there at the converted convent. Kate was over the moon. "Oh my god, the art we saw today was *amazing*! I *love* Italy! A bottle of their wine here comes out to less than two dollars!" She giggled at her own jokes and rocked in her chair; Brandon's hand was glued to her thigh. His face relaxed into a smile only intermittently. Kate turned to Eli. "While you were running, they showed us the big huge wooden vats where they stomp the grapes! They were going to let us try, but Brandon wouldn't do it," she said, giving her boyfriend a playful shove.

"That's gross!" Brandon said. "I don't want to get my feet in all that!"

"Hopefully the employees wash their feet before they stomp," said Eli.

Kate watched as Grace bent over to clear a nearby table. "I bet you'd eat grapes from between her toes, Eli," Kate laughed.

He nodded. "I bet I would."

"You should totally fuck her!" said Kate in a voice boosted by wine and high spirits. Several people at the table turned, but Grace was just out of earshot.

"*Kate!*" Brandon hissed. "Keep it down. Please?"

She tisked at him. "Well he *should*! I would kill for her body!" An uncomfortable silence between the three of them ensued; Eli examined the ceiling. Finally Kate broke the silence. "This mouthy drunk girl is going to go have a cigarette outside." She rose and made a facetious curtsy toward Brandon. "Would my prude and judgmental boyfriend like to join me?" Brandon got up and followed her out of the dining hall, shooting a pained, forced smile over his shoulder at Eli.

Eli drained his glass of wine and stared a while at the dregs left in the bottom. He poured another, and looked up to see Grace through the swinging double doors of the kitchen, taking off her serving apron and pulling her long black hair out from a headband. Eli downed the glass of wine and followed her out of the dining hall.

Eli called to her as she began to climb the stairs to the employee quarters. "Hey," he said. "Grace - Thanks for the running advice. I tried that route over the hills you told me about. It was beautiful."

She paused on the steps and turned to face him. "I'm glad," she said blankly.

"So…are you doing anything later?" Eli asked. "Would you like to get a drink in town or something?"

Her dark eyes seemed to see everything and show nothing as she listened to his invitation. Without returning his smile, she agreed. "Okay," she said. "My studio is at the top of these stairs to the right. Why don't you come up in about an hour?"

Climbing the staircase an hour later, Eli heard the sound of a violin. It was a high, sweet sound, like a single drop of honey on the tip of the tongue. The door of the studio was open. Eli stepped tentatively into a huge room with twenty foot ceilings and high windows that let in the last light of evening. He leaned against the doorway and listened as Grace, sitting with her back to him, eyes closed in concentration, finished practicing and replaced the instrument to its case. He put his hands together in applause after the violin's echo had faded away. "You play beautifully," he said.

She turned around to see him. Maybe the hint of a smile played on the corner of her mouth. "I have a lot to learn," she said. In one corner of the giant room, behind ornate oriental folding dividers, she had a simple cot and dresser with her things. Her roommate, not present, had a similar set-up in the opposite corner. The lower halves of the high walls were covered with art: pencil and charcoal drawings, acrylic paintings, watercolors. One particular series caught Eli's attention: abstracted faces, female and male, old and young, of different cultures, painted in garish, surreal, tempera colors. They were like finger-paint death masks, revealing haunted souls caught in a limbo between living and extinction. The faces sagged with premature age; the eyes stared with burning intensity, but seemed to see only betrayal and horror. Their twisted mouths called out in silent protest.

"Wow," said Eli. "Are these yours?"

"Not these. They're Elena's. She works with me in the kitchen."

"They're really good," said Eli. "But they're so…sad."

A pale young woman with a sturdy build, a pageboy haircut, and a bottle of wine in her hand walked into the studio. She smiled easily at Grace. "I can't wait to get to the bottom of this bottle!" she said. "We better get another on the way out. You won't believe…"

"Elena," Grace interrupted her gently, with a tilt of her head to the visitor just out of sight behind her. "This is Eli." Elena froze and stiffened. He stepped forward with a big grin and his hand out; she looked away as she shook hands with evident discomfort. "We're taking a walk," Grace said to Eli. "Join us?"

The three of them headed out to an abandoned chapel on a nearby hill. Elena chatted rapidly at Grace as they walked a tree-lined dirt road up a gentle slope. She hovered and circled and herded Grace up the hill, physically screening out Eli like a basketball player. Eli walked behind with a wry smile on his face. He'd been hoping for a party of two. It was obvious Elena was in love with Grace. He could hardly blame her.

They arrived at a tiny rustic stone chapel framed by a spectacular panorama of the valley and the lush countryside beyond. The wine was delicious, and the sunset over the valley was spectacular. Eli couldn't get a word in edgewise as Elena flitted frantically around the dark-haired beauty, speaking the private language of female friendship with alcohol-induced exuberance. Grace stood on a promontory overlooking the valley, eyes closed, half-empty bottle in her hand, arms spread against the gold and rouge sky, the sun illuminating the bronze skin of her bare limbs. Elena was transfixed by her every move, like a devoted congregant in awe of a priestess in communion with unseen spirits, and laughed with incoherent delight. Eli leaned against the stone church wall with arms folded.

"I should go," he said at last.

"Oh," said Grace, giving him her full attention for the first time since Elena entered their shared room. She handed him the bottle and he took a drink.

"Just tired, you know," he said. "We have an early train tomorrow." Grace met his eyes, but again he could read nothing. "Thanks for the walk," he said. "It's beautiful. I'll find my way back."

Back at the dorm, Eli found Brandon and Kate smoking in the courtyard. He helped them finish a bottle of wine, and then another, as the sky phased through the last embers of sunset into a gentle and dreamy dusk and finally into soft, velvety night. Most of the conversation passed him by; after a while Kate's monologue blended into a high-pitched song in the background of his mind, with Brandon's occasional deadpan baritone interjections as counterpoint.

Eli excused himself and went up to his room to write by a bedside lamp as his roommate slept. He let the image in his mind turn to fantasy as he wrote: Grace standing on the promontory with all of Tuscany bathed in sunset colors below her; her skin glowing and a beatific smile on her face, in a rhapsody like an old-time silent movie star; levitating up into the clouds on the gentle wind, arms outstretched like a triumphant female Christ. Finally he turned out the light, but the little movie — highly embellished and with Elena edited out altogether — kept playing over and over in his mind. Finally he got out of bed.

In shorts and a t-shirt, Eli climbed the stairs and walked down the hall on silent bare feet. He stood outside the door of the studio and made himself still to listen. Immediately he heard the sound of loud, labored snoring. He debated in his mind if Grace's sleek body could be the source of that racket; he felt sure that by all the laws of heaven and nature it could not. He rapped gently on the giant old door of the studio with two knuckles, just loud enough for a waking person to hear. He waited but heard nothing except the snores. He knocked again. This time he heard rustling sheets and creaking springs. Light and shadow flickered under the door; bare feet padded toward him. "Grace?" he said in a loud whisper.

She opened the door with a sheet wrapped around her body and placed her hand over his mouth. She beckoned him inside and closed the door behind him. Silently he followed her across the studio, lit by the flickering, jumping flame of a single candle, to Grace's cot in her little partitioned space. "Lie down," she said into his ear. She didn't have to tell him twice. He lay on top of the cool white sheets, watching Grace as she turned her back to him, dropped the sheet and put on a t-shirt. He let his eyes linger over the curve of her lower back and her firm, round bottom in plain white cotton panties as she changed. She climbed into bed with him in the small cot and sat up hugging her knees. He lay on his back, hands behind his head, looking up at her. The candle made a crazy show of shadow and light on the high walls of the big open room behind her.

"I wasn't sure if you'd be sharing a cot with Elena tonight or not," he said.

"Ha!" Grace said. "She's tried once or twice." A particularly loud snore resounded from Elena's corner of the room, followed by a muffled whimper and the sound of shifting limbs. After a moment the snoring resumed its ponderous rhythm. "Don't worry," Grace said. "She'll sleep through anything after all the wine we drank."

"I hope you don't mind me wandering up here. I just wanted to apologize for how I acted earlier."

"Apologize? Why?"

"For sulking."

"I didn't think you were sulking. I thought you were just tired."

He shook his head. "Sulking. I had hoped it would be just the two of us. You know, get to know each other a little."

She smiled faintly in the darkness. "Well, we can get to know each other now."

She told him her story. She was twenty-five and came from Los Angeles. She'd gone to school and earned a graphic design degree that brought her a well paid advertising job, but she walked away in disgust after a year. "I felt like I was prostituting myself," she said. "These hands were made for better things."

"Hm, I'd better investigate," Eli joked, taking one of her hands in his and examining her slender, strong fingers in the candlelight. He felt the urge to kiss them but restrained himself. "I agree," he said, letting her hand rest on her knee again. "Definitely made for better things."

A friend had given her a lead on the dormitory job, and she'd taken it as a sort of self-imposed artist's exile. When she wasn't cooking or serving, her lovely fingers were free to draw and paint and coax heavenly sounds from the violin. The dormitory, the studio, Italy itself was a dream space where Grace was reinventing herself. "The voices are different here," she said, pointing to her skull. "Have you noticed?"

He laughed and nodded. "I have noticed," he said. They switched postures; he propped himself up on one hand while she relaxed and lay back, black curly hair tumbling down around her head on the pillow. He leaned in to kiss her; she casually raised an elbow to block him. They laughed. "The elbow block – that's new," he said. "Real economy of effort there."

"You like that?" she asked, placing her fingertips on his lips, where she allowed them to linger just an extra moment. "It's your turn. Talk. Are you an artist?"

"No," he said. "Maybe. I don't know yet."

"Who are you then?" He didn't know. He told her everything. He told her about Gwen. She peeled back his skin with her questions, layer by layer, with perfect empathy and piercing insight. He watched her face as she stared up at the ceiling, where the dying candlelight's show had slowed to a languid pulse, like water lapping the shore of a placid lake. *Where is she now? Do you think you'll see her again? Do you believe in God? When did you learn Buddhism?* And, simple but cutting, *What do you want?* Elena's haunted faces stared accusingly at him from the wall.

"I don't know what I want," he said. "To feel something. To figure out who I'm supposed to be." He mustered a smile. "I don't know who I am, but life is for learning."

Grace's eyes softened. Eli leaned in and kissed her, softly. She let him, for a moment, and a moment longer, then pushed him away. He felt her fingers trembling against his chest and he heard the tremble in her voice too. "So, you came all the way to Europe to kiss a Mexican girl?" she said.

"I've kissed one or two at home," he said. "I'm here to make love to you."

All of a sudden the interrogation was over. Grace pulled him back to her and kissed him. Her face was flushed, hot. Their mouths and tongues locked together; Grace swung her thighs over and straddled Eli's body. He pulled her t-shirt off over her head. Suddenly she stopped grinding on his body and pushed him down on the bed. "Damn it!" she swore.

"What's wrong?" He spotted a tiny sliver of moon in a little window high above her head.

"Timing," she said. Her proud face looked crestfallen.

He brushed her thick black hair back from her forehead with his fingers. "I don't mind. If you don't mind. I don't mind at all."

In the morning, Eli awoke to the sound of Grace's voice in his ear. "Elena is in the shower. You have three minutes to get your butt out of here." He sat up obediently and rubbed the sleep out of his eyes. The studio was flooded with sunlight. Elena's sad gallery of faces greeted the new day with predictable dismay. "Hurry up, I have to get these sheets into the laundry before I go to the kitchen," Grace said, hooking her bra together behind her back. Eli stood up and began pulling his clothes on. He saw on the white bed sheet a thin, curved crimson outline of Grace's pretty backside on every spot where he'd had her: a constellation of red crescents against a pure white sky. Grace yanked the sheet off the bed, gathered it up in her arms, and left the studio with a single look over her shoulder at Eli.

Chapter 38

SHINY BROKEN THINGS

Bobby smacked his cigarette pack anxiously against his palm - *thwap-thwap-thwap*. He walked with his shoulders hunched as if against the cold, but it was warm out, warm enough that he perspired under his fisherman's hat and plaid wool shirt as he strained to keep up with Xavier's long strides in weathered black combat boots down Colfax Avenue. The giant street punk put his thumbs in his suspenders as he walked, surveying the street scene with a cocky, practiced eye. His spiked mohawk added almost a foot to his already imposing height. "Check it out, man," said Xavier, pointing at graffiti on a wall. "My tag. Pretty sweet, right?"

Bobby admired his handiwork. "On the side of the cathedral? Fuck yeah. I approve."

Xavier pointed to a bench. "Let's chill over here and scope it out. This is usually a hot corner. We should be able to score here before long."

They sat down. Bobby stared up at the gothic spires of the cathedral, straining towards a distant heaven in the blustery baby blue sky of Colorado spring. "You know Brandon and Eli are in Europe right now looking at the real thing?" Bobby said.

"No shit? Wow, man. What about Alexander? You heard from him?"

Bobby pulled out a cigarette and lit it. "He's in Seattle. I've got his number. He wants me to come out. Says he can get me a bar gig easy. Says he's trying to get a new band going."

"For real?" He laughed. "The Naked Way. That was some shit, man. They're just a legend now. They were, like, underground superheroes! I mean, between you and me" - he frowned and leaned close — "I think they would have made Nirvana look like pussies. Know what I mean?" Bobby winced and shrugged. Xavier went on. "Like, they would have kicked Pearl Jam's ass, you know what I'm sayin'?"

"I never know what the hell you're saying, Xavier." Bobby smoked his cigarette and stared straight ahead. "So you're sure we can score on this corner?"

Xavier nodded. "Yeah, no worries. Maybe my guy isn't out yet. It's only eleven in the morning." They scanned passersby for a connect, but nobody looked up to meet their eyes. A steady unbroken stream of homeless men shuffled up the hill from downtown, past the stately gold-domed Capitol. Some stopped to sleep on the Capitol lawn, stretching out on the grass under the well-trimmed trees. "Where the fuck do they all come from?" Bobby asked no one in particular. "It's like every broken down cowboy yokel and drunk Indian from here to North Dakota is living on the streets of Denver now."

"Like birds," Xavier said. "Migrating north for summer."

Bobby kept his eye on the passing crowds. "Some of these guys have it all worked out," he said. "Look at this fucking guy and his rig." He pointed at a man pushing a tricked-out shopping cart rattling up the street, packed with aluminum cans and newspapers and assorted junk of every kind with an old battery-powered transistor radio strapped to the side. The cart had a blue tarp rigged over the top for shade and protection from the rain. Its owner walked just a little taller than the other homeless men on the street. "Just like a suburban mom on her way back from the mall in a huge SUV full of consumer crap with a George Bush sticker on the back," said Bobby.

Xavier laughed uncomprehendingly. "Say what?"

"Look at him," Bobby said with a wave that blended contempt and admiration. "Shiny broken things collected from dumpsters, promenaded up and down the street. That's all we know how to do. That's all we know how to be." He turned his head, covered one nostril, and blew out the other into the gutter. He wiped his face on his crusty sleeve. "America is burning. The police beat the shit out of Rodney King for no good reason and now the whole country is burning down to the ground."

"Dude, you're getting really heavy with it," said Xavier. "I don't even like, read the newspaper, but I'm pretty sure those riots ended a while ago. When's the last time you ate something? I know a church that gives out cheese sandwiches..."

Bobby rocked back and forth on the bus stop bench. His nose ran and his hair was matted. "They asked me if wanted to go to Italy with them. Fifteen fucking hundred dollars! Not including spending money!" He shook his head and snorted and looked up at the golden sun over the city. "We gotta fuckin' score," he said to the disc in the sky. He turned back to Xavier. "Where is your fucking guy?"

Xavier turned the question around. "What about that girl you hang out with sometimes? The hot one, dude. She's all super-smart and businessy but she parties too. Bethany. We can ask her. Like as a back-up plan. Just in case. She can score, right?"

Bobby frowned and crossed his arms like he was hugging himself. "I can't ask her for shit," he said to his shoes through gritted teeth. His eyes hardened and he turned to look back up at Xavier. "And how the fuck do *you* know that she can score dope?"

Xavier's massive shoulders tensed and he frowned at Bobby. Then he shook his spiked head and shoved his hands in his pockets and looked the other way. "Whatever. It doesn't matter, dude."

Bobby pulled his worn fishing cap low over his eyes and turned back to scanning the steady stream of people drifting past. "Look at these young guys going by in dirty jackets with sleeping rolls over their shoulders and that desert highway look still in their eyes," he said. "I swear, if you wait a few minutes, you'll see the same kid go by, only ten years older, thirty years older: the same dirty, ripped jacket, the same old baseball cap, maybe green instead of orange this time, the unwashed hair sticking out in gray streaks, he's got a limp he didn't have last time. Still carrying that huge bag over his shoulder. Where could they all possibly be going? Isn't there an aunt with a spare back room for them somewhere?" Xavier laughed. Bobby ignored him and ranted on. "What if they finally made it home? Soft pillows and clean white sheets of salvation and mercy, the whole deal. What do you think they'd dream about, that first night?"

"I don't even know what home is," Xavier said. He poked Bobby in the chest with a giant finger. "What would *you* dream about if you made it home?" he asked.

Bobby pushed the finger away. "I'm never gonna dream that dream," he said. "I can't go home."

Xavier's face contorted with emotion. "Me neither," he said. He suddenly scooped up Bobby in a gigantic bear hug. Bobby endured the overwhelming embrace, wrinkling his nose at the bigger man's smell and the feel of his sandpaper stubble against his cheek. Finally Xavier released him. "Hey man," Xavier said, rummaging through his pockets, "take this. It'll help you when you're feeling sad." He passed Bobby a small locket on a chain. "Go ahead, open it," he said. Bobby pried it open with his thumbnails to reveal a tiny picture of the Virgin Mary.

"I'm not fucking religious," Bobby said.

"It doesn't matter," Xavier said. He put a big paw on Bobby's shoulder and leaned in too close. "Just talk to her," he said, filling Bobby's senses with his rancid breath. "It doesn't matter if you believe. Just say the words. Ask her for help, like a little kid who doesn't know any better. She makes it better, I swear." He gave Bobby a hearty pat on the back. Looking across the street, he saw a familiar face. "That's him!" Xavier said. "Quick, give me that ten spot." Bobby fished a crumpled bill out of the front pocket of his flannel and handed it over. Xavier took it and bounded across the dirty boulevard, dodging traffic as he went.

Bobby stared down at the battered old locket in his palm. "Fuck Italy," he mumbled.

Chapter 39
THE HIDDEN CHAPEL

Grace and Eli ran together. She led him through the valley beneath their little walled city on a hill, up and down steep ridges and dirt roads, between little country estates and vineyards and green peasant fields where the plow still deferred to the shape of the land and not the other way around. She knew all the dogs in the valley by name – in Italian.

Afterwards they stood panting in the courtyard, hands on knees, catching their breath. Grace reached out and goosed Eli, who laughed and jumped. "You have a pretty ass," she said.

"Are you objectifying me?" he demanded with mock outrage.

She bit her lip and looked him up and down. "Hell yes." He put an arm around her waist and pulled her into a deep, sweat-drenched kiss; she gripped his behind with both hands. The first drops of a gentle afternoon rain fell on their heads. Grace broke off the kiss. "Can we go to your room?" she asked him.

He shook his head. "Roommate. He was writing letters when I left."

Grace frowned. "Elena is painting in the studio," she said. Suddenly her face brightened. She put her finger to her lips, took Eli by the hand, and led him into the building and down a back hallway. She stood on tippy toes to reach a key hidden above a doorframe. The door opened into a suite of seldom-used offices; each showed less sign of recent use than the last.

"I had a dream like this once," Eli said.

Grace smiled at him. "Help me move these boxes," she said, pointing to a stack blocking an obscured door. They cleared the boxes and with effort, Grace pulled open the heavy wooden door, revealing behind it a small abandoned chapel. The old building had been a convent, after all.

The little chapel imitated the style of the great Italian cathedrals, only in garish school-house miniature. High windows illuminated pale yellow walls hung with plastic cherubim and scaled-down, amateurish copies of iconic paintings by Renaissance masters; dust motes swirled overhead in lazy beams of light. Christ looked down placidly on the scene from a rustic wooden crucifix. The pews were full of dusty boxes and piles of assorted stuff; the chapel had long been relegated to use as storage space.

The two of them wandered among the room's forgotten treasures. Eli took a stack of old framed prints and photographs from a pew where it lay among stacks of boxes and books. The frames held 1920s class pictures of angelic children with their somber teachers, artistic woodblock prints of flowers, Holy Mothers radiating light, sepia photo portraits of people long dead. The black and white faces stared back at Eli, radiating longing, love, nostalgia. As he went through the stack of pictures, the sequence of random images, one after the other, seemed full of mystery and wonder, as if they were finally remembered from a forgotten life or revealed to him in a slowly-unfolding mystical trance.

Eli thought of the image of Gwen he carried in his wallet: the expired ski pass with her picture that she gave him on the curb to remember her by the day they parted. If he left it in this cosmic archive of memory - if he were to just casually drop it into one of the old boxes of photos and papers - maybe in fifty or a hundred years someone would find it and think "such a lovely girl" or "strange that an old ski pass from Colorado, USA, halfway around the world, is here in this abandoned chapel hidden in the back of a dormitory in Tuscany." Nothing more. The joy and pain that the face had brought to Eli would be gone, passed out of the universe forever, transfigured into pure frozen image.

But the ski pass stayed in Eli's wallet. Grace was behind him, around him. He set down the pictures and felt her arms clutching him, her breasts pressing into his back, her breath in his ear, her wild black hair on his cheek.

"I think I've dreamed of this place too," she said. They pulled each other in a heap down onto the dusty chapel floor.

Chapter 40
TEN THOUSAND PERFECT NOTES

The art history class returned from a day trip to Rome in high spirits. Extra bottles of wine went down with dinner, and more after that. As the sun went down, an Italian DJ set up a powerful sound system in the courtyard and began playing 80s rock records: a dance party for all the different student groups at the dorm. Americans abroad with access to cheap and abundant alcohol can only keep up a front of good behavior for so long. *Toga party! Toga! Toga! Toga!* was the chant from the Denver contingent. They went to their rooms, took off their clothes, ripped the bedding from their cots, and reassembled in a large party room adjacent to the courtyard in their new party attire.

It was decided to stage a *pietà* – a sitting Mary cradling the body of Jesus deposed from the cross – after the Michelangelo statue they'd seen that day at Saint Peter's Basilica. "Brandon, you should be Jesus!" lisped Kate, hanging around his neck. She'd belted her toga and folded it just so, making it extremely flattering to her little body. Eli's eyes drifted down over her tan, bare shoulder as she leaned against Brandon, drunkenly tugging on the sheet draped over his bare chest.

Brandon smirked. "Eli would make a much prettier Jesus," he said with a sporting tip of his cup. Soon Eli was splayed, corpse-like, in the lap of a drunken female classmate, suppressing laughter while cameras snapped. Two dozen toga-clad classmates danced around them, singing ironic praises and hosannas, laughing and waving their hands in mock adulation that grew to genuine ecstatic abandon. Other Italian and American party-goers joined in the improvised ritual with wine bottles held high. The sound system blasted The Police's *Message in a Bottle*. The revelers danced and chanted in unison: *Sending out an SOS! Sending out an SOS!*

As the party wound down Brandon had the worst of it; he passed out on a couch in the corner. Kate, just as drunk but somehow still standing, kissed him on the forehead and straightened his toga and put a blanket over him. "I have to make sure no one tries to get to Brandon's magnificent penis," she slurred, laughing. She turned to Eli with a look of triumph. "I did it! I drank him under the table! I'm always the one who face-plants at the end of the night! I win!"

Eli gave her a high-five. "Congratulations, *bella*," he said. She grabbed him by the elbow and pulled him outside, saying "I have to smoke, come with me." She fumbled with her lighter as they stood on the veranda in the cool Mediterranean night. The DJ was still playing, but the dance party had devolved into small clusters of guys and girls lingering in pockets of darkness away from the festive lights strung across the courtyard. Eli stared at Kate's lips as they wrapped around her cigarette. "Oh my god, Eli," she said, releasing a puff of smoke to the sky and snapping him out of his trance. "Can you believe the things we saw today? Sculptures by Michelangelo?"

Eli began to sing. "Michelangelo indeed could have carved out your features…"

Kate giggled. "What are you singing?"

Eli smiled and shook his head. "Never mind."

"I'm taking the train to Paris to see my sister this weekend!" Kate said. "You'll keep Brandon company while I'm gone?"

"Of course!"

"You know what he and I did last night when you were with your little love bird?" said Kate. "He told me he wanted to take me somewhere special and that I should get dressed up. So I put on my little cocktail dress, stockings, heels - the nines. He put on his suit jacket with the skinny tie" – she fanned herself theatrically – "so fucking hot! But he wouldn't tell me where we were going. We walked down the cobble-stone streets – which is fucking difficult in heels! - to this adorable little church. It was a classical music recital. He had this big shit-eating grin on his face. He thought he'd come up with a pretty classy little date. Everyone was decked out in beautiful clothes – the Italians are incredible dressers. So we go inside and sit down, and there are so many kids. Slowly we realize it's a children's recital. Brandon has been practicing his Italian, and he read a notice in town for the concert. Only his Italian wasn't good enough to pick up that it was little kids performing! He was so mad and embarrassed. He thought he'd taken me to this swanky gig. But it seemed rude to just get up and bolt, so as the lights went down I made him stay.

"The first performance started and it was a kid about six years old - the parents rushed up to the front with their video cameras, the whole thing. Brandon was seething. I squeezed his hand and told him it was cute but he stayed pissed for a while. He kind of slid down in his chair, you know how he does. But I started to kind of get into the show. At first it was these little tiny kids playing the simplest little songs. I could see all the little girls were in love with the music teacher who introduced them and sat with them while they played. And of course there we were dressed like these decadent American rock and roll assholes with all these aunts and grandmas and grandpas there to see little kids play piano. We got a few looks. It was hilarious, really, but Brandon didn't think so at first.

"So anyway, the kids got older as it went on, and the pieces got better, more complex and sophisticated. I'm no classical music expert. But some of this stuff was pretty deep shit, you know? Twelve and thirteen year old girls. Brandon started to get interested again. He sat up straight. He got really into it. These girls were pulling off some beautiful music, and all of a sudden Brandon is sitting on the edge of his seat and clapping for these kids.

"So finally the last girl comes up. She was about fourteen or fifteen. Seemed very shy and nervous, didn't smile. She sat down and just charged into this incredible piece of music." Kate turned to Eli and he saw the fire flashing in her bleary eyes. "Her fingers flew across the keys," she continued, "and I had this vision - that her soul was going up and up through this, like, waterfall of music - these impossible interlocking chords, it was like they were raining down from the sky and crashing onto her piano and out over the whole room. The sound in this tiny little church was incredible!

"So the girl all of a sudden gets this wicked smile, like a mad scientist. Like, she can feel the control at her fingertips. The magic is just pouring out. She's driving the thing home, to this insane climax. Just as the applause starts to well up in the audience, she loses her concentration in her moment of triumph and flubs the last closing measure. One bad note, the girl lets out this awful cry of pain, and the whole house of cards came crashing down. There was a huge gasp from the crowd, then everyone applauded anyway - you never heard so much applause, it was like thunder! But the girl was inconsolable." Kate teetered as she reached for her drink; she put her hand on Eli's bare chest to steady herself. He felt her fingers slide over his chest. Kate recovered her balance and continued, looking up at Eli with her deep brown eyes.

"The poor thing sobbed her eyes out, right there on stage," she said, breaking eye contact and shivering at the memory.

"But nobody took it harder than Brandon. I turned to look at him and it was like he'd been shot. I wasn't sure if he was upset for the sake of the music itself or for the girl. Or both. We found little a bar around the corner afterward and got hammered. The more we drank, the more he went on about it. 'They've been playing music in that church for eight hundred years,' he kept saying, 'and they'll be playing music there another eight hundred years after we're gone.' He sat there gripping his whiskey glass like he'd just come from a funeral. He kept saying 'a single broken note after ten thousand perfect ones — just one bad note!' over and over. I kept trying to tell him I understood but he just shook his head with this crazy look in his eyes. He said, 'One bad note after ten thousand perfect ones, do you know how that feels?' I was like, 'No, do you?' I swear, he loves music so much it makes him half insane sometimes."

Kate let out a dramatic sigh and slumped against the wall. Eli looked out over the courtyard and noticed two figures moving in the shadows. After a moment he made out the figure of the DJ leaning back in a chair while a girl knelt in front of him. "Oh my god," said Kate. "One of those hookers from Texas is giving him a blow job." She threw her head back and laughed. The figures in the shadow were still for a moment, then resumed. "Holy shit," said Kate. "Now I've seen it all." She emptied her red plastic cup full of wine in a gulp. "What do you think it all means?" she asked him. "About Brandon and the piano recital, I mean - not the blowjob."

Eli was quiet for a long time. "I think it means he's got something in him and it's got to come out," he finally said. "No matter how long it takes, no matter how much how much it hurts, it's got to come out. For better or worse, it's going to keep coming out the rest of his natural born life."

Kate pouted. "Shouldn't I be enough for him?"

"He's crazy about you, Kate," Eli said. "He's all yours. He's a moody son of a bitch but he's never going to walk away from you, I can tell you that much. He's lost something he really loved. It changed him. I know he doesn't want to go through that twice. But he's going to follow the music forever."

"So he's not a serial heart-breaker like you?" She smiled her Marilyn Monroe smile at Eli; her perfect pearly white teeth gleamed in the moonlight.

"You wound me, madam!" said Eli, pantomiming an arrow to his heart, slumping from the pain of it.

She raised her eyebrow skeptically. "You're Saint Sebastian now?" she asked.

Eli shook his head. "I've already impersonated one great work of art tonight, that's plenty," he said. Kate kissed him on the cheek, just a moment too long, and went off to drag Brandon to bed.

Chapter 41
LAWN FURNITURE

"Camille, I appreciate your concern, but we're both adults. He's a partner at the firm. I don't think anything bad is going to happen." Bethany cradled the phone on her shoulder awkwardly as she touched up her lipstick in her bathroom mirror. With effort, she reached behind her back and zipped up her little black dress. "Yes, he's very good-looking. He gets up at quarter to five every morning to go to the gym before he comes in to the office." She pushed a button on her stereo system and a moody, shimmering electric guitar sound played from the speakers. A throbbing rhythm locked in behind it and soon a soaring, romantic male voice floated on top.

"Hell *no*, I haven't told my mother about him," said Bethany into the receiver. "She wants to send over a team of psychiatrists or have me institutionalized every time I mention an older man, you know that." She checked the fit of her cocktail dress, pushing her breasts together for effect. "Having said all that, do you think plunging neckline with cleavage is appropriate? Too much?" Her high heels clicked on the floor as she walked to the kitchen. She opened a bottle of red wine and poured herself a glass. "I bet you're right, he *will* appreciate it." Bethany heard a sharp knock at the door. "That must be him. I have to go. I'll call you tomorrow and tell you how it went." She hung up the phone and took a last look in the mirror, straightening her hair and dabbing at her lipstick with a tissue.

She undid the lock and opened the front door to find Bobby waiting outside. Compared to her picture-perfect glamor he was a mess: curly hair uncombed, a week of sandy stubble on his unwashed face, dirty t-shirt, army-surplus shorts, and battered kid's backpack over his shoulder. But his big brown eyes shone bright for Bethany.

"Surprise!" he said.

Bethany covered her face with her hands. "Bobby, no! Can't you call before you just show up?"

Bobby's grin melted into a hurt puppy-dog eyes expression. "Nice to see you too, beautiful." He looked her up and down. "What's the occasion?"

"It's just bad timing. I have a friend coming over. He's taking me to a party."

"A party, huh? Well that's a lucky thing, I have party favors right here!" He pulled a little plastic baggie full of white powder from his pocket and dangled it in front of her.

Bethany's stiff posture slumped. "Goddamn it, Bobby. One of the partners of the firm is picking me up in ten minutes. And I haven't done that shit for months."

"You'd better let me in and get the straws quick, then." Bobby said.

With a sigh of exasperated surrender, she stepped aside and let Bobby into her apartment. He plopped down on the couch while she rummaged in the kitchen. "It's going to have to be wine, that's all I have in the house," Bethany said from the kitchen.

"How in-control of you," Bobby said. "I'm sure everyone at your AA meeting would be proud." She ignored the remark and placed a bottle on the coffee table with a glass for Bobby. Then she came back with a small mirror, a razor and two straws cut in half. "It's been months, huh?" he said skeptically.

"Bobby, if you're going to show up and get me wrecked ten minutes before I go out with my boss, you can't be an asshole about it."

He dumped out the coke on the mirror and began chopping it up with the razor. "Fair enough," he said. He made four finger-length rails and handed Bethany a straw. "Ladies first."

"Chivalry lives," Bethany said. She brushed her hair back over her bare shoulder and leaned over the coffee table to snort up a line.

"It's the end of the world," Bobby said. His big soft eyes were bloodshot. He gripped the arm of the couch as if hanging on for dear life. "There's nobody I'd rather party with before the shit hits the fan than you."

"What are you talking about?"

"America is burning. Don't you read the news? The Rodney King riots. The economy is crashing. And the only guy they can find to turn it around is this Bill Clinton joker? Have you heard him *talk*? He sounds like he wants to sell me a used waterbed or something."

"Bobby, the riots have been over for two months. Life goes on. How long has it been since you've slept?"

He ignored the question and bent over the coffee table to honk a line, half up each nostril. He tilted his head back and snorted, then resumed his tirade. "You see this new talk show guy they have during the day?" he said. "Jerry Springer, I think his name is? Now *that* is the end of the world. Trailer trash throwing chairs and fighting about who knocked up who in the Hillbilly McInbred family. It's the fall of the Roman Empire all over again."

"What are you doing watching daytime TV? Did you lose that new job?"

Bobby's eyes narrowed as he took a long gulp from his full wine glass. "Wait a minute," he said, pausing to identify the music on the stereo. "Is that the Naked fucking Way? I try to show you a good time at the end of the world and I have to share you with that fucking gigolo witch doctor?"

Bethany put her palm to her forehead. "Alexander is gone," she said. "Let him go. The Naked Way doesn't exist anymore. They're not the 'next big thing,' anymore," she said mockingly, making air quotes with her fingers. "Time marches on." She sighed and sipped from her wine glass. "This song just makes me feel nostalgic, is all."

"Nostalgic for what? The back seat of a parked van at six in the morning with a pimp and one of his drugged-out groupies?"

Bethany drew a sharp breath and her eyes bulged in anger. But she stopped herself short and exhaled. "Listen," she said in a low, calm voice. "We'll talk another time. He's going to ring that bell any minute and I'm not going to let you get me upset. Drink up and finish that line, then you have to go."

"A partner in the firm, huh?" Bobby winked at her. "Nice ropin', sis. This ain't your first rodeo, is it?"

"I'm a step down from a secretary there, Bobby. How's it going to look if I'm not gracious when he tries to be my friend?"

Bobby shook his head. "All these men. Why is it never me? Couldn't it… couldn't it ever be me?"

Bethany's eyes softened. "It's always you, Bobby. Always. Just not like that. And what '*all these men*'? I don't think I appreciate that very much."

Bobby leaned closer, his eyes twitching with emotion. "I know you like none of them ever could, Bethany. You know that. We hit rock bottom together. I've been through everything with you. I knew you when you were giving blowjobs in the parking lot at the mall to get money for drugs. None of them could ever know you like that. Not even Alexander."

"Give me a fucking break!" she exploded at him. "You make it sound like that freak was my soul mate. And Bobby, I don't *want* anyone to know me like that! I don't wear my pain like fucking a suit, like you do. And, Bobby - you're scaring me. You look like shit. I'm worried about you, all this living on the edge of the moment shit. It was brilliant when we were seventeen. Or at least it seemed like it then. But rebelling against our parents is over now. We have to move on to something, make something of our own."

"You think I'm *rebelling* against my *parents?*" He shook his head. "What about *your* family?" he asked pointing at her with the coke straw for emphasis. "Is that what you're running from?"

"*Nobody knows about that,*" Bethany growled through gritted teeth. "And I'm not running. The past is the past. Let the dead bury the fucking dead."

Bobby raised an eyebrow. "You're quoting the bible to me now?"

"You're not the only one who read the classics, mister." Bethany frowned and looked at her watch. She grabbed a straw and snorted another line. "I remember that paper you wrote about Greek philosophy and the New Testament," she said. "It was brilliant. You won a scholarship or something for it, right?"

Bobby laughed out loud. The anxiety melted away from his face for a moment. "Five hundred bucks," he said. "I scammed the registrar at City College into giving it to me in cash, then I un-enrolled before they could figure out I didn't get my high school diploma. That was quite a weekend."

"Bobby, you could go back. To school, I mean. You're so fucking smart."

"And do what? Teach? That was always my fantasy. We'd have a little house. I would teach totally inappropriate literature to kids all day - Bukowski and Kerouac and Dorothy Parker and James Baldwin - you would do whatever you do all day, and come home to a house that smells like my chili. I make amazing chili. I'll cook for you every night. Sound good?"

Bethany laughed. "Your chili is fantastic, I must admit. But I thought you were dead-set against dreary suburban life."

"For you, I'd make certain exceptions," Bobby said. "For you, lawn furniture."

Bethany put her hand to her heart. Bobby watched her slender fingers spread over her chest just above her cleavage. "I'm touched by the profoundly bourgeois sentimentality represented in your own personal symbolic vocabulary by lawn furniture," she said. "Thank you, Bobby."

He just smiled; for once the stream of words failed him. The moment stretched on an extra beat. Bethany's hand stayed over her heart. Her mascaraed eyes fluttered. Bobby leaned forward and kissed her painted lips. She let him. Her brittle posture relaxed into the kiss. Bobby held her face in his hands, pulling her closer across the coffee table. Suddenly he knocked over a glass with his elbow, spilling wine onto the mirror and the table and the carpeted floor beneath. "Bobby, dammit," Bethany said. "Shit!" she ran to the kitchen for paper towels to clean up the mess.

"Look," Bobby said. "Look how the coke soaks up the wine. It's kind of beautiful. It looks like blood."

Bethany sopped up the spill. "Fuck. I'm going to have to have the carpet steam-cleaned." She let out an exasperated groan. "This is crazy, Bobby. I'm sorry, that was a mistake. You have to go."

The scowl returned to his face. "You can run all you want, Bethany. But nobody knows the real you. Nobody but me. You go from man to man to man like you're running from something. Now you're back to Daddy figures. Maybe bad boys will be back in season again in the spring…"

In a blur, Bethany slapped him across the face. The sound was like thunder. "You make me sound like a fucking whore!" she hissed. "I'm a free woman, I do what I want. I'm not running from anything. And I don't sleep with every man I have dinner with, asshole!"

"You just pick and choose the real winners," Bobby spat.

"*Get out!*" she shrieked. Bobby scraped what coke he could salvage from the mirror back into the baggie. "Take your shit and do not darken my fucking door again!" Bethany yelled. He stormed out without a look back.

Bobby rode the elevator down to the first floor of Bethany's apartment building. The double doors slid open and Bobby passed a guy who looked to be in his late thirties getting onto the elevator. The man smiled mildly. He was handsome, with broad shoulders, a sprinkle of gray around the temples and an expensive-looking suit. "Toxic waste spill upstairs, very dangerous," Bobby said. "Save yourself!" The man frowned as the elevator doors closed on him. Bobby popped an unlit cigarette in his mouth and laughed, spinning out the front doors and into the night.

Chapter 42

NO, LIKE A HUMAN BEING

While Elena worked her shift in the kitchen, Grace drew Eli in the big studio on the second floor of the old dormitory building. She directed him to a cushioned palate near the bed, where he sat cross-legged. Grace set up a drawing table and made preliminary sketches, very fast, her dark eyes flashing from his body to the page to his body again, the pencil in her hand a blur across the paper. "Take off your clothes," she said. He did. The afternoon light poured in through the high windows. Suddenly Grace swept the sketches to the floor and pulled a giant sheet of paper from a roll in the corner onto her desk. "Now choose a position and sit still, I'm ready to start," she said. Eli shifted to find a center of gravity. He took a meditator's pose: spine straight, legs crossed, left palm on top of the right in his lap, ends of his thumbs touching. Grace frowned. "No, like a human being," she said.

Eli laughed. He stretched out his legs and leaned back on his elbows, trying to look relaxed. "I guess I'm a little self-conscious posing," he said. She made no reply except to furrow her brow and tilt her head this way and that, seeing his form from different angles, not meeting his gaze with her own. What did she see? A naked boy in her room, a silhouette of heat against the cool white linen, an arrangement of graphite strokes on her drawing paper?

Grace finished the first drawing and put it aside to make way for a clean sheet. "Do something, move around," she said, squinting. Eli clowned, flexing his biceps, then putting his arms in front of him to fly through the air like Superman. The artist let the hint of a smile touch her face. "Come on," she said. He hugged one knee and let the other leg rest on the palate. Grace began her sketch with a flurry of strokes on the page. Eli watched her face. She was brilliant, articulate, sensitive and self-aware.

She was amazing in bed. And yet, he didn't feel what he thought he should. Her face was beautiful — but it wasn't *the* face.

Grace finished her second sketch and pulled it aside to rest atop the first. She stood up, hands on her shapely hips, and looked down at Eli. This time she met his eyes. In the flash of an instant he felt she could see right through him — into his loss, his lust, his dreams, into his very soul.

Her face brightened. "I have an idea," she said. She walked to her improvised bedroom and rummaged through her dresser. She returned with a blue bandana. She knelt next to Eli and tied it gently but firmly around his eyes, giving him a little kiss on the cheek as she pulled the knot behind his head: a blindfold. "Maybe that will help you relax," she said.

Eli slumped back into the soft cushion of the palate. The sounds of Grace's pencil flying and her paper rustling echoed in the big room. Eli felt his body becoming weightless. Blindness was liberating. He felt her eyes on him. There was a stirring between his legs. Soon he was posing for Grace with a raging hard-on. The sounds of her drawing continued, even more frantic than before — then suddenly stopped. He heard her feet softly padding across the floor, then felt her hand on his shoulder. She pushed him down onto the palate, then swung her long leg over, straddling him.

Chapter 43

THE POSTCARD

Students poured out of the air-conditioned tour bus into the street in front of the Leaning Tower of Pisa. They mugged for the camera in front of the tower, pretending to hold it up with great effort. Two students were missing from the group. The professor asked Eli where Brandon and Kate were. He shrugged behind his shades. "I thought Kate was supposed to be back from Paris by now," he said. "I haven't seen Brandon since he went to get the mail last night. He took my Walkman! Maybe he went to meet Kate, but that wasn't the plan."

Brandon was in Rome. He was standing on a street corner, just outside the busy central train station. Porters and tourists and cabbies jostled him and cursed him in several languages. He was groggy and disheveled and his hair was a spikey mess. After getting Kate's Eiffel Tower postcard after dinner the night before, he turned around and ran, ran across town to the little train station. He'd missed the last train to Rome for the night, so he half-slept on a bench outside the station to catch the first thing smoking at dawn, with the vague idea that he'd make the connection to Paris from there. He boarded the train to Rome full of determination, but as he read the postcard – covered on one side by Kate's tiny, prim, precise handwriting - over and over on the three-hour ride, his determination turned to despair and paralysis.

He went inside and looked at the ticket counter for trains to Paris. He counted his lire and made calculations, then he read the postcard yet again. He sat down at the coffee bar and ordered nothing, frightening the old man behind the counter with his hard sneer and his black leather jacket and his sleepless red eyes. He took out Eli's Walkman, borrowed for his evening walk and stashed away in the jacket pocket. He put on the headphones and pressed play. Eli had The Naked Way's demo tape in the Walkman. *Son of a bitch*, he thought. Brandon walked out of the station and stood on the street corner, oblivious to the crush of crowds rushing by. The occult, churning, rhythmic introduction to the song *Seduction* filled his head. Brandon remembered the drum pattern, played it in his mind, saw every move on the drum kit as if the last show had been yesterday. He turned his back on a newspaper peddler who was yelling at him to get out of the way of his customers on the busy corner. He turned up the volume on the Walkman until it hurt his eardrums. Then he read the postcard again.

Dear Brandon,

Hello darling. Paris is amazing! It's everything I thought it would be and more! I feel like Europe is my own private Disneyland! I guess that makes me an ugly American, doesn't it? How ironic!

Sweetheart, I have bad news for you. I met a wonderful man on the train to Paris. He's smart and funny and speaks four languages. His name is Isaac. He's a jeweler, and he owns a whole block of flats right on the Seine. We fell in love the moment we met and we haven't looked back. I'm putting this in the mail to you now from a precious little café where everyone knows him. Then we go to meet Isaac's parents for dinner. He already showed me the family chapel where we'll get married. Never thought you'd see me become Catholic, did you? Haha.

I may never go back to America. This is my dream, Brandon, I hope you understand. I know this is harsh but I'm telling you the whole truth in hopes that you'll understand some day. I believe that everything happens for a reason. People change so that you can learn to let go, things go wrong so that you appreciate them when they're right, and sometimes good things fall apart so better things can fall together. I'll always remember the fun times we had, especially when you were playing with The NakedWay. That was special, Brandon.

You can keep my things in the room or throw them away. I have my passport, Isaac will replace everything else.

This is Goodbye,

Kate

Brandon had read the postcard at least a hundred times by then. *The Eiffel fucking Tower*, he thought, turning it over to the picture side. He tore the postcard up, letting the pieces of Kate's girlish neat penmanship fall to the Roman sidewalk. *I just want to play the fucking drums right now*, he thought. He felt the heft of the wooden sticks in his hand; the action on the foot pedal to his kick drum when he knocked out a quick triplet fill: *boom-boom-boom*. But he couldn't play. So he walked.

He walked past broken ancient columns and medieval cathedrals. He walked in front of darting motorbikes and honking taxis; if they wanted to run him over, they could. He walked past military police strapped with machine guns and past hooded bishops and priests from a hundred countries. He walked past newsstands full of pornography, with teenage boys siting on the sidewalk shamelessly pouring over the pages. He walked past painted, unsmiling Italian women, dressed to the nines for a Monday morning. They didn't meet his searching, hungry eyes. With his high school Spanish and tourist Italian, he tried to decipher the ancient Latin carved into the walls of the old Roman buildings. Arabic graffiti in the alleys and side streets seemed mysterious and vaguely threatening. He listened to Alexander's voice raging in his head through the headphones until the last echo of the last song faded out. He flipped over the tape in the Walkman. Eli had recorded the John Coltrane Quartet on the other side — *A Love Supreme*. Typical esoteric Eli cosmic crap.

By the time the sun was high in the sky, Brandon had reached the Spanish Steps. His face was covered in sweat, but he wouldn't take the black leather jacket off. He stood and looked around at little groups of teens or families eating their lunch on the steps or throwing coins in the elaborate Baroque fountain. He realized he hadn't eaten anything since dinner the night before. The crazy jazz music swirled and wailed and crashed in his head. *This is the greatest drumming I've ever heard*, he thought. *Who the fuck is this drummer?* He felt faint. The sunlight seemed to penetrate his body, to pass right through his organs. He looked up defiantly at the blazing fireball in the sky until colors danced and the light began to blind him. *I have to check my ID*, he thought. *It will tell me who I am.* He noticed a Japanese tourist pointing a camera at him as he took his wallet out; he sneered his meanest rock and roll sneer until the man moved along.

Brandon looked at his passport in the bright summer noon glare. *Still me.* Cool mist from the fountain carried on the breeze to touch his face. His legs felt weak; he allowed himself to sink down to the Steps. He struggled out of the bulky leather jacket, letting it rest on the old stone next to him, and he wiped the sweat from his face with his plain white t-shirt. The Coltrane opus rumbled to a close. Brandon took off the headphones. A little ways below him on the Steps, a kid with an Eastern European accent and an acoustic guitar led a dozen or so others in a sing-along of *We Are the World*.

Kate hates that fucking song, Brandon thought. *Even more than I do.* He hung his head and sobbed.

Chapter 44

A TIME-OUT FOR YOUR MIND

Eli and Grace walked down the narrow, winding streets paved with stone to an old café in the heart of the walled city. They held hands, like a couple. Eli had firm handshakes and game Italian phrases for the men who greeted Grace along the way. A few of the town's dogs scampered happily underfoot. Purple neon halos crowned statues of Mary and Jesus in a little street-side alcove shrine. Cool dusk in the Tuscan summer was like heaven falling slowly, slowly from the sky.

The café was called *The Velvet Underground*. A pickup band of earnest local amateurs played covers of British and American rock and R&B standards. "Accents and all, they aren't half-bad," Eli granted, putting his beer down to clap as the band finished its set with a passable *Bad Moon Rising*. Grace squeezed his knee under the table.

"So tell me, Mr. World Traveler Art Student," Grace, said. "What's your favorite work of art you've seen over here so far?"

"Wow, how do I narrow it down?" Eli said. "Well, we went to a town called Volterra," he said. "They had a little museum with some Mannerist paintings. You're the artist, ever study about the Mannerists?"

Grace nodded. "They were working at the height of the Renaissance when Italy was invaded and Rome was sacked. They used classical forms to portray fear, uncertainty, grief, anxiety." She became animated, talking with her hands like a native. "They leaned toward the grotesque; contorting bodily proportions, using impossible colors, playing tricks with geometry. They were irrational and subjective."

Eli smiled at her evident passion for the subject. "You know your stuff, beautiful." He gestured at the waiter for another round. "We saw this fantastic painting, maybe you know it. A green Christ with red hair being taken down off the cross. A 'deposition,' they call it."

Her face lit up. "You saw Rosso Fiorentino's *Deposizione dalla Croce!*" she said. She slapped his hand playfully. "I'm jealous as hell! I love that painting! It was like the Renaissance turning post-modern, turning itself inside out. The distorted, bulky, discolored body, the eerie twilight, the smile on his face. It was decadent as hell! So surreal!"

"Yes, the smile," Eli said. "In every other painting I've seen in this country, the object is to show Christ in as much torture and anguish as possible. But in this one, he was the only one who wasn't suffering. The disciples all looked traumatized, the women were crying. But he was at peace, like he transcended the body, passed beyond good and evil." Eli laughed abruptly. "Brandon and Kate were blown away too. Kate was totally mesmerized. It was like the first time she did acid all over again."

Grace looked shocked. "You guys do drugs?"

Eli shrugged off the question. "Kate got all weepy and started talking to the painting." He said. "Saying, 'now I understand!' Tears running down her face. She forgot where she was, I guess, because she reached out to touch it! Put her fingers right on the canvas, practically speaking in tongues. Alarms went off, and we got hustled out by security guards. Brandon was so pissed and embarrassed, so of course they had a big fight down the hall in the museum while the professor spent twenty minutes convincing the security people to let us back in."

Grace shook her head. "That little Kate is quite a piece of work! Did they make up?"

"Oh, of course. Their whole relationship is drama and make-up sex."

"Well that's good. Maybe we should go out with them some night. A double date."

"Sure, if you don't mind watching the one-woman show up close and personal. She went to Paris for a long weekend to see her sister who's studying there. But she hasn't come back yet and now Brandon is gone. I shouldn't be worried, right? He probably just went to romp around France with her for a few days and just didn't say anything."

"I'm sure they're fine," Grace said. "So Eli," she said, playfully unbuttoning the top button on his shirt, "what's next for us?"

He shrugged. "I don't know. Do people do shots in Italy? Or is there some-where else – another bar you want to go to?"

She poked him gently. "No, silly, I mean…us. I think you're amazing. I'm com-mitted here until spring, but I don't know where I'm going after that. Denver sounds nice. I have cousins in Pueblo." She looked deeply into his eyes, an imploring look. "I think I'm falling in love with you," she said.

"Oh, Grace," he said. He took her face in his hands and kissed her tenderly. "I love you too. I think you're amazing. But..."

Her glowing face dropped. "But?"

"No, I mean - Grace, you caught me off guard." Eli turned red and his voice grew flustered. "I told you about Gwen..."

"You told me she was out of your life and you'd never see her again!"

"And that's true! But I'm...recovering. I didn't...I don't know if I can really be with anybody right now."

Grace leaned forward, an incredulous look on her face. "Can't *be* with anyone? You've *been* with me quite a bit these last couple weeks." She locked him to an angry stare. The soft, loving brown eyes of a few minutes ago turned to black stones.

Eli grabbed her hand. "And it's been incredible, I've loved every second with you. It's been like...like an instant flashing by that we were stealing. I just thought it was understood. We're *here*" – he spread his arms to embrace the whole boot of Italy - "this isn't real life...this is like time out of mind, like a fantasy world..."

"Excuse me?" she yanked away her hand. "Self-absorbed asshole! This is *real*." She wrapped her knuckles on the table. "*I'm* real. This isn't a...what did you call it? A time-out for your mind?"

Eli put his elbows on the table and covered his face with his hands. "I would be the luckiest guy in the world to wind up with you, but I don't even know where I'm going to be in a year. Or even in a few months. I'm trying to find myself, I'm trying to write. I was stripped down to the bone, now I'm just trying to follow the spirit where it takes..."

"Oh shut *up*, for fuck's sake!" she screamed. The café fell quiet; a trumpet player warming up on stage put down his horn. Grace stood up and commanded the full attention of the crowd as she dressed Eli down. "Who *are* you, anyway? What do you *do*? What do you stand for? You think my body is a port in a fucking storm for you?" She picked up her beer glass from the table and tossed its contents in Eli's face. The patrons erupted in howls and cheers.

Grace leaned in close as Eli wiped the suds out of his eyes. "You can't just smooth talk your way through life! You have to *do* something...make something! And you can't just fuck your way through every woman you meet. Some of us have *hearts*." She turned on her heels and stalked out of the bar.

Eli sat dripping wet alone at the table; he pushed the sopping mop of hair back out of his face as the chorus of laughs subsided. A few Italian guys gestured for him to join them at the bar. They slapped him on the back and got him a towel. They bought him drinks, and with their limited shared vocabulary and numerous hand gestures and pantomimes, commiserated about women.

Eli struggled to make his new friends understand exactly what part of the U.S. he came from. "Colorado?" they repeated to one another with polite shrugs. Finally Eli hit on the right reference: "Red Rocks - U2, *Under a Blood Red Sky* video," he enunciated carefully in English. Their eyes lit up with recognition; merriment ensued; more drinks were ordered. Eli looked down to see one of the town's dogs, a little brown mutt, curled up asleep at his feet.

On his drunken walk back to the dormitory in the wee hours, Eli stopped at the grotto with the purple neon halo Jesus and Mary. He crossed himself, clutching at the little leather pouch hanging around his neck, and sunk down to the sidewalk where he sprawled against the wall beneath the little shrine. The dog from the café padded up and began licking his face. The stars danced and the crescent moon winked at him from the indigo velvet sky above.

Chapter 45
GWEN'S DIARY - FALL 1992

I only kissed Connor once. At first.

We had lots of time to kill at work. When I first started there, it took me about ten minutes to get him to stop acting like my "boss." Like I was really going to put up with that shit. But it was easy, we had a lot in common. Same kind of families. We talked about boarding school. Funny stories, people we both knew. First times. Who was on drugs, who was secretly gay, who was fucking a teacher to get grades. He made me laugh so hard. I could never talk about that world with Eli. He would roll his eyes and call me an elitist. Or say my dad is a capitalist pig, or whatever. Connor went to Phillips Exeter. It's a very prestigious school.

The first time I kissed him was at this kegger at some gorgeous million dollar condo right on the ski slopes. Rose-colored marble and crystal chandeliers and everything, and then crushed up beer cups and empty Mountain Dew bottles with chew spit in them. And stupid rich kids smoking cigarettes and trying to pose but too drunk to stand up. I think I was one of them. I definitely was. Eli has no idea how much I love cigarettes. He would hate it.

So Connor and I were smoking and talking on a dark balcony at this party and the moonlight was making the snow glow on the slope below us. The moon was pretty full and I hadn't eaten anything all day but I'd been drinking right along, so I was pretty buzzed. I think my head was spinning. I remember that I was leaning against a wall holding a wine cooler and the Chili Peppers were playing on the stereo. I realized that if Connor tried to kiss me, I'd let him. Connor is an idiot but his parents are important people and his sunglasses cost $175. He knows where he comes from and his name means something.

When Connor kissed me, it was kind of abrupt. I guess it was ok. He has really thin lips. I don't think they have any feeling in them at all. It's like he has a congenital disease where he doesn't have nerve endings in his lips. He just kind of mashed his face into mine.

But. He wore cologne. I missed that. His cologne reminded me of my dad's. I let him keep kissing me. Even though he kissed me and I let him and I kissed him back…it was wrong. I guess. Because of Eli and everything. But I knew it was only temporary with Eli. Like I could ever in a million years bring Eli home to Mom. Or even to Dad and his new wife. Not too fucking likely.

Even though Connor was kind of a horrible kisser, I liked it okay. His cologne reminded me of home, and sailing especially. I felt like myself again. Not the girl I was trying to be for Eli. Me. Just the old me. I didn't come to Colorado to fall in love. I came out to ski and party!

When I was with Eli, I had so many crazy feelings I didn't know who I was anymore. When I'm with Connor, I don't feel anything. It's much easier that way. I don't know why I told Eli all those things about my past. Somehow, when that kid touched me, I turned into a puddle and everything just came pouring out. Things that I don't even know if they're true or not. I guess I was trying to scare him away. Everyone loves me on the outside. I thought if I showed him my insides, he'd be smart and get scared off. So he wouldn't get hurt. But for some fucked-up reason it just made him love me even more.

Connor almost caught me having phone sex with Eli one time. My stupid fucking roommates let him in without telling me or even knocking on my door to give he a head's up or anything. He opened the door and I had my hand down my pants but I just played it off like whatever. I actually told him I was talking to my mom and could he wait in the living room for five more minutes? Eli got me off and then I told him some lie too and got him off the phone.

Me and Connor did it once while one of Eli's tapes was playing. He must have made me twenty mix tapes. Connor didn't get it and kept trying to put on Jimmy Buffet or the Dead or something, but I wouldn't let him. One of Eli's tapes had a song by that band his friends had, he couldn't stop talking about them. I think they were called The Naked Guys? No…The Naked Way. When the song played it was like I was back in that little apartment, closed off from everything, in a little bubble safe from the world. I made Connor rewind it like five times in a row. At least I was a big girl and didn't cry while we were doing it like I almost always did with Eli.

It was okay with Connor. His thing was like, curved. I guess it was okay. After I got tired of the Naked Way song, I reached over to turn off the tape. Connor tried to put on some other tape, but I said no music. He was like, what's the big deal? But I didn't want to hear his crappy music and I didn't want Eli's tape on anymore. Music is too emotional sometimes.

So I told Connor to tell me more boarding school stories. After a while that made me feel more relaxed again. So I started playing with him. But I made him keep telling me stories while I did. He was annoyed as hell but he did what I said and he got hard and stayed hard. We got in the shower, and it smelled kind of like leather. The soap and the steamy hot water and our bodies. I think I liked it. I know I did. It smelled like lavender and leather and sailboats and home.

Chapter 46

SEATTLE

Alexander climbed two flights to the studio apartment above the pawnshop in the old brick building. He limped, favoring his left leg. He carried a little brown paper bag and several envelopes he'd retrieved from the mailbox.

"I'm home, dear!" he called out facetiously to Bobby as he opened the door to the apartment. "Did you miss me?" The only reply was from a stray cat they'd taken in, a crippled old gray tabby with one eye who made a plaintive mewing sound from a cardboard box lined with an old t-shirt where he was curled up. Alexander put the grocery bag down in the little alcove that passed as a kitchen. "And hello to you, Popeye," he said to the cat. "I remembered your food this time. Jack Daniels, cigarettes, cat food. Nature is fulfilled in all her ends. Isn't that right, Bobby?" Bobby still made no reply. Alexander waved a hand at him dismissively. "See how you ignore me and break my heart?" he asked in an arch Jewish-mother voice. He over-filled a bowl with cat food and set it on the floor; Popeye leapt from his bed to eat.

Pushing aside piles of dirty plates and dishes, Alexander cleared a space on the tiny counter. He rinsed out a shot glass with a picture of the Space Needle on it and poured three fingers of Jack. He sat down at the little card table, covered with books and full ashtrays and drug paraphernalia, and picked up a book from the stack closest to Bobby. "*Steppenwolf* again? I thought we agreed Hesse was bad for you." He lifted the shot glass in a toast. "To your health, Bobby!" He downed the shot in a single gulp, and poured out another. "We received some letters from our friends, Bobby," he said, holding up the envelopes. "Shall I read them to you?" He cleared his throat. "Here's one from Camille. The salt of the earth, that one. And an absolutely depraved hellcat in bed, let me tell you. Anyway. Camille says:

"*Dear Alexander,*

Haven't heard from you since your first postcard when you got to Seattle. How is everything going? Are you guys still heading up to Alaska to find work when fishing season starts? I know we haven't been pen pals but Bobby doesn't write back any more so I thought I'd try my luck with you. Denver is back to being a vortex of nothing. It feels like nothing has happened since the band broke up. It's freaking 1993? That sounds like a science-fiction year, not a real year. The scene is totally dead now. Ever since 'grunge' hit big, all the rock shows are the same: a bunch of fresh-faced little white kids I've never seen before in plaid shirts and wool hats. Nothing seems fresh or creative anymore. All the bands do that whisper-to-a-scream shit. Some of the lead singers even try to front as sensitive feminist guys like Cobain. Almost makes me miss your whole phallus worship act. At least it was honest.

Brandon is on about his fourth new band since you guys split up now. Eli hasn't been the same since that girl broke his heart. He seemed happy for a while right after they came back from Italy, but now he just sits around The Marketplace all the time writing in his notebook. Wait, that is the same. He seems more serious about it now, but he won't show anybody what the hell he's writing.

A, how is Bobby? I worry about that kid like you wouldn't believe. Give him my love. Are you singing? Writing? We heard you're doing a project with one of the guys from Screaming Trees, is that true? You have a gift, you son of a bitch. Use it.

I'm with Bethany now. Yes, you read that right. There's your masturbation material for the night. I finally crossed over to the other team, just like you always said I would. Sometimes Bethany cries half the night. Did you ever hold her through night while she weeps and shakes, telling her a hundred times that the horrible things her father told her about herself weren't true? Did you tell her you'd be there for her forever? Or did you just fuck her and leave her cold? You didn't cause her problems but you sure didn't help any. Your bullshit with me is water under the bridge, but I could tear your eyes out for how you treated Bethany. Even if she brought it on herself. I don't know how long it will last for us. But I love her.

I hope you're looking out for Bobby at least. He idolizes you for some goddamn reason. Please write and tell me you guys are okay."

Alexander put the letter down. "Darling Camille! If you're in the market for female flesh, there are some less complicated kitties than Bethany to play with out there! But that one was worth the trouble. You never did find out for yourself, did you Bobby? It's ok, boss. I reconnoitered for you!"

He held up another envelope. "Well now, here is a real passion flower if I ever saw one…Amelia. 'Alexander,' she writes,

"Little Alexia is almost two now. It's amazing how much she looks like you. I think she wants to be a singer. She sings along to the music in the car. My mom heard her singing to the Divinyls. You know, 'When I Think About You I Touch Myself.' Of course Alexia had no idea what it meant, but Grandma freaked out and bought her every Debbie Gibson and Tiffany CD in the store. Some Disney crap too.

You are a stupid fucking idiot for missing her growing up. She's beautiful, Alexander, and she's ours. What the fuck is wrong with you? She asked some man in a store the other day if he was her Daddy. I cried behind the wheel the whole way home. I tried to hide it but she asked what was wrong, so I told her I had a stomach ache. I hope you're proud of yourself. You've left a trail of lies and broken hearts and destruction behind you, with nothing to show for it. Maybe you'll find a new band in Seattle, but I just don't give a fuck anymore. My mom has been calling around to lawyers about going after you for child support, but I told her don't bother. You'll never have two fucking nickels to rub together, unless you're taking them from some poor stupid woman. Like me.

"Jesus Christ, the sound of violins is deafening, enough!" said Alexander. He crushed up the letter into a paper ball, which he threw at a bunch of garbage bags and empty beer bottles on the floor in the corner. The paper ball sent flies buzzing from the trash pile. He poured another shot and swiped idly at a fly that got too close. "Fucking Amelia," he said. "Who does she think I am? Ward Cleaver? Fucking Father Knows Best?" He downed the shot. "Look," he said. "She sent a picture of the little brat." He flipped the polaroid snapshot through the air at Bobby; it hit him in the chest and fell to the floor. "Alright Bobby, I'd like you to take dictation for me, if you would. You've always had such marvelous penmanship. Here goes:

"Dear Camille,

So sorry to hear Denver has reverted to a desert wasteland in my absence, but I'm not surprised. Trying to get a new band together. But I haven't heard back from the bass player and drummer I met the other night. Possibly because Bobby hasn't been very good about answering the phone and taking messages the last couple of days."

He wagged a finger at Bobby and tisk-tisked. "Ready for the next one?"

"Dear Amelia,

You'll be lucky if that child grows up with any of my talent. Who knows who her Daddy really is? Probably that blue-haired freak from Twice Jilted. Your parents have money from here

to the moon, what the fuck are you worried about? Maybe you can still trick Barry Fey into marrying you. Best Wishes, Love Muffin."

He looked up at Bobby with his tart, mocking grin. Bobby's faint shadow moved against the wall as the late afternoon sun shone pale and tired through the tattered blinds. "I must say it's unnerving the way you spin around and around without saying a word like that," Alexander said with a sigh. He leaned back in his chair and put his feet up on the table, sending a stray beer can clattering to the floor. "Who'd have thought it. Our Bobby, another junkie driven to despair by German philosophy and Russian novels." Bobby's body spun slowly. It was hanging by a rope around his neck from the ceiling fan. The languid rotation of the fan stirred the dust motes dancing in the air slowly, slowly. "That's quite a knot you made there, Bob. Were you a Boy Scout?"

Alexander shuffled around the apartment, dragging his bad foot, throwing a few things into a duffel bag. "I'd cut you down," he said over his shoulder, "but I don't want to mess with the scene for the nice policemen. DNA and fingerprints and all." Bobby's sad brown eyes stared into space as he went round and round, making a hopeless appeal to Alexander each time his body rotated to face his friend.

"Damn it, brother," said Alexander. He stood in the middle of the room, at eye level with the hanging corpse. "What the fuck did you go and do it for? I thought we were having most excellent adventures! Am I supposed to go to Alaska alone now? Selfish fucker. Weren't you getting enough pussy? I could have set something up for you, all you had to do is ask. Squeaky wheel gets the grease, Bobby." He fingered Bobby's heroin works on the table. "Speaking of pussy, I made the acquaintance of a lovely young thing at the bar down the street. Meeting her again later. She looked like a partier. Lots of tattoos, too much mascara, droopy eyelids. You know the type." He put the needle and the drugs into his bag. "You don't mind if I dip into your stash, do you? To entice the young lady and all. I'm going to need a new place to stay, can't have too much leverage with these little birds. As if my super-human wang wasn't enough, you know?"

Popeye the cat rubbed up against Alexander's leg and purred. He bent down and patted the cat's head. "You're on your own now, little guy." The cat looked up at Bobby's boots slowly spinning overhead. He meowed curiously and batted tentatively at the boots with a gray paw. Alexander shooed him away. "A little respect for the dead, Popeye? The man has been hanging there for two days, for god's sake." He packed his notebook in his bag and put a couple of full beers from the fridge in his jacket pocket. He drained the bottle of Jack and left it empty on the counter, then wiped his mouth on his sleeve. He slung his bag over his shoulder and shook his head. "Another tortured slacker genius kills himself," he said. "So trendy, Bobby. You never were the trendy sort." He reached around Bobby's neck and undid the clasp of a chain with a locket, and put it in his pocket.

Alexander picked up the old rotary phone hanging on the wall and dialed 9-1-1. He let the receiver drop as an operator answered. The phone swung gently from side to side as he limped out the door of the apartment, closing it shut behind him.

Chapter 47
APRIL 5, 1994

Babylonia opened her deep brown eyes wide. She listened to the silence for the sound of her child stirring. Hearing nothing, she closed her eyes again and relaxed. Her manicured fingernails, black with tiny white polka dots, dug into the bright red sheets. She released the fabric, then clenched again. The tip of her tongue traced the shape of her lips. She opened her eyes wide again and stared up at the ceiling. Her eyelids fluttered rapidly. Her chest rose and fell, then abruptly stilled as she drew in a sharp, deep breath. She let it out with a gasp, and began panting. Her legs stiffened and her eyes rolled back into her head. She turned her face into the pillow, her mouth open in a silent scream. The feeling began deep inside her, in the root chakra, and then spread like needles of light up and down her limbs to all the extremities: pierced nipples, fingertips, even her scalp tingled. Her toes curled. Her back arched, heaving her breasts dramatically, and finally she came. She covered her own face with the pillow, letting it absorb the sound of a deep guttural moan. Her legs quaked and her breath found a different, more syncopated rhythm as the orgasm reached another level.

Finally she'd had enough. She grabbed him by the hair and tugged. He looked up from between her legs with a self-satisfied smile. He put two fingers to her mouth, offering them for her to taste. She playfully slapped them away. "Stop it," she said, still catching her breath. She lit a cigarette and fell back on the pillows. She took a long, luxurious drag, and with her other hand toyed with her silky black hair, twirling it idly around a long, delicate finger. "Somebody tell me, why did I stop fooling around with you back then?" Babylonia blew a smoke ring to the ceiling and smiled up at him as he climbed into bed next to her. "Glad I ran into you again. I seriously forgot how good you are at that. God damn, boy!"

Eli laughed. "Practice makes perfect," he said. "I think you forgot how good I am at lots of things." He savored her naked body, running his fingers up and down from her belly button to her mouth and back down again to her thighs. He thought she was even more beautiful without all the elaborate make-up.

He had run into her with her friend and her kid at the grocery store an hour earlier. She looked almost like the girl next door, fresh-faced and hair back in a pony-tail, dressed down in jeans and a t-shirt with a denim jacket. He helped carry her groceries home. The friend left. She put the kid down for a nap. They went to bed.

"Stop it, you're going to make me horny again!" she said, slapping his hand away. "I have to get up and take a shower and get ready for an appointment."

"Oh yeah? What about this?" he asked, placing her hand on his boxer shorts.

"This," she said, smiling and squeezing him firmly, "will be *amply* rewarded when I get back – if you'll be a doll and stay here with him while I go? With traffic there and back, three hours tops. He may not even wake up, he was up with me most of the night."

"I can read to him," Eli said. "He has books, right?"

She gave him an appreciative stroke. "You would? You're so sweet. You know, he still isn't talking. I read to him all the time, but it just isn't clicking yet. I'll cancel the babysitter."

"He's almost four now?"

She let go of Eli's anatomy and got out of bed. "Just turned. He was born on the last day of the zodiac. His dad always thought that was a big deal. Anyway, I'm trying to save money to take him to a specialist."

Eli nodded. He lay back, savoring the rich violet and amber smells of Babylonia's perfume on the sheets. The whole apartment was an extension of her style: red and purple silk tapestries on the wall; jewelry boxes and little cases full of her exotic treasures; an old, tattered Sisters of Mercy poster above the bed.

Babylonia turned on the shower in the tiny bathroom adjacent to her bedroom. "Make yourself at home," she told Eli. "It'll take me a bit to get ready, this guy likes the full Betty Page thing. Here." She tossed him the remote to the little TV on her dresser. He turned it on, but watched her reflection in a long dressing mirror instead as the hot water began to steam the windows and she stepped into the shower one long, shapely, alabaster leg after another. Eli clicked the remote leisurely, settling on a rerun of *Star Trek: The Next Generation*.

She returned to the bedroom after her shower in a blue silk kimono with her hair wrapped in a towel on top of her head. Eli's face was screwed up in a grimace and his eyes were glassy. "What's wrong?" she asked.

He nodded toward the television. "Kurt Cobain killed himself."

"Are you shitting me? Selfish son of a bitch. I'm not surprised." She stood transfixed for a few minutes by the TV news bulletin recounting the story. "He has a daughter, you know."

"I know."

She shook her head as she moved around the room, lighting a half dozen candles. Dusk was gathering outside her windows. "Stupid fucker," she said. "They fucked everything up anyway. *Bleach* was good, but after that they turned everything so *pop*." She packed a small black travel bag with an assortment of items: furry handcuffs, a little bottle of lube, and a paddle that clearly wasn't for ping-pong. "That fucking bitch Courtney Love killed him, what do you wanna bet? Or drove him to do it. She has crazy for days."

"Maybe," Eli nodded. First Bobby, now this. "I can't believe he did it. A hundred Nirvana clones up and down the radio dial, so he kills himself."

Eli pretended not to watch as Babylonia sat and did her hair and make-up in front of the mirror at her vanity table. Kurt Cobain's face flashed again and again on the muted television; the same three-second clip from the *Smells Like Teen Spirit* video ran with the news teaser at each commercial break. Eli's eyelids grew heavy. The opium smells of Babylonia's perfumes and oils and incense filled his senses and he slipped in and out of shallow sleep. He dreamed he was sleeping under a Christmas tree, wrapped up snug as a present under the soft, holy lights.

When she was done, Babylonia stood and twirled. She was the living picture of the famous pin-up girl. She bent down and kissed Eli. "Three hours tops. If he wakes up, just tell him Mommy will be home soon. He'll understand. There's an old acoustic guitar in there. If he freaks out, just play him a few chords. He loves it."

After she left, Eli put on his jeans and pulled a pen and notebook out of his backpack. He'd almost filled another one. He thumbed through the pages of free-writes and poems and bits of narrative and fragments of disconnected verse. Letters to Gwen never sent. A reconstructed conversation with Bobby. Lyrics for a song he'd tried to write with Brandon. Prose-poem sketches from the trip to Tuscany.

It was all crap. Sentimental, bloodless crap. He'd have to start all over again, dig deeper, find a new voice, shed off one more layer of skin. *What else could I write? I don't have the right.*

He opened the notebook to a fresh page and put the pen to paper.

I don't want this century anymore. I don't want the next one either. A future of endless possibilities has no meaning for me now. I only want this...

A sound from Morrison's room interrupted him. Eli got up and poked his head in. The kid was awake and out of bed. His hair was a curly blonde mess. If he noticed Eli, he gave no sign. He had the guitar face down on the floor and he banged on it like a drum with both his fat little hands.

AUTHOR CHRIS HENRY

The Naked Way is Chris Henry's first novel. Chris lives in Denver, Colorado. In previous incarnations he has worked in progressive politics, real estate and academics. He loves music, history, and comedy. You can find Chris on twitter, facebook and Goodreads.